S0-AIV-976

Praise for the Kenni Lowry Mystery Series

"Fabulous fun and fantastic fried food! Kappes nails small town mystery with another must-read hit. (Also, I want to live in Cottonwood, KY.) Don't miss this one!"

— Darynda Jones,
New York Times Bestselling Author of *The Dirt on Ninth Grave*

"Packed with clever plot twists, entertaining characters, and plenty of red herrings! *Fixin' To Die* is a rollicking, delightful, down-home mystery."

— Ann Charles,
USA Today Bestselling Author of the Deadwood Mystery Series

"Southern and side-splitting funny! *Fixin' To Die* has captivating characters, nosy neighbors, and is served up with a ghost and a side of murder."

— Duffy Brown,
Author of the Consignment Shop Mysteries

"This story offers up a small touch of paranormal activity that makes for a fun read...A definite "5-star," this is a great mystery that doesn't give up the culprit until the last few pages."

— *Suspense Magazine*

"A Southern-fried mystery with a twist that'll leave you positively breathless."

— Susan M. Boyer,
USA Today Bestselling Author of *Lowcountry Book Club*

"A wonderful series filled with adventure, a ghost, and of course some romance. This is a hard book to put down."

– Cozy Mystery Book Reviews

"Kappes captures the charm and quirky characters of small-town Kentucky in her new mystery...a charming, funny story with exaggerated characters. The dialect-filled quirky sayings and comments bring those characters to life."

– Lesa's Book Critiques

"With a fantastic cast of characters and a story filled with humor and murder you won't be able to put it down."

– Shelley's Book Case

"Funny and lively...Before you blink your three chapters down and your trying to peak ahead to see what happens next. Fast moving with great characters that you wish were real so that you might be able to visit with them more often."

– The Reading Room

"Kappes is an incredible author who weaves fabulous stories...I can't wait to see what she comes up next in this series."

– Community Bookstop

"I am totally hooked. The people of Cottonwood feel like dear friends, and I enjoy reading about the latest happenings...The story is well-told, with plenty of action and suspense, along with just enough humor to take the edge off."

– Book Babble

AX TO
GRIND

**The Kenni Lowry Mystery Series
by Tonya Kappes**

FIXIN' TO DIE (#1)
SOUTHERN FRIED (#2)
AX TO GRIND (#3)
SIX FEET UNDER (#4)

AX TO GRIND

A KENNI
LOWRY
MYSTERY

TONYA KAPPES

HENERY PRESS

AX TO GRIND
A Kenni Lowry Mystery
Part of the Henery Press Mystery Collection

First Edition | September 2017

Henery Press, LLC
www.henerypress.com

All rights reserved. No part of this book may be used or reproduced in any manner whatsoever, including internet usage, without written permission from Henery Press, LLC, except in the case of brief quotations embodied in critical articles and reviews.

Copyright © 2017 by Tonya Kappes

This is a work of fiction. Any references to historical events, real people, or real locales are used fictitiously. Other names, characters, places, and incidents are the product of the author's imagination, and any resemblance to actual events or locales or persons, living or dead, is entirely coincidental.

Trade Paperback ISBN-13: 978-1-63511-247-4
Digital epub ISBN-13: 978-1-63511-248-1
Kindle ISBN-13: 978-1-63511-249-8
Hardcover ISBN-13: 978-1-63511-250-4

Printed in the United States of America

Jack Keller—
Always reach for that dream.

Chapter One

"What exactly are we looking for again?" Finn asked, rubbing his hand through his hair. He stood in the corner of the bedroom of Hattie Hankle with a wooden Louisville Slugger in his hand, his face clouded with uneasiness.

"Just tap the bat on the floor a few times," I said, my head stuck up under Hattie's bed, only to find what looked to be at least a hundred crumpled-up plastic grocery store bags, rolls of paper towels, and toilet paper that filled every single inch of space under the bed's box spring.

"Get, you critter," I said a little louder than normal so Hattie could hear me from the other side of the shut door.

"Get away," Finn repeated, tapping the bat on the hardwood floor a few times. "Seriously, what kind of critter again?" His eyebrows rose.

I tugged the bed skirt down and stood up, brushing the front of my sheriff's uniform off in case I'd gotten some dust bunnies on me.

"Critters." I smiled. "You haven't gotten to experience a Hattie Hankle call."

I sat on the edge of Hattie's bed and patted my hand on the flowered quilt that lay on the mattress. Finn sat next to me. Living in a small town like Cottonwood, Kentucky, there were many calls that probably weren't necessary for the sheriff to respond to, but the citizens pulled their weight around our small town and that was one thing that made us special.

"Hattie lives here in the bed and breakfast. She doesn't have any family, and she can't live on her own. She has some special needs. My poppa always said Hattie would always be childlike, which wasn't a bad thing, because she would never know the evils of the world. She's been living in the Inn as far back as I can remember. She thinks there are critters running around her room." I grinned. "I know it sounds crazy, but she calls dispatch and I come here and pretend to catch them or tell her I've run them off. It satisfies her for a couple of months."

"A couple of months?" Finn's jaw dropped along with his shoulders.

"Every time it's something different. Plus, I feel a little bad for her, and it's nice to sit and chat for a while." I shrugged and stood up. "She doesn't get much company, I don't think. Or at least that's what I've heard."

Meaning the little bit of idle gossip that generally circulated during my weekly girl's night out Euchre game.

Even though Finn had been a deputy in my department for a couple of months and he'd mostly gotten used to the small-town life here in Cottonwood, it was still entertaining to watch his reactions to some of our more colorful citizens.

"Did you get it?" Hattie asked from the other side of the bedroom door. "Is there a lot of blood?"

I walked over to the door and jerked it open. The bottom of the long window curtain with the same flower pattern as the quilt swung out and rested in a billowy cloud of fabric on the floor.

"Well?" Hattie tilted her head to one side to listen. Her gray hair, styled like a football helmet, didn't move—a sure sign she'd been to her weekly hair appointment down at Tiny Tina's, Cottonwood's only salon and full-service spa. And by full-service, I meant massages with stones that came right out of the Kentucky River that ran along our small town. Somehow Tiny Tina's passed those rocks off as fancy.

"The critter is all taken care of," I said, leaning in close to her ear when I noticed she wasn't wearing her hearing aids. "Where are your hearing aids?"

"My ears?" She jerked around and took a few shaky steps into the small living area, where she had a matching taupe loveseat and couch. The room opened up into a small kitchenette with a round table that had two chairs across from each other. The table was set as though she were about to have company, but that was what most of the tables in Cottonwood looked like. It was the proper thing to do in the South.

Of course, my table wasn't. Instead it was piled high with old community coupon papers and junk mail. Not Hattie. There wasn't a thing out of place. Every time I'd come to visit her, it was spotless.

Slowly Hattie's head turned toward me. Her eyes squinted in a furtive manner. "I bet that critter took them."

"I'll be sure to let Darby know," I said to ease her mind. Darby Gray owns The Inn and has always been the one I knew of that took good care of Hattie.

I glanced back at Finn, who was still sitting on Hattie's bed as if he were trying to process what he'd just witnessed.

No doubt his mind was running around itself wondering what on Earth he'd gotten himself into, probably having second thoughts about recently taking the deputy sheriff's position.

"Did you get a look at that thing?" Hattie let go of her cane and lifted her hands in the air, forming them into claws. "Big claw hands and big teeth." She chomped her teeth together. "Did it hiss at you?"

"I don't know," I said, turning back to Finn. I smiled. "Officer Vincent was the one who caught it and threw it out the window. Did it hiss?" I teased Finn.

"Like a snake," he said, playing along as he walked over to us.

That was one thing that I liked about getting to know Finn, not only through our job but also on a personal level. He could go with the flow, and he was quick and witty. All qualities that made him so appealing.

"I'm glad you got you a new sidekick," Hattie said, pointing her bony finger at Finn. "You take over Lonnie's job?"

I was a little surprised Hattie remembered that Lonnie Lemar had retired as my sheriff's deputy.

"Yes, ma'am." Finn nodded and rocked back and forth on his heels. "I'm happy to be here in Cottonwood."

"Who's your kin?" She blinked owlishly.

"My who?" Finn asked.

"Your kin folk," I said, finding it a little disturbing how cute he was when he was confused. "Hattie, you'll have to excuse Finn. He's from Chicago. Finn, Hattie wanted to know who you're related to around here."

"A northerner, huh?" She nodded. "No wonder."

"No wonder what?" Finn asked.

"No wonder you're the talk of the town." Hattie's eyes fluttered. "You're a handsome thing."

Hattie Hankle might be hard of hearing, but her eyesight was just fine.

As Finn's face reddened, he shifted and dropped his head. "That's nice of you to say. Thank you."

"Aw, Hattie," I teased. "Who's going around telling you about our friend Finn here?"

It was fun to aggravate him and put him on the spot.

"Paige told me," Hattie said, speaking of Paige Lemar, an employee at the bed and breakfast. Hattie nodded with a big grin on her face. She elbowed me. "You might think about this one."

"Are you ready?" My head jerked up. Hattie Hankle trying to fix me up was my cue that it was time to leave. "It was nice to see you, Hattie." I took a step toward the door.

"You aren't staying for a cup of afternoon coffee?" Hattie asked.

"Not today." There was no way I was going to hang around— even though the sheriff's department had been quiet for a few months—and listen to Hattie Hankle inform me on what a cute couple Finn Vincent and I would make.

My mama had already mastered that task, and I could barely stand listening to her. And she was my mom.

"Let us know if you have any more problems with those critters." I opened the door.

Finn followed me, put his hand on the open door, and held it for me.

"And a gentleman at that." Hattie nodded a few slow times and drew her lips into a tight smile.

"Have a great day." I stepped out into the hallway of the Inn.

"That was rude," Finn said with a look of amusement on his face after we'd stepped out into the hall.

"What was rude?" I asked, glancing over Finn's shoulder to make sure Hattie had shut her door. Sometimes after I left, she'd forget to and then wander around into other people's rooms at the Inn.

It was part of her childlike ways, but I had a hard time explaining to customers at the Inn when they'd call me because there was an intruder in their hotel room when it was only Hattie. She was harmless.

"You didn't agree that I was a gentleman," he joked, pulling the corners of his lips up slightly.

"Ha ha." I rolled my eyes, barely missing knocking down a guest on our way down the hall.

The smell of paint tickled my nose. The note taped on the wall warned of the freshly painted walls. The new powder blue color went well with the bamboo wood floor. There were six rooms on this floor and two suites on the third floor.

"What about you being the talk of the town?"

"Who is Paige?" he asked.

"Paige Lemar. Lonnie's wife." We stopped at the top of the staircase to let a few guests pass us. "She's the Inn's housekeeper."

"You want to go grab a bite to eat?" Finn asked on our way down the staircase to the first floor where the registration was located.

For a split second I thought about it. But there was no way I could cancel my weekly Euchre night with the girls. I'd much rather be spending the time with Finn, even though the conversation would be about work.

I looked into the gathering room in the front of the Inn to see if Darby was in there. She wasn't. Only a few guests were sitting by the fireplace. Just the sight of the flaming logs made me excited for the best season in Kentucky. Autumn.

Maybe Darby was outside. I wanted to let her know about Hattie's missing hearing aids.

"I'd love to, but I can't." I shrugged off the light fall breeze that sent chills along my arms when it hit my neck after we walked out through the screen door. "Euchre." I patted my belly. "You know there will be good food there."

"Let me know if they decide to let guys in." He winked. I gulped. "Maybe another time. See you in the morning at the ceremony?" he asked.

"Sounds good." I stood on the top step and watched him head toward his car.

He sucked in a deep breath and, with his chin up in the air, looked around the landscape. The prism of trees that blocked the view of the Kentucky River behind the Inn had painted the landscape in orange, yellow, and red leaves. This was the perfect time of the year in Kentucky. Mid-seventy degrees during the day and mid-fifties at night. The nippy evening air told me fall was in full swing and soon all the trees would paint a beautiful canvas across Cottonwood.

"I love Chicago, don't get me wrong, but this." Finn's arms stretched out in front of him. "This is amazing."

Both of us stood there enjoying the view with silence between us. It was fun seeing him take in the fall scenery for the first time since he'd moved to Cottonwood.

He waved me off on his way to his Dodge Charger.

I stood on the front porch of the Inn until I saw the taillights of his car round the corner before I turned to go back into the Inn to find to Darby.

"Duke, where did you come from?" I asked my bloodhound, who was lying in a sunny spot on the wood porch floor. I'd dropped him off at home after I'd gotten the critter call from dispatch.

"Where'd you come from?" Kiwi, the Inn's green macaw

mascot, clasped his claws around the wire of the domed bird cage that stood at the end of the porch. His head bobbed up and down. "I came from Beryle's and couldn't find the book. Couldn't find the book. Glad she's dead."

Chapter Two

"Stay, Duke," I instructed my dog, who was too busy sniffing new smells to even greet me. I wanted to make sure he didn't scare Kiwi before I could question the bird.

He was a great dog—if it weren't for him taking a bullet for me in the line of duty a few months ago, I wouldn't be here. Tomorrow the town was going to give him an award. It was a pretty big deal around these parts, and word around the street was that everyone was going to be there. Even Lonnie Lemar, my ex-deputy that had come out of retirement to run against me in the next election.

I glanced around the large porch to see if anyone else was around and might've heard Kiwi, but there wasn't. Pops of white, yellow, pink, lavender, red, and bronze mums were strategically placed around the porch and down the steps. They seemed to frill themselves in the last bit of the day's sun.

"Hi, Kiwi." I walked over to greet the bird. "What did you say about someone dead?" I questioned the bird like it was going to tell me.

"Hi, Kiwi," Kiwi repeated. The bird was good at repeating and I had no idea why on Earth I thought I was going to be able to question him.

"Glad who is dead?" I asked the bird, hoping he'd repeat what I thought I'd heard.

"Hi, Kiwi. Cold out here." The bird lifted one claw in the air and sent a wave of ruffled feathers up his neck.

"It's almost too cold out here for you." I ran my hands up and down my arms to ward off any more goosebumps before I poked my finger through the cage and pet him on his tiny little head. He bobbed up and down with delight.

"There you are." Mama's voice floated to me with the breeze.

She stood behind the screened front door inside the Inn.

The hinges on the old door creaked when she pushed it open and it smacked closed behind her.

"Mama? What are you doing here?" I asked.

"Since I won the cook-off, all sorts of local restaurants have asked me to cook something for them." She tapped the *Vote For Lowry* pin stuck proudly on her chest. "Now, don't you worry that pretty little head that I produced with this here body." She dragged her hand down her body, starting at her head and ending at her toes. She was good at reminding me where I'd come from, like I didn't know. "I'm still working for your election. Free of charge, I might add."

"Thank you, Mama." I was grateful that Mama had taken over my re-election campaign. I just wasn't sure if she was hurting or helping, since she was going around either pushing my re-election propaganda on the citizens or threatening them. Either way, Mama was very persuasive. "Did you pick up Duke?" I asked, though I already knew.

Mama had a key to my house, and she let herself inside whenever she felt like it. It was a bit of a privacy issue, but it was typical of family in a tight-knit community.

"I did." She sashayed down the porch toward me and eased herself into one of the many rocking chairs Darby had strategically dotted along the front porch of the Inn. "His little brown droopy eyes just tugged on my heart after I'd spent all morning over there using your oven."

"You used my oven?" I asked.

"Honey, I had to get my hot browns cooked so your daddy stayed at our house keeping an eye on those while I got my Derby Pies cooked at your house." She acted as if I should know her calendar. "I knew I was going to see you at Euchre, so I just brought him along."

"Good evening, Kenni." Darby had ambled around the Inn with a basket full of colorful leaves that'd already fallen off the trees. Her brown hair was swept up in a knot on the top of her head. Her almond-shaped brown eyes stared at me for a moment before she turned to my mama. "Your Derby Pie is the talk of the Inn. I'm going to need about five more for tomorrow."

"I have plenty that I made today and put in the freezer. I'll put them on the windowsill tonight to thaw and you can warm them at three hundred and fifty before you serve them. You know a little scoop of vanilla ice cream on top of that warm pie is just a slice of heaven."

Don't get me wrong, Mama had always made good country homemade suppers when I'd lived at home and even when I'd come home during college visits, but I never knew she could win a cook-off.

"Perfect." Darby sat down on the porch's top step and scooted all the way up to the wood railing to let some arriving guests pass by. "I can taste it now." She licked her lips.

"Business must be good." I noted the flurry of activity.

"Didn't you hear?" Darby's forehead puckered. "Beryle Stone's estate is being auctioned off this week."

"Really?" I was a little taken aback. Beryle Stone was a famous author who was from Cottonwood.

Estate sales around these parts were a dime a dozen. I tried to recall if I'd heard through the grapevine about Beryle's auction, but I couldn't remember. There was so much gossip flung around, my immune system had gotten used to it and I was good at drowning it out.

The estate wasn't far from the Inn and it too overlooked the Kentucky River. Probably the best view of the river in Cottonwood. "I thought that place was dilapidated. I wonder what state she finally decided to spend the rest of her life in."

It wasn't as if Beryle Stone was young.

"The state is six feet under," Darby said. She pushed herself up to stand. "You've been living under a rock, Kenni Lowry."

"Six feet under? Beryle is dead?" I gulped and looked at Kiwi.

"It's been the talk of the town for a while now. Ruby Smith is rumored to be the executor of her estate." Darby seemed to know more than rumors.

"Executor?" I asked, a bit shocked. "Ruby Smith and Beryle were that good of friends?"

I found that strange since I'd never heard Ruby mention Beryle. I was sure it was all over town, especially since Beryle was a big-time author. Unfortunately, I'd never read anything she'd written nor did I have time to visit the gossip circles Mama and Darby were participants in.

"I hate to hear this." There was a tug of sadness on my heart. It was a shame to hear when anyone passed. "Was she sick?"

"Must've been. She's dead, ain't she?" Mama said. Darby simple shrugged.

"There was an announcement in one of those fancy estate sale papers and online about her items being sold. Most of the Inn's guests are all the people who are here to get their hands on one of Beryle's things." She leaned in and whispered, "It's rumored that Beryle has a tell-all manuscript that was only to be auctioned off after she died."

"Juicy." Mama's brows lifted as she vigorously rubbed her hands together.

"A tell-all? Like how to be in love, or what?" I asked, knowing that Beryle had been famous for her romances and feisty love scenes the women in Cottonwood swooned over. Even Mama.

"Oh, your daddy and I could use some of that feisty love." Mama's shoulders did a little wiggle. I rolled my eyes out of disgust.

"I heard it's about her life and some buried secrets." Darby's tone was a little too excited. Her brows lifted along with her smile.

Mama's nose crinkled. "Interesting." Mama's voice dripped with a southern drawl.

"Buried secrets?" This was starting to become very suspicious.

"Uh-huh." Darby slowly drew her chin down to her chest and stared at me under hooded brows.

"I'll definitely have to go to my auxiliary meeting this week to get the scoop on what Beryle Stone had over on someone." Mama perked up like a steaming pot of coffee.

"I don't ever recall hearing anything about Beryle Stone other than she was a nice woman." I didn't like all the gossip.

"Even nice women have buried skeletons." Mama winked.

"Now, Mama," I warned. "Don't be going and packing any tales where there is no tale to pack." I patted my leg and Duke came running up the steps. "Anyways, I checked on Hattie. All the critters are gone. She didn't have her hearing aids in either." Mama and Darby snickered. "Duke and I are going to head on over to Tibbie's. I'll see you over there." I gave my mama a hug. "Let's go, Duke."

"I guess I better get in here and shut up the windows. It's gonna be a cold one tonight." Darby brushed down the front of her shirt and picked up the basket of leaves.

No doubt in my mind she was going to use those leaves in some creative decorating technique. The Inn had the perfect touches to make it nice and cozy.

I waved goodbye to Darby on my way to my Jeep Wagoneer, and I couldn't help but look at Kiwi. No doubt I'd heard the bird correctly repeating something one of the Inn guests had said, though I did think them saying they were glad Beryle was dead seemed a little harsh.

Duke jumped in the passenger side with his head stuck out the window, the chilly night air pinning his ears back as we sped down the old country road back into town.

"How was Hattie?" The voice sent my heart galloping inside my chest.

My eyes peered into the rearview mirror. An uneasy feeling smacked my gut.

"I'm back," the ghost of my poppa, the ex-sheriff of Cottonwood, said as he arched a sly brow.

Chapter Three

The tires screeched to a halt. My hand gripped the wheel. Duke turned himself around to face the backseat, wagging his tail at the sight of Poppa's ghost.

"Where have you been?" I asked. The feeling of death crept in my soul and settled with an empty feeling in my heart. "As soon as we got the Godbey case settled, you vanished. It was like you died all over again."

It'd been almost six months since Owen Godbey was found dead and Poppa had come back to be my ghost deputy.

"It just happens that way." Poppa ghosted himself up in the front seat next to Duke, making it a little tight. "We're learning as we go."

"What does that mean?" My eyes narrowed. "You mean that for you to be my guardian ghost, there has to be a crime committed?"

"I'm not sure. It seems that way, though." He shrugged.

"Are you telling me that there has been a crime committed?" I asked and looked down at my shoulder where my dispatch walkie-talkie was strapped. "Because I haven't heard a peep out of dispatch about any shenanigans going on around here, other than Hattie Hankle's critter."

Poppa smacked his knee and cackled. The wrinkles around his eyes deepened as the smile grew across his face. He brushed his fingers through his thinning gray hair, fixing the stray strand that had escaped from the comb-over.

"You mean to tell me that Hattie Hankle is still claiming she's got critters?" he asked.

"Yes. She's gotten a little more eccentric." I chose my words wisely. I knew that she and Poppa had been good friends and were probably the same age.

"She's a bird," he joked, using the endearing term we called people who were a little on the odd side. "But that doesn't give me reason to be here."

"Maybe we're wrong." I bit the edge of my lip, hoping there wasn't any crime brewing in Cottonwood. "I'm so happy to see you."

"Me too, Kenni-bug." Poppa shifted to face the windshield and put his thin-skinned hands in his lap.

Hearing him say my childhood nickname chased away the chills of the season and warmed me inside and out.

"We've got Euchre tonight." I threw the Wagoneer in drive and pulled off the shoulder of the road. "How long have you known Hattie?" I questioned, trying to push Duke's ninety-pound body into the backseat with my right elbow.

He loved Poppa and, for some reason, he could see Poppa's ghost.

"Long time." His brows furrowed. "I don't recall exactly when we met, but she's been there a while. I'm sure Darby can tell you. It was awful nice to take her in."

"Yes, it was." I continued into town to Tibbie Bell's house. I wasn't sure why Poppa was there; all I knew was that I was happy.

The comfort of Poppa's ghost presence had become a reality a little more than a year ago when Doc Walton was found dead and someone broke into the jewelry store. I had a hard time believing that Poppa had come back in ghost form, much less that he'd come back to help me solve any and all crimes that had or were going to take place in Cottonwood. It'd taken my parents a long time to even accept that I was in law enforcement, but when I ran for sheriff of Cottonwood, it nearly put Mama one foot in the grave. So the little secret about Poppa coming back probably wouldn't sit well with her or the other residents of Cottonwood. They'd think I'd done lost my marbles, so I kept Poppa's ghost a secret.

Over the past few crimes, Poppa and I became a team again, like old times when he was sheriff and I was a kid. We'd sit around and come up with all sorts of scenarios on who committed crimes like putting together a puzzle. Of course, Mama threw a fit that Poppa would encourage such behavior for a young lady, and she took to the bed when I entered the police academy. Mama could be a bit dramatic now and then.

Tibbie's house was on Second Street, off the town branch that was a left turn off Main and a right turn off Oak. We affectionately referred to it as the town branch due to the fact there was a creek that ran right through the middle of that part of town. In fact, most of the houses were built behind the creek and you had to drive over a little concrete bridge driveway to get to them.

Luckily, Tibbie's house was a small ranch that sat in front of the branch and parking was prime along the street curb.

"Woo-wee." Poppa looked outside the window. "Looks like a lot of gossip is going to go on in there tonight."

I put the Jeep in park and bent my head down to look out Poppa's window.

"Looks like you're right."

I eyeballed Lulu McClain and Stella standing on the front porch. Both women loved to gossip, and by the way their heads were pushed together and their lips were moving, they sure had something to say about someone.

Before I got out of the car, I reached in the back for my bag where I kept an extra set of civilian clothes. There was something about my sheriff's uniform that stopped the henny-hens from squawking.

The "henny-hens" was what my friends and I lovingly called the old gossipy women. Mama was a hen. I'd learned from Poppa that if I showed up in my uniform, the gossip ceased, but when I put on my civilian clothes, I was one of the girls. They flapped their lips, and you could learn a lot from flapping lips.

"Evening, Sheriff." Stella ambled inside the house after she greeted me and I nodded back. Lulu nodded too.

"Hi, Lulu." Duke and I walked past her and headed inside Tibbie's house.

The house smelled heavenly. It was the one night of the week where the women tried to outdo one another with their cooking. They took pride in the slightest of compliments.

Everyone was gathered in the front room on the left where Tibbie always set up the card tables for the food and drinks. The sound of chatter and laughter echoed off the walls. Next to the front room was the small powder room. Duke headed for the food, and I went to change.

"I just can't believe that after all these years we're going to know the truth about what happened out at the Stone estate." I heard a muffled voice through the air-conditioning vent while I changed. "Now, you know I'm a God-fearing woman," Instantly I knew it was Stella. She loved calling herself that, which only meant to me that it made her feel better to gossip. "And I'm not packing tales, but I heard that Ruby Smith was the executor." Her little bit of information was greeted with a collective groan.

I hurried and got my clothes on. It did pique my interest to see exactly what truth she was talking about that was buried in the Stone estate and why it was such a shock that Ruby Smith was the executor. Beryle Stone was the biggest thing that'd ever come from Cottonwood. Obviously, Ruby hadn't arrived at Euchre yet or I'd have heard her voice. Of course, these women were only going to gossip about it until Ruby got here.

Quickly I threw my uniform in my bag. My stomach was growling and my curiosity was up. I needed to feed them both.

"This looks so good." I stood at the first table and grabbed a plastic plate.

The table was filled with at least three Crock-pots full of something delicious. The next table had four different casseroles and the last table had oodles of desserts. If I didn't feel Mama's eyes on me, I'd have gone straight to the dessert. I was in no mood to hear her lecture me on how I didn't get enough exercise and I ate poorly.

"What are you ladies talking about?" I asked after I'd moseyed on over to Stella and Toots Buford.

"You know," Toots chomped on her gum, "just the usual gossip that don't mean nothing."

I nodded and plucked a grape off the fruit plate and tossed it in my mouth. Stella didn't miss a mark.

"You hear about the Stone estate going up for auction?" she asked.

"Why do you have to gossip with the sheriff?" Toots clucked and rolled her eyes.

"It's Kenni." Stella gave me a sideways glance. Obviously she needed to make herself feel better about telling me because she followed up with, "She might know something. I bet they're going to need extra security."

"I heard some rumblings about it," I said and cocked my head to the side. "What did you hear?"

"Well, I heard Beryle Stone died and her estate is selling her stuff," she said.

"That's juicy gossip?" I asked, looking at Toots. "People die every day. Sounds like nothing to me." I shrugged. "Now, if you know who the executor of her estate is, that would be juicy."

Stella opened her mouth but quickly shut it when Toots gave her the wonky eye. So Stella just slowly shook her head.

"Come on." Toots smacked her lips together. She elbowed Stella. "Let's go pick out our table. Maybe our teams can play each other first."

I rubbed my hand over my chin, wondering what those two were up to. They whispered back and forth. Before they turned the corner to go into the room where Tibbie had set up all the Euchre tables, Stella glanced back at me. Toots still held a grudge against me from when I accused her of killing Doc Walton. After I did catch the real killer, I'd apologized to her, but she wasn't going to have anything to do with me. She was a grudge holder and everyone knew it.

"I guess you must be starving after hunting critters all day."

Jolee snickered, bringing me out of the long slow stare Stella had disturbingly given me.

"How on Earth did you hear about that?" I asked and glanced over at Mama, knowing that she'd done spread it all over town. "Never mind." I shook my head at my best friend. "How is business?"

"It's great, but that mama of yours sure did do a number on me." Jolee owned the On the Run food truck. She had a pretty neat business, actually. She had gotten permits from all sorts of places over the county where she could just pull up and open shop. She even parked right outside of the church after Sunday meeting with fresh coffee and donuts for all the members.

"You're talking about her winning the cook-off, aren't you?" I rolled my eyes and she nodded. "I was so shocked that she entered. I had no idea."

"Ben Harrison apparently knew she could cook. That sneaky dog." She looked down at Duke. "No offense, buddy."

Jolee had really started On The Run to bug another restaurant in town owned by Ben. They'd had the competition cook-off between their two restaurants. Mama was on Ben's team and she won, which meant that he won. Something Jolee wasn't too happy about. But if anyone asked me, I thought Jolee had a hankering for Ben that went beyond just friendly competition.

"He's a cutie." My smile spread across my face.

"Yes, he is." She bent down and patted Duke even more.

"Not Duke." I hesitated, wondering if I should even broach the subject. "Ben." And it was out there just like that.

Jolee straightened up and put her fists on her hips.

"You have lost your mind." She huffed. "He is a thorn in my side, Kenni Lowry."

"He's a cute thorn and he's single and you are going to be thirty soon," I teased.

"Now you just sound like your mama." Jolee fidgeted. "Come on, let's go beat these old henny-hens."

The interesting thing was that Jolee didn't protest too much, so I had an inkling she'd thought about the idea of her and Ben too. But I kept my mouth shut the rest of the night. At least until we went up against Ruby Smith and Stella.

"You getting excited about tomorrow?" Ruby asked and offered the Euchre deck to me to cut.

"I'm not cutting my luck." I knocked on the top of the stack. "Yes, I am excited for Duke." I reached down next to me and patted my trusty hound dog.

She offered the cut again and again I declined.

Around here we were a tad bit superstitious about a few things, and cutting the deck while playing Euchre was one of them.

"But I hear you've come into a bit of luck." I looked at Ruby to see her reaction.

It was Stella's reaction that threw me. She yanked her forearms off the table and placed them in her lap.

Most of the time when I interacted with people, I observed their body language. It was a job habit that'd spilled over into my personal life as well.

"What are you asking me, Kenni Lowry?" Ruby fluffed the edges of her spiky red hair nervously with her fingertips before she picked up the deck and started to deal out five cards each to the four of us.

Stella suddenly became interested and grabbed the edge of her chair and scooted the legs closer to the table, leaning in.

Jolee's eyes shifted between Ruby and me.

"I guess you'll have a lot of business at the store with all the people coming in to bid on the estate sale." I was creative with my wording to get to the heart of the matter. It was all in how you opened the door to the conversation with these women. If you seemed genuinely interested, they'd talk all day.

"I was out visiting Hattie Hankle at the Inn and that place was hopping." I drew my five cards in and arranged them according to suit. "And Darby told me that the old Stone place was going up for sale. I was shocked. I hadn't heard that Beryle had passed."

"We got the call about a week ago at the church office for

Pastor to go to the Stone Estate." Stella's elbows rested on the table. Her hands held the fanned cards in front of her face, her eyes glancing over the top of them. She shifted them across the table to look at Ruby. "When he came back, he told me about the quickie memorial for Beryle Stone on the property."

Since Toots wasn't there to stop Stella's loose lips, we might hear some real gossip.

"I might as well give you a bite, because y'all are fishing." Ruby threw her cards down on the table. "Beryle and I were third cousins once removed. I know it's distant, but she ain't got no more family. Now that she's dead, they came looking for next of kin, and guess who?"

Stella eased back in her chair, taking in every bobble, quip, or sigh that escaped Ruby. I was sure she was taking notes for future gossip circles.

"I don't think there's much out there. Hell," Ruby tapped her finger on the table, "that place of hers is all run down and almost falling in on itself. What do I want with it? Nothing." Her chin tucked to her chest. "According to Wally Lamb she'd had it all planned out. I'm just doing my part to follow through. After all, we might be distant relatives, but we are family. You know as well as I do that family sticks together. Good times or bad." She shook her head. "No gossip here."

"She was the biggest celebrity out of Cottonwood," Stella said. "Naturally there's going to be gossip. And the money that goes with being a famous person."

"And I bet she got royalties or something from all those books." Jolee shrugged.

"I done signed all the paperwork for any royalties or money from the sale of anything of Beryle's; it's going to a charity that she's been giving to for a while now. Wally Lamb already drew the papers up for me and signed them." Ruby spat. "I didn't even know about it until after she was cremated."

We all drew back in shock. Rarely was anyone from Cottonwood cremated. It was almost an afterlife sin not to be buried in the Cottonwood Cemetery right on Main Street.

"Oh, shut up." Ruby flung her wrinkly hand at us. "That was her wish, not mine. Besides, could you imagine if she were to be buried here? These people are going nuts over a few junky things in a rundown house, not even the fresh body of the woman. And that's all I'm going to say about that." She pointed at Stella. "So when you go gossiping about this, you tell them you heard it straight from my mouth."

"Well, I never." Stella threw her cards down on the table and jumped up, knocking her chair to the ground before she stormed out of Tibbie's house.

"I guess we heard it from the horse's mouth." Poppa did a little giddy-up and neighed like a horse behind Ruby.

I tried the best I could not to laugh, but it was too hard to keep it in.

"What is wrong with you?" Jolee shushed me, only making me laugh more.

"Not a thing." I leaned back in my chair.

My belly was full and the night was still young. And this was the way Euchre usually ended—with one player yelling at another.

Chapter Four

"Good morning, Betty," I greeted Betty Murphy the next day when Duke and I walked into the sheriff's office, located on Main Street in the back room of Cowboy's Catfish restaurant.

It seemed a bit unusual to most people outside of our tiny town to have a one-celled sheriff's department in the back of a food joint, but it worked quite well for us with our small bit of crime up until recently.

"Well, look at him." Betty popped up out of her chair and drew her hands up to her mouth. "Doesn't he look distinguished?"

"Yes, he does." I looked down at Duke and the bow tie I'd strapped around his neck. "It took me all morning and nearly knocking over a pot of coffee to get him to keep that thing on."

"You have to look good for your close-up, Duke." Betty reached into the treat jar on her desk and walked over to give him one. "Are you excited?"

"I am," I said. "Duke couldn't care less."

Duke's medal ceremony for saving my life was this morning. The whole town was going to come out for the presentation, followed by a reception put on by the Sweet Adelines in the basement of the Cottonwood Baptist Church.

"You look good." Betty's head tilted side to side, taking a good look at my face. "Well-rested even. A little pink in the cheeks."

"You know," I smiled, "I do feel good. There hasn't been any crime. I'm getting to bed on time, actually eating a little better, and I do have on a little makeup."

Normally, I threw my clothes on, brushed my teeth, and pulled my hair into a ponytail. I figured I better put on a little makeup since I was going to be standing in front of everyone at the ceremony.

I failed to mention to Betty that I was eating better because Finn and I went out to eat a lot and I generally ordered something good for me since he was a healthy eater.

Speaking of Finn...

"Are you ready?" He came through the door between Cowboy's Catfish and the sheriff's department holding two cups of coffee. He had on a pair of blue jeans, out of his normal khakis, and a new brown sheriff's shirt neatly tucked in, with his gun holstered around his waist. "Here you go. Betty didn't want one."

He held it out to me and I took it, trying not to look into his big brown eyes. I grabbed a couple of dog treats off of his desk that he kept there for Duke and stuck them in my pocket. Duke was going to need them during the ceremony.

"There is a lot of attention being thrown at the dead author," he said and walked over to his desk, but not without petting Duke first. I certainly didn't seem to have the same effect on him as he had on me. "Did that woman come in here yet?"

"What woman?" I asked, taking a sip of coffee.

"A woman named Cecily called earlier asking to speak with the sheriff about some extra protection for the Stone estate sale." Betty picked up her glasses off of her desk and put them on. She read off a sticky note, "She says she believes that someone is going to cause some trouble for the sale and wanted to make sure the sale and items in the home were safe."

"Has she seen the home?" I chuckled and took another sip.

Stella had mentioned extra security for the sale. Was it a coincidence that she knew Cecily was going to request this? What did Stella know? Obviously more than she let on at Euchre.

"I told her that it wasn't in the best condition, but she insisted that she was going to come down here and talk to the sheriff." Betty held the sticky note out and I walked over to get it.

"Cecily Hoover," I read the name, looking at the out-of-town area code and number. "I'll call her back after the festivities. From what I understand, Ruby Smith is in charge of the estate, so I'll ask her about this Cecily."

"Sounds good." Finn shuffled through a few of the papers on his desk. "Since it's quiet around here, I'm sure I can go over and help out. So feel free to offer my assistance."

"Thanks, Finn." It was nice to have a deputy who liked to help.

When Lonnie was deputy, I had a hard time getting him to go anywhere, and now he wanted to run against me. I grabbed a couple of *Vote For Lowry* pins off of my desk. I pinned one on my shirt and bent down, pinning one on Duke's bow-tie.

"You ready?" I rubbed his head and he got up. He loved going for rides. I looked around at Betty and Finn. "I guess I'll see y'all over there?" I asked.

Both nodded their heads.

"Good luck, Duke." Betty patted his head on our way out the door.

I'd parked the Wagoneer in the alley behind the office. Duke was all too eager to jump in, only Poppa was sitting in the passenger seat. Duke jumped in the back, wagging his tail at Poppa. I'd always heard that animals and children were sensitive to spirits. Now I knew it. Duke loved being around ghost Poppa just as much as he had loved being around the living Poppa.

"Well? Anything going on?" Poppa asked, probably wondering about any new crime, since that seemed to be the only time he was around.

"Not a thing." I shook my head and pulled out of the spot, heading down the alley and taking a left on Walnut Street and stopping at the stoplight.

The weather had taken a chilly dip overnight and left a gray sky, which wasn't going to dampen my mood.

"Betty did say that a woman from the Stone estate had called about more security, which was something Stella mentioned." I took a left on Main Street once the light turned green.

"Security? Did she say why? It's not like they had something worth stealing. They had money, but they were really simple people from what I remember," Poppa said.

I slid an eye at Poppa. "If you aren't doing anything, maybe you can go out to the Stone estate and look around for me. See what's going on."

"What am I looking for?" he asked.

"I'm not really sure. Something that would warrant someone watching the house," I suggested. "Just let me know what I'm going to find before I get there so I'm prepared."

"All right," Poppa agreed. "I'll head out there after the ceremony."

There were some people milling around Main Street, window shopping in some of the boutique shops' display windows, especially Ruby's Antiques. They had to be out-of-towners here about the Stone estate because I didn't recognize any of them, and I pretty much knew everyone in Cottonwood.

I nodded and waved while they stared at Duke and his floppy ears hanging out the back window of the old Jeep.

After I'd taken a left on E. Oak Street, I found a parking spot right in front of the Rock Fence Park, named after the dry stone rock fence that was built around the park.

All over Kentucky, these walls were built in the 1700s. For some reason they'd always been called the Slave Walls of Kentucky, when in reality they were built by Irish-immigrant stone masons. Regardless, I'd always admired the hard work of someone who had laid the stones freehand with no mortar. It was now a Commonwealth of Kentucky law that you couldn't remove or harm a dry stoned wall.

But the law didn't prohibit Mama from standing on one. She was teetering on top with a megaphone in her hand and screaming, "Vote Kenni Lowry for re-election!" She had my poor old daddy handing out buttons to anyone who dared give him eye contact.

Jolee didn't let the opportunity pass her by either. She was parked on Second Street selling food out of On The Run.

"Mama, get down from there," I urged her. "This is a

respectable ceremony for Duke. We can campaign later." Mama kept yelling as if she didn't see Duke and me standing on the sidewalk underneath her.

"Daddy." My eyes grew and my jaw clenched.

"You think I can do anything with her?" He shook his head and shoved a *Vote For Lowry* pin in someone's hand when they walked by.

"That's my girl." Poppa beamed with pride, standing on the jagged wall next to Mom. If he was living, I was sure as shinola he'd fall off and break a hip.

"At least you could've worn a pair of nice pants." Distaste for my sheriff's uniform was apparent in the tone in Mama's voice. "At least let Finn Vincent see you in something girly." Her nose twitched. "Well, I'm glad you decided to wear a little makeup."

My eyes lowered and for a moment I thought I'd threaten to arrest her. Only what she was doing wasn't grounds for a charge. I let out a deep sigh and patted my leg for Duke to follow.

I put the sound of Mama's amplified voice in the back of my head and walked up to the stage where the summer concert series was held. It was all decorated with red, white, and blue balloons, an enlarged photo of Duke that I'd given them, and a podium. Behind the podium there were four folding chairs.

Mayor Ryland and City Clerk Doolittle Bowman stood next to the stage, going over the ceremony. When they saw me, Doolittle waved Duke and me over.

"Now," she looked down her long nose at me and then at Duke, "I'm going to say a few words before I introduce the Mayor, who will then say a few words before he gives Duke the honorary medal."

"Sounds good." I nodded.

When we turned back around, almost all of the folding chairs were already filled. It was so nice seeing all the citizens of Cottonwood come out and support not only Duke, but the sheriff's department.

"The seats are for me, the mayor, you, and Officer Vincent,"

Doolittle pointed out. "You and Duke can sit at the end so he'll have room."

I nodded again. Off in the distance, Finn and Betty were making their way through the crowd that was getting larger by the minute. Betty just shoved her way through, while poor Finn was stopped by every woman in the county. They all had big grins planted on their faces and goo-goo eyes. I couldn't blame them. The likes of him wasn't around these parts—that was why Mama was so desperate to hook Finn and me up.

"Are you Sheriff Lowry?" A woman, with her hair pulled back in a low ponytail wearing a black skirt suit that practically hung off her shoulders and a pair of brown-rimmed glasses, stared at me.

"Yes. I'm the sheriff." I smiled to try and break the serious look on her face.

"I'm Cecily Hoover. I left a message with Betty Murphy for you to call me." She used the pad of her forefinger to push the glasses up on the bridge of her nose. "We need to talk about the security for the Stone estate."

"Betty did give me the message, but I had to be here first." I glanced over her shoulder and noticed everyone had taken their places on the stage, including Duke, who was next to Finn. "Do you mind if we talk about this after the ceremony?"

"Actually, it'll only take a few minutes." She blinked rapidly. "I need to make sure someone stays at the house twenty-four seven until the auction. The secret manuscript will be sought after, and I'm afraid it might be stolen."

"Stolen?" I asked. "A book?"

"Hello, Sheriff." Paige and Lonnie Lemar walked past us. Both of them looked at Cecily and me.

"Good morning," I said, finding it odd that Lonnie wanted to come to a ceremony where my dog was getting an award.

Cecily cleared her throat.

"I'm sorry. About the book," I encouraged her to continue.

"It's not just any book," she whispered, shifting her eyes side to side. "It's a tell-all that probably shouldn't see the light of day."

"A tell-all about people around here?" I questioned and she slowly nodded.

"Yes." There was a mysterious tone to her voice.

"Exactly who are you?" I asked.

"I'm Cecily Hoover, Beryle's assistant. Was her assistant." Her eyes watered. She swallowed hard. She sucked in a deep breath to get her emotions under control and said, "The book?"

"Why don't you go get it then?" I asked what seemed like a logical question and a reasonable way to solve the issue.

"I don't know where it is." Her eyebrows arched above her glasses.

"If you don't know, then how are people supposed to buy it?" I asked.

"I don't think anyone should buy it since the publisher technically owns it. This way the estate won't have to pay back the advance, and the money can go to the charities." Her lids covered half of her eyes.

"This warrants you wanting some security?" I questioned again.

"Beryle said that if it got into the wrong hands before it was sent off to her editor, then some bad things could happen..." Her voice trailed off.

"Have you seen it?" I asked.

"Yes. But she has hidden it or something. I can't find it anywhere." Stella and I both looked over at the stage when the speakers screeched as Doolittle took the podium. "I've heard rumblings that people know about it. Her words about it getting into the wrong hands really have me worried that someone is going to come looking for it before we can find it." She drew her hands up to the string around her neck and fiddled with the key that dangled from it.

It was one of those keys that I'd seen teenagers wear as jewelry.

"The estate sale is in a few days. Surely that's enough time to find a book," I said, wondering what secrets Beryle Stone was hiding since she really didn't live here most of her life. "Besides, why are you taking it upon yourself to find it when Ruby Smith is the executor? I mean, she is after all Beryle's third cousin or something."

Carefully I watched her body language. It was one of my favorite classes taught at the academy. One's body language told me a lot more than the words that came out of their mouth. Cecily Hoover knew more than she was telling me.

"Sheriff Kenni Lowry," Doolittle's voice echoed over the speakers bolted to a tripod on each side of the stage, "and Duke."

The crowd clapped.

"I'll meet you at the estate when I'm finished here. In about an hour or so." I waved my hand in the air letting her know give or take a few minutes. I'd find that book come hell or high water.

"I'll be there." She stared at me.

"Sheriff Kenni Lowry," Doolittle said with a little more oomph in her voice, "and Duke."

I walked past Cecily.

"Don't wait too long. We're running out of time." Cecily Hoover's words hit the back of my neck and pricked it with goosebumps.

I stepped up onstage and waved to the crowd before taking my seat next to Finn. Duke came over and sat down next to me. Doolittle introduced Mayor Ryland.

"Who is that?" Finn's shoulder leaned close to me.

"Cecily Hoover." My eyes gazed over the tops of the crowd's heads until they stopped at Cecily.

She crossed her arms and leaned up against a tree. She looked as if she was looking for someone. A couple of times her head bobbed to the right and left as if she seen something that'd piqued her interest.

"It's with great pleasure," Mayor Ryland said, though I knew it was killing him to give Duke this award when he was behind Lonnie Lemar coming out of retirement to run against me, "I am here to give the Paws of Distinction Award to Duke."

The crowd clapped and was brought to their feet when I stood up and Duke stood up next to me. He followed me up to the podium, where I gave him the command that Finn had recently taught him.

"Shhh." I ordered him to stay still while Mayor Ryland Velcro-ed the ribbon with the medal dangling on the end to his collar. What he really wanted was the treat I'd taken out of my pocket.

The mayor and I shook hands with Duke sitting pretty between us.

"Look here, Sheriff, Mayor." Edna Easterly from the *Cottonwood Chronicle* stood at the edge of the stage with her camera pointed at Duke and me. She had on a brown fedora with a big orange feather hot glued to the side of it. There was an index card with the word PRESS written with a black Sharpie. Her hunter-green vest looked like something she'd gotten from the Tractor Supply store in the fishing section. She had pens and notebooks hanging out of every pocket. "Smile for the camera."

A few clicks later and a couple more congratulations, I scanned the crowd for Cecily while Duke basked in the lavish rubs of hands and a few scratches behind his ears along with some treats from the treat jar sitting on the stage in his honor.

Edna had even separated Duke from me to get a few photos alone. I swear he looked like he was smiling.

I looked over and saw Cecily and Darby Gray on the other side of the rock fence standing on the sidewalk.

"Do you understand me?" Darby stood nose to nose with Cecily, who surprisingly didn't back down. "This town has a right to know before some outsider buys it!" Darby's voice escalated.

Cecily thrust her arms to her sides, palms fisted. "Neither you nor anyone else in this town are going to get your hands on her manuscript. It belongs to the publisher."

Darby leaned in. I couldn't hear what she said, but her lips were moving and her jaw was tense.

"Over my dead body!" Cecily turned on the balls of her feet and stalked down the sidewalk.

Chapter Five

The higher-than-normal-pitched conversation between Darby Gray and Cecily Hoover quickly stole the spotlight from Duke. But it didn't stop Mama from taking her spot on top of the stone wall with the megaphone up to her mouth while Daddy stood next to her handing out the *Vote For Lowry* pins. While everyone hung around to get a photo of Duke before they headed over to the church undercroft for the reception, I walked over to get a cup of coffee from Jolee.

"What was all of that about?" Jolee asked Lonnie and Paige Lemar, who just so happened to be in front of me in line.

"I don't know. One thing I do know is that we need more law and order in this town." Lonnie's chin twisted to touch his shoulder, making sure I noticed him and what he'd said. "I'm telling you that I know how to stop those types of disorderly conducts and it's not by just ignoring them."

Paige Lemar grabbed the two cups of coffee and gestured for Lonnie to move along.

"Lonnie, Paige," I said. "Have a wonderful day."

"I have a feeling this town is going a little nuts." Jolee pointed to the side door of her food truck and left her part-time worker to tend to the line of customers.

Duke and I met her over there and she gave him a treat, like she always did, and gave me a cup of coffee.

"I gave you the extra strong blend. I figured you might need it today." She bent down and gave Duke a nice rub behind the ears before she took a look at his medal. "Look at you getting your own award."

"Thanks for the coffee," I said after she stood back up. "You're right. Everyone is talking about the Stone estate. I haven't heard anything about Beryle Stone in years."

"She went into hiding years ago after her big novel was made into that movie. She said she didn't like the spotlight." Jolee tugged the hairnet off of her blonde hair, letting it fall down around her freckled face, making her green eyes stand out even more.

"How do you know that?" I asked.

"The smut magazines in the checkout line at Dixon's Foodtown." Jolee loved those tabloid magazines.

"Puh-leeze." I rolled my eyes.

"I've heard that this tell-all has some secrets that will embarrass a very prominent person in the community. I'd love to get my hands on it. If it's half as good as her novels, it'll be a bestseller." She rubbed her hands together. "Apparently she was close to finishing it. She'd been living here for a couple of months without anyone knowing."

"That was in the magazine too?" My brows furrowed.

"Edna Easterly." Jolee nodded back towards the park.

I looked around, and there was Edna, with her pen in one hand and her notebook in the other, jotting down all sort of notes as Ruby Smith flapped her lips.

"She said that after she heard they were having the estate sale, she began to look into Beryle Stone's past. She claims some things don't add up around here and she's going to get to the bottom of it." Jolee smirked and tossed her hair over her shoulder. "I just don't know why people can't leave the dead alone."

"Me either." My brows knitted in a frown. "Me either."

I looked over at Poppa. He stood next to Mama with a big smile on his face. Seeing him made me a little nervous. It wasn't that I didn't love being with his ghost. I did. I'd take any way to see him since his death, but I couldn't help but shake the feeling there was a reason he was here. Only because the past few times I'd seen him, it was due to the fact he was here to help me solve a murder. There weren't any murders in Cottonwood right now, and something made me think there was a shoe about to drop. Whose shoe?

I looked around at the crowd.

I patted my leg. "Come on, Duke."

"You know, it's probably all gossip like most stuff around here," Jolee said. "We only have four days until the estate is sold and all is said and done. After that, the henny-hens will move on to something or someone else."

"I'm afraid this might be a long four days," I said, looking back over to where Edna had been replaced by Mama, Lulu, Mrs. Kim, and Toots Buford, all of them talking at once and probably over the others.

The fall sun was slowly disappearing behind a gray cloud, adding a light breeze. The chill wasn't just in the air, it was also deep in my bones.

"I'll see you over at the reception." Jolee disappeared back into her truck and gave one last call for fresh coffee.

After a short drive back down to Main Street, Duke and I, along with Poppa, parked in the church parking lot. Stella was on the sidewalk in front of the steps that led down to the undercroft directing everyone where to go, as if people didn't already know.

"For he's a jolly good fellow," the people who'd already gathered at the reception sang when Duke and I walked in.

Tibbie Bell and Katy Lee, another good friend of mine, greeted us with a bone-shaped cake. They set it on the ground in front of Duke, and he didn't waste any time gobbling it up.

"Patty's Pet Pantry," Tibbie said, pushing back her brown hair behind her shoulder. Katy Lee stood next to her smiling. She wore her long blonde hair in loose curls that cascaded down her back, giving me hair envy. It was easiest for work that I kept my shoulder-length honey blonde hair up in a ponytail.

"Patty did a great job," I said and couldn't help but laugh when Duke looked up, green food coloring on his nose.

Patty Dunaway was the local animal expert. She was a dog walker and she boarded animals, baked treats, and sold fun animal items in her boutique store.

"The human cake is over there." Tibbie pointed in the direction of the tables that were lined with food where the Sweet Adelines had taken their posts to serve.

I moseyed over to the tables and took a look at the food. The room was filled with chatter and laughter. I got a few nods and confirmations that I had people's votes as I passed by. I nodded and smiled and let Duke have his day. I couldn't help but notice Darby had a filled plate and was sitting at a table in the back. She was alone, probably not for long, so I took the opportunity and walked over to her.

"Thank you for coming." I sat down across from her. Her plate of food sure did look good.

"I wouldn't've missed it for the world." She used the edge of her fork to cut a piece of the Derby Pie before she stabbed it with the tines. "Duke is a good boy." She lifted the fork in the air, the piece of pie dangling. "He saved you, didn't he?"

I smiled. "That he did."

There was no sense in beating around the bush, and she might tell me to jump off a bridge since it was really not my business, but I wanted to know. After all, it was my job to keep the peace. At least that was how I justified being nosy.

"Do you know Cecily Hoover?" I asked and folded my hands, placing them on the table in front of me.

"Cecily who?" she asked without making eye contact with me.

"Cecily Hoover," I said again and couldn't help but notice how she used the fork to move the food around on her plate.

"Nope. Don't know her."

"Really?" I asked and leaned back in my chair. "Because it sure did look like you knew her at the ceremony."

"Is that her name?" Darby put her fork down.

"Don't let me stop you from eating." I looked at her fork.

"I've lost my appetite." She pushed the Derby Pie away from

her. "Why are you asking me about that woman? Did I do something wrong?"

"No." I shrugged. "I just want to make sure everything goes smooth with the estate sale. She notified me that she's worried about something going wrong, so I'm just following up on what I'm seeing."

"You didn't see anything. I asked her a question about the sale and she didn't want to answer. That's it." Darby stood up and grabbed her plate. "Have a good day, Sheriff."

My eyes narrowed as I watched Darby walk away. She chucked her plate in the garbage and headed out the door. I'd definitely hit a nerve.

"What was that about?" Finn asked, putting a piece of cake down in front of me.

He pulled out the chair next to me and sat down with his own piece of cake.

"Thanks." I dragged the plate to me. "I needed this." I took a bite and let it melt in my mouth. I sucked in a deep breath through my nose. "I don't know what that was about, but I do intend to find out."

"Does this have to do with the estate sale?" he asked.

"I think so. I'm not sure, but Cecily Hoover was adamant that we needed to have security because she claims there's a tell-all manuscript out there that will spill town secrets." I chewed on my words. "Cecily said that she didn't know where it was."

"Has she read it?" Finn asked a really good question.

"She said Beryle wouldn't let anyone read or see it. I told her I'd come out to visit her at the estate." I tapped the table with the butt end of my fork.

"Do you want me to go out there with you?" he asked.

"Nah. You stay around here in case Betty needs you." I stood up. "I'm going to go on over to the Stone place and see what exactly this Cecily knows."

"Great idea, Kenni-bug," Poppa appeared and called me by my nickname. "I just left there. Maybe two sets of eyes will be better than one, because I didn't see much. Definitely lived in."

I shivered.

"Are you getting sick?" Finn asked.

"No. Why? Do I look pale?" I put my hand on my forehead and realized I probably didn't apply my makeup right.

"No, you look great. But you shivered," Finn said.

I was a little taken aback that he noticed such a small action.

"Did I?" I tried to play it off since the shivers were caused by the appearance of Poppa. I swear I felt it in my gut that something was wrong. "I'm good. I'm out of here."

Duke and I thanked everyone for coming and said our goodbyes as we made our way out of the undercroft and out into the drizzling rain.

"I'm glad the rain held off," Poppa said once we'd gotten in the Wagoneer. "Now let's go find that tell-all."

"Do you know anything about it?" I asked. "Maybe you do and that's why you are here. So we can prevent it from seeing the light of day."

"I don't know anything about a tell-all. Beryle and I were friends, but I never read a thing she wrote." Poppa completely blew my theory up. "Maybe I'm here to help prevent a crime, like I did before you saw me."

That was possible. During my first few years as sheriff there was zero crime. It wasn't until I saw Poppa's ghost that he told me that he'd been scaring off any would-be robbers and criminals, until there were two crimes committed at once. Even ghosts couldn't be in two places at once.

Maybe he was here to make sure everything went smoothly with Beryle's estate since they were friends. It was true, we didn't know all the rules or even if there were rules about his being here. He only knew that he was here to be a guardian while I was sheriff and he just so happened to be around whenever there was a murder. An uneasy feeling curled deep in my gut. He was there for a reason. For someone. But who?

Chapter Six

The Stone estate was just a couple of acres over from the Inn. The actual property was probably going to bring in a couple million dollars. It was prime real estate that not only had land, but also a nice view of the river.

The trees this time of year were beautiful, but the tree line next to the river where the trees fed off the rich limestone was gorgeous. It was like a painted picture with the vibrant fall colors of orange, yellows, reds, and deep purples.

"It was nice going by there earlier since it's been a few years. Brought back a lot of memories." Poppa straightened his shirtsleeves as he shifted around the passenger seat to get comfortable, forcing Duke to jump in the back. "I'd forgotten how pretty the drive up to the house was."

He was right. The large oak trees stood like soldiers lining the black-topped drive, at least twelve deep on each side.

"I bet it sure is pretty when the sun shines," I noted, thinking about the dreary day.

"It's gorgeous." Poppa leaned back as he told me about a memory. "This was Beryle Stone's family house. Her parents were gone a lot with her younger sister, who sadly passed away when we were seniors in high school." The edges of Poppa's lips turned down as if he were remembering the sad event. "Anyways, we used to play tag right along these trees. Freeze tag was what we called it."

"I played freeze tag with my friends." I had forgotten all about that childhood game where we ran around and the person who was "it" tagged you and you had to freeze in place. The only way to get unfrozen and back in the game was when someone who wasn't "it" crawled through your legs.

The memory brought a smile to my face, matching Poppa's smile. I enjoyed listening to his stories.

"How did her sister die?" I asked. It was the first I'd ever heard that there was another Stone sister.

"You know," Poppa shrugged, "I really don't know. We were teenagers and Beryle never really wanted to talk about it. The only thing she did say was that her sister was considered mentally slow. But I thought she seemed like a little sister."

"That's so sad." I couldn't imagine the pain the family had gone through losing someone so young.

"We had a lot of fun growing up." Poppa's eyes drew up to the large white brick house that was covered in crawling ivy. Most of the shingles were off the roof. The large water fountain in the middle of the circular driveway had pretty much deteriorated and was in shambles. The weeds and bushes next to the house had grown up past the front windows. The barn, a little distance away from the house, was literally caving in on itself.

It was a shame. I'd heard how beautiful it was in its time when it was kept up.

"Beryle left Cottonwood after we graduated. At her daddy's funeral, I asked her about the estate. She said she'd keep it but wouldn't be returning to live here because there were just too many memories. By that time, she'd gotten famous and there was really nothing left here for her. At least that's what she said." He tipped his chin my way. "Even though I never read anything she wrote, I loved listening to her stories. She knew how to tell some doozies. You never knew if she was telling you a fib or the truth." He shook his bony finger at me. "Once she wrote to me telling me that her editor said there was a fine line Beryle had between reality and fiction that made a good writer. I guess that editor was right."

I noticed a car parked in the front along with the box truck that Ruby Smith used to transport antiques to and from her shop. I parked the Wagoneer next to it.

Two burly men were coming out the front door carrying a chest of drawers and heading towards the truck.

"It sure doesn't look like someone's been living here." I opened the door and got out. "Come on, Duke."

Most times I didn't take Duke into people's houses if I didn't know them or thought they'd mind, but with the condition this house was in, Duke was just fine to go in with me. Especially if Cecily really did sense some sort of danger, it was good to have Duke by my side.

I rested my hand on my holster and pushed the cracked front door open with the toe of my shoe. "Hello, Cecily?"

Duke stood next to me. The fur on the back of his neck stood up a little more than normal.

"I hear some voices." Poppa ghosted himself through the door and into the house.

I waited for a minute and when he didn't come back, I waited a moment longer in hope he'd warn me of any danger. We were still getting used to each other and how we worked as a team in the ghost deputy, human sheriff department. So far we were working out the kinks, but like any new working relationship, it was going to take some time and probably a lot more cases.

I took the first step over the threshold and Duke followed alongside. The dim chandelier hanging from the ceiling added some light and had a little help from the matching sconces dotting each side of the long narrow hallway. The wood floors creaked with each step we took. Poppa's head stuck out from an opening down the hall a little, and he gestured for me to come there.

Surprisingly, the house was in great shape. In fact, much better shape than the outside. I looked into a couple of the rooms as I walked down the hallway and noticed the upgraded lighting and furniture. It did look like someone had been living there.

"I'm not going to say a word," the familiar voice of Cecily Hoover came from the room where Poppa's ghost had stuck his head out.

"You have to tell me where the manuscript is. I'm the executor and I want to get as much money for Beryle's charities as possible. Nowhere in the paperwork is it stated that you are to have a job, so you can gather your belongings and get out," Ruby Smith demanded.

I stood in the hallway to listen in before I made my presence known.

"Beryle Stone didn't want it that way, and that's the way it's going to stay. The manuscript will go to the publisher." Cecily's voice hardened. "I'm going to stay until the end of the sale to make sure the editor gets it."

"Let me tell you something, missy." Fire was brewing in Ruby and making her ill-tempered. I knew that she was boiling inside because she didn't call anyone missy unless she was about to blow. "Around these parts we take care of our people. I don't know about that New York attitude you got, but it ain't gonna fly around here."

Ruby's accent was coming out like it did when she was angry.

"If you think for one minute that I'm gonna let you and anyone else in this town disrespect Beryle's legacy and what she wanted to do with that manuscript, then you have another thing coming. Do you understand me?" Cecily said.

Ruby threatened back, "I will stop this estate sale with one call to Wally Lamb. So get out of my way because I'm going to tear this house to shreds to find the manuscript with or without your help."

My eyes rolled skyward. I should've known that Ruby would use Wally Lamb as her attorney. If it had anything to do with money, Wally Lamb was knee deep in it.

"You will find that manuscript over my dead body," Cecily said, followed up with the sounds of a little shuffling.

"Alright, Duke. Let's get into this one." I gave Duke the go-ahead to enter. When there was an "over my dead body" threat being thrown out, I figured I might as well make my presence known. "Hi, ladies," I greeted them just before the two of them put their hands on each other.

Both of them turned, wide-eyed with their mouths gaped open at the sight of me.

"I'm sorry if I startled y'all." I smiled and walked into the room. "Oh." I took a step back. "Did I walk in on a private conversation?"

"No, no." Ruby shook her head. "I'm here to take inventory of some of the antiques since I'm the executor. I need to know what exactly is going to go up for sale and what is going to go to the antique shop for another fund Beryle had set up. I've got some of my workers here to take some items now so the buyers who are already in town can come down to the shop and look."

"And I was helping her." Cecily planted the fakest smile. Like those ones you see on the Miss America pageant contestants.

"It didn't sound like either of you were helping each other." I looked between them.

"We have an understanding." Ruby nodded, her nose crunched when she smiled. "Cecily, it was nice to meet you. I'm sure you will enjoy your stay at the Inn." The soles of Ruby's flat shoes clicked across the hardwood floor. "Kenni." She nodded on her way out of the door, but not without petting the top of Duke's head first.

I sucked in a deep breath and waited until I heard Ruby's shoes off a good distance. I couldn't help but notice that Cecily looked fried.

"I thought you were staying here." I recalled her telling me she was when we were at the ceremony.

"I am." Her words were as flat as the look on her face. "I'm just glad you're here so you can keep an eye on the place." She brushed her hands together and took a few steps toward me as if she was going to walk out the door.

"Wait a second." I put my hand out before she made it past me. "I'm not here to watch over anything. I'm here to take the secret manuscript and take it to my office for safekeeping. I don't think anyone will try to come into the sheriff's office to steal anything."

"I told you earlier I don't know where it is," Cecily said. "I don't know where Beryle put it."

"I know I asked you earlier, but did you physically see the

manuscript?" I asked, feeling as if I'd just wasted my time driving out here. "Are you sure it's even real?"

"Yes, it's real. She worked on it every day. I saw her working on it." Cecily drew her lips together. "She didn't tell me what was in it, and she didn't let me see it. She just said that she had to tell her story."

"Did she tell you her story?" I asked.

"No." Cecily didn't seem to offer any information unless I dragged it out of her.

"You said you were her assistant. What exactly did you do for her?" I asked.

"I've been with her for five years now. I traveled with her. I lived with her, mainly to keep her company. I know what her wishes were, and I'm asking you to help me keep this place secure until we can find it," Cecily said.

"Like I said earlier, there are only a couple of people in our department; I'm not sure if I can spare the resources. You can call in a security service. I'm trying to assess the danger." I twisted around. "There doesn't seem to be anyone here beating down the door. Ruby Smith is just doing her duties as executor."

"Beryle never mentioned her. I was surprised when Mr. Lamb told me about her."

"How long have you been here?" I asked.

"A couple of months," she said.

I took a seat next to her, but Duke stayed at the door. "You are asking for the sheriff's help. You are trying to evade any questions I ask in order to make an informed decision on whether or not to send someone here because of a supposed manuscript. You're going to have to give me something to make me believe someone is going to come here and steal it."

"I told Beryle I'd keep her secret safe, but now that's she gone..." Her voice broke. "From what I could tell, she was healthy and happy. She'd been working on a tell-all because she said that she needed money and this book would be her biggest yet. She had a meeting set up with her publisher in a week to discuss the book and her advance."

"I thought she had plenty of money," I said.

"I thought so too, but when she told me she needed money, I didn't ask why. It wasn't my place. My salary came from her publisher. She was a very private woman. And when she died in her sleep, I just couldn't believe it. I called her lawyer, and he looked at all of the requests she'd put in her will and has carried them out. I'm just here until after the estate sale." A tear trickled down her cheek.

"How did she act over the past week or so?" I asked.

"She was happy. Happy about living back here. She'd take long walks and disappear for hours. Happy about this book. That's when she insisted on fixing up the house and changing things around. It was a lot of fun. We painted a few rooms and brought some of her old furniture back to life. I showed her Pinterest and we got some ideas from there. She didn't want anyone to know she was here, so she sent me to get all the materials."

"Why didn't she want anyone to know? Her friends would've loved to see her." It was a burning question, unless Beryle had put something really terrible in her tell-all that would prevent her from wanting to face her friends.

"I don't think she had many friends." Poppa appeared next to the window. "She wasn't a busybody like the rest of the old women our age. She was a good person. I'm not sure what her big secret was about."

I tried to keep my attention on Cecily as Poppa kept yammering on.

"She was in the early stages of doing a big book release here after it was published. She was going to announce her retirement and that she was moving back to Cottonwood full-time." Cecily sat on the couch with her legs crossed. "She talked about how this house inspired her to write when she was a young adult. She loved Cottonwood so much that she wanted to come back and live the rest of her life here. She said she had a lot here, but from what I could tell, it's just this house."

She gulped. A tear fell from the corner of her right eye. She reached up and wiped it away.

"Even the small memorial service didn't do her justice." Her voice cracked.

"It was so hush-hush." I said.

"Yes." She nodded and pushed a tear to the side of her face. "It was her wish to just have Preacher Bing say a little eulogy."

"It's just like Beryle to want to go out peacefully and quietly. She was such a wonderful person." Poppa ghosted himself into the room. "She never bothered anyone."

"When did you say that Beryle died?" I needed to know for sure. I was definitely going to the church to see what they knew. I was sure Stella knew more than she was letting on.

"It'll be a week tomorrow," Cecily said.

She reached over to the end table next to the couch and took something out of the drawer. She handed me what looked to be a memorial card to honor Beryle's life.

"Would you like a cup of coffee?" she asked and stood up.

"That'd be great." I looked down at the memorial card after she'd left the room. Poppa stood over me. "Would she really not want a funeral?" I whispered to him.

"She was pretty private. She never had a lot of friends, she never gossiped, and she never went to the school events. She just wanted to hang at her house."

"Then what in the world is in her supposed tell-all that would need to be protected until it's sold?" There was something that didn't add up.

"I have no idea. We didn't keep in touch that much. She would send me a postcard from here or there, but she rarely came back to Cottonwood, that I know of." Poppa went to the opposite side of the room when Cecily came back in.

She was carrying a tray with two ceramic mugs and a carafe of coffee along with some creamer and sugar.

I handed her the memorial card in exchange for the coffee mug.

"Anyone else at the memorial that you might've forgotten?" I asked taking a sip of the black coffee.

"Cream? Sugar?" I waved her off. She fixed her coffee and answered, "It was me, the preacher, and her editor, who flew in and out for it."

"And you really don't know what she was writing?" I asked.

"I told you, no. In fact, her editor asked me if I knew where it was. She said that Beryle never let her read it either. They'd given her an advance based on her track record."

"You didn't find it?" I asked and took another drink, trying to read her body language to see if she was lying.

"Why do you keep asking me this? I told you earlier and just a few minutes ago that I have no clue where it's at and that I need security." Cecily was getting a little testy from my friendly interrogation.

"I have to make sure there's a real need for me or my deputy to provide some sort of security." My instinct told me that she wasn't lying.

She curled her bottom lip under her front teeth. Her eyes darted between mine nervously. "I'm afraid that Beryle might've been murdered."

"Murdered?" I asked, my voice high-pitched. She caught me off guard.

"Murdered?" Poppa stood in shock. "Who would want to murder her?"

"I just have a feeling." Cecily put her hand flat on her stomach. "She was healthy, but she suddenly dies in her sleep?"

"Sheriff Lowry, you there?" Betty Murphy's voice chirped through the walkie-talkie.

I held a finger up to Cecily and excused myself into the hall.

I pushed the button on the side of the walkie-talkie strapped to my shoulder. "Go ahead, Betty."

"There is an emergency on Walnut Street." Her voice escalated with each word.

"Can you tell Deputy Vincent to take care of it? I'm out at the

Stone estate." It was nice to be able to count on another deputy to help out.

"I'm sorry, Kenni. I already sent Finn to the Graves' place where there was a trespasser," Betty said. "I think you better hurry. It's a gun-slingin' from what I can get from the girl."

"Gun slinging?" I asked. "I'm on my way." I clicked off the walkie-talkie and poked my head back in the room. "Duke." I patted my leg and Duke came. "Cecily, I'll have to come back either tonight or tomorrow to figure out what we can do about this missing manuscript. And this accusation of Beryle Stone being murdered."

There was no time to hear Cecily's complaining. After rushing out of the house, Duke jumped in the Wagoneer before me. I rolled down the window.

I grabbed the old beacon police light from underneath my seat and licked the suction cup and stuck it to the roof off the Jeep.

"There's a gun slinging going on in town." I pulled the gearshift into drive and peeled out of the driveway, but not without looking in the rearview mirror, where there was a very unhappy Cecily Hoover staring back at me. Poppa was next to her, staring at her with his ghost eyes.

I shivered.

Chapter Seven

The rattle of the Wagoneer didn't dislodge the image of Poppa's eyes from my mind, nor did the blaring siren or the blue and white flashing lights that danced in the shadows of the fall-colored trees that lined the old country road on my way back into town. Heck, not even the thought of dueling neighbors had my blood stirred as much as Poppa's stare.

Still, I had a job to do, and neither Cecily nor Poppa had committed any sort of crime. The feelings I was having were probably just unanswered questions that I left behind after Betty called me.

Just like a small town, the cars on the road in front of me pulled over to let me pass, but not without speeding behind me once I'd passed them so they could keep up and get to the scene to see exactly what was going on. It shouldn't have annoyed me like it did because my dad used to do the same thing with me in the car. If a firetruck or Poppa passed with their lights on and the siren blaring, we followed right behind, anticipating what happened just so we could gossip about it later.

Instead of taking Main Street all the way into town—I knew all the downtown shops would be busy with the tourist and supper crowd—I took a right on Chestnut and a quick left on York until I made the right turn onto Walnut. I didn't have to try and figure out exactly where the dueling neighbors were located since there was a small crowd gathered in the yard and right in the middle was my mama yapping in that dang bullhorn.

I pulled up to the scene and put the Wagoneer in park. The dispute was between Daryl Young and Gilly Bates, both young men and both completely political. It wasn't a secret which candidates they were each backing. The billboard signs told me.

"Get him, Gilly!" Mama shouted, standing next to a *Vote for Lowry* sign that was as big as the *Welcome to Cottonwood* sign that sat on the edge of town.

"I'll shoot. I'm a law-abiding, gun-toting citizen." Daryl Young, who just so happened to be Lonnie's grandson, stood next to the sign pointing his rifle at it. He jerked his hand up in the air. "I've got my permit right here."

"You stay," I instructed Duke. The last thing I needed was for him to get in the way and get shot. I stuck my hand out of the window and flipped the old beacon siren, something else I'd gotten from Poppa besides the love of keeping the law.

The path of nosy neighbors parted.

"What's going on, fellas?" I stopped next to Mama and grabbed her megaphone right out of her jeweled fingers.

"I'll be. You don't treat your mama that way," she scolded me.

"Sheriff, I'm sorry, but you know I ain't for you. I'm for my pappy, and this here zealot said I was going against the church by voting for him." Daryl was at least trying to be respectful. "Then he went and got this big billboard from her." His pointer finger jutted toward Mama. "Who just so happened to have it delivered."

Huffs and puffs came out of Mama's mouth as it opened and closed before she finally decided it was best to keep it shut.

"Shush, Mama." I swung a glare at her that told her to behave. "I'm sorry, Daryl. Please go on."

"Then I politely asked him if he wouldn't mind moving the sign a little more toward his house so I could see down the street and wave at my neighbors walking by from my porch swing." Daryl pointed to all the locations he was referring to. "He refused, so I called up my pappy and he had a sign delivered."

I glanced over at the sign. It said *Committed to Making Cottonwood Safe* with a big photo of old Lonnie Lemar on it. A groan escaped Mama's lips and I gave her another you-better-be-quiet look.

"If he thinks my wife wants to look at his puckered-up face every morning when we have coffee on our porch, he has another thing coming to him." Gilly gestured between him and his wife with Mama nodding profusely beside them, a look of disgust on her face.

"I can't help it that she didn't put her mug on her signs." Daryl pointed to me. "Not that you ain't pretty, Kenni. It's all politics."

"Thank you, Daryl, but I'm not here to be political. I'm just here to do my job." I looked back at Gilly's wife. "Darlene, you got some coffee on?"

She nodded.

"Why don't you go on in and grab a couple of cups for me and the guys here. Everyone else is going to go home since there's nothing to see here," I said to the crowd, shooing them away.

Darlene rushed up her steps and inside her house.

"Now, Gilly, you go on and put your gun in the house, and you do the same, Daryl," I instructed both men, who eyed each other to see who was going to move first. "Go on now," I encouraged them. Out of one corner of my eye I saw Finn pulling up, and out of the other eye I saw Mama trying to sneak up Gilly's front porch steps.

"Mama, you go on home and I'll deal with you later." I wagged a finger at her.

"Kenni, you don't go treating your mama that way in front of the whole town." I didn't know how she did it. She scolded me with words that sounded as sweet as a canary's song with the prettiest smile on her face.

"Mama, don't make me put you in the back of that Wagoneer and haul you down to Cowboy's Catfish where I'll put you in that cell and leave you all night long," I warned.

No way did I try to disguise my words with a smile and a happy tone.

"I birthed you." She cocked a brow.

"You did a mighty fine job." Finn walked up behind us.

"You staying for coffee?" Darlene asked Finn from the porch.

"Yes, ma'am, I'd love a cup." Finn took his hat off his head and mussed up his hair.

"Mama, you've outdone yourself with this little fiasco. You're going to be the reason I don't get elected if you keep acting crazy." I took her by the elbow to escort her to her car.

She jerked her arm away and trotted off at a show horse's pace. I didn't have the time or energy to keep up with her. I hated to admit it, but Mama had more energy than a two-year-old child. I stood there and watched to make sure she got into her car and drove down the road. Away from me.

"You come on by Ben's for some of my beans and cornbread special," she called out the window. "Toodles!" She waved her fingers in the air before pushing the gas pedal.

"I see everything is under control," Finn said after I'd walked back up to the porch, where everyone seemed to be sitting and enjoying the coffee Darlene had fixed.

"We'll see here in a minute." I walked up the steps and took the warm cup of coffee from Darlene.

"If I remember, you like a couple scoops of creamer." She smiled, knowing that she had it exactly right. "Have you a seat before you burn yourself."

"You do make great coffee." I took a sip and sighed loud enough so she knew I enjoyed that first sip. "This coffee is good to warm me up on a cold day."

I leaned on the railing and situated my hip so I faced both men.

"Gilly, I appreciate the support." I looked at him and then turned to Daryl. "I appreciate your right to vote for whoever you want, but in this case," I lifted the cup to my lips and took another sip, "both of you are going to have to take down your signs."

"What if I don't?" Gilly blew up like a puffer fish, but settled down when Darlene tapped his shoulder.

"Then you're breaking the law and I'd have to take you to jail," I stated simply. "Your sign is against Cottonwood's sign regulations, which you should know, because if I remember correctly, you were a good campaign manager for my poppa. And campaign signs can only be eight feet wide and two feet high."

"And you have a damn billboard," Daryl scoffed.

"So do you!" Gilly's chin and chest jutted out.

"Settle down." I took another sip to give them a minute to stew. "If you agree to take these signs down by tonight, I won't fine either of you."

"How much is the fine?" Daryl asked.

"I don't know, but I can ask Betty Murphy right now or haul you on down to the jail." My voice was stern.

"Fine." Gilly crossed his arms across his chest. "But I like my sign."

"Do you still have that farm on the south side of town?" I asked Gilly.

"I sure do," he answered with pride. "Got the best deer hunting stand out there you ever saw."

"Your sign can go out there," I suggested. "The law states that there can't be a sign that large in a city or neighborhood yard. And Daryl, you can put your sign out on your mom and dad's property." I wanted to make sure I could give them both options. "We've all been friends and neighbors for a long time, and I know better than anyone that elections are very personal. But it will come and go. Our friendships are what's important."

I did the best lying through my teeth I could. It took everything in my body not to pull my own gun out and put bullet holes in Lonnie's sign, but since I was the law, I had better abide by it.

There was a faint grin on Finn's lips as he stayed on the bottom step sipping his warm coffee.

"Gilly," Darlene was soft spoken, "I think Kenni is right. Now you go on out there and take the sign down." She patted him on the back to encourage him.

Gilly stood up and gave Daryl a nice long stare.

"Go on." Darlene nudged him.

He reached down for his tool bag and grabbed a wrench, then took his sweet time walking over to the billboard. Daryl set his cup on the floor next to the rocker and placed both hands on the rocker arms, pushing himself up to stand.

"Well, I guess I can go take mine down too." He turned to Darlene and said, "Thank you, Darlene. Your coffee was as good as ever."

"You are welcome." Darlene smiled. "You know, we've been neighbors for a few years and have had a lot of fun. I'm glad we got this solved."

"Me too." He returned her smile. "Sheriff." He nodded.

"Thank you, Daryl." I held my hand out for a nice firm handshake before he too headed to his house to take down the billboard of Lonnie's face.

"I think my work here is done," I said. "I've taken up enough of your time."

"Nah. I knew Gilly was going to make Daryl mad. They'd been arguing for days on why we shouldn't be voting for you, but Gilly loves your mama and daddy so much that he won't even think to hear of any nonsense about you not being sheriff," Darlene said.

"We are very lucky we have passionate citizens. And I appreciate your vote." I gave a slight wave. A few words of goodbye were exchanged between Finn and Darlene.

"I'll get me a small yard sign." Gilly waved us off to our cars.

Finn and I stopped shy of the Wagoneer.

"Did Betty call you too?" I asked, since Betty had told me he'd already been dispatched on a call. One I was glad I didn't get because the stink from the sewage plant that sat right behind their neighborhood would've ruined my supper.

"I heard it over the dispatch and came out to make sure you didn't need backup." He grabbed the handle of my door and opened it for me. He was quickly learning the southern gentlemanly ways of Cottonwood. "You want to grab a bite to eat?"

"Sure. Mama said something about beans and cornbread at Ben's." I made the suggestion and tried not to look into his big brown eyes, a distraction I didn't need. I got into the car, pushing Duke to the passenger side.

Finn reached across me and patted Duke on the head. I'd have liked to blame my lightheaded feeling and the dip in my stomach on being hungry. Let me just say that Lonnie Lemar never wore good-smelling cologne. Being this close to Finn made my heart twist and turn.

"I'll meet you there." Finn slammed the Wagoneer door after he finished patting Duke. He tapped his hand on the open windowsill.

From my side mirror, I watched him get into his Charger. I pulled the siren off the top of the hood and put it back under my seat before I pulled out onto Oak Street with Finn driving closely behind me. Ben's was located on Main Street, and we scored a couple of parking spaces along the curb.

Ruby's Antiques was still busy, which didn't surprise me since she was displaying some of the antiques from the Stone estate, and she'd taken the opportunity to advertise it on a big sidewalk A-frame chalkboard.

"She's drumming up business." Finn pointed across the street once we were standing out on the sidewalk in front of Ben's.

"She sure is," I muttered, still wondering what was going on between Ruby and Cecily, remembering their confrontation just a little while ago. Whatever it was, it wasn't pleasant. But it was no business of mine. Not yet anyway.

Finn opened the door for Duke and me to step inside of Ben's. The smell of fried cornbread made my mouth water. It went so well with Mama's brown soup beans. Everyone loved Mama's beans and always wanted to know what her secret was. She always said a little of this and that, but truth be told, she used about a cup of Crisco in the soup. Fattening but delicious.

We took the seat up near the window with a view of Ruby's. I wanted to keep an eye on the place in case Cecily showed up with something from the estate. My curiosity was on high alert.

"To what do I owe the pleasure?" Ben Harrison greeted us with paper menus. He had his shaggy brown hair tucked up underneath his backward baseball cap. His usual hairstyle. Ben was definitely the best-looking guy in Cottonwood, and the most eligible, until

Finn Vincent came to town.

"I hear you have the best beans and cornbread around town." Finn was learning real fast how to talk to the citizens around here. He was losing that hard exterior he seemed to have when he'd first come to Cottonwood.

"You've been listening to the Lowrys, haven't you?" Ben knew Mama had gotten to Finn. "I have to say they are pretty darn good. That's why I won the cook-off with your mama on my team. I knew she could cook, and she was my secret weapon."

"Then we will have two bowls and a plate of cornbread. I'll have a Diet Coke." I lifted the paper menu up in the air for Ben to take.

"Water for me." Finn handed him his menu.

"Speaking of the cook-off..." I couldn't help myself. "Have you talked to Jolee?"

"No. Why? What did she do?" He cocked a brow. "Is this concerning that permit question I had about Duke's ceremony?"

"What question?" I asked.

Ben was always questioning whether or not Jolee had the right paperwork to park her food truck. I always made sure she did.

"Nothing." Ben shook his head. "What about her?"

"Don't you think it's about time y'all put your differences aside and maybe saw things a little differently?" I wasn't as good at the matchmaking stuff as Mama. But Ben and Jolee were two of my good friends, and they were perfect for each other.

"I'm never going to understand cooking out of a Winnebago," Ben said.

"Not about cooking." I hesitated. "About becoming friends."

"We are friends, just competitive ones," Ben replied.

"Man, I think she means more than friends," Finn said.

I was a bit shocked Finn actually knew what I was saying. I smiled.

"Kenni Lowry, you've lost your marbles." Ben glared at me before he headed back to the kitchen to put our order in.

"How did you know what I was talking about with Ben and

Jolee?" I asked Finn, fiddling with the edge of the rolled-up napkin with the silverware wrapped up in it.

"I know you better than you think." Lightly he drummed his fingers on the table, a slight grin tipping the edges of his lips and a gleam of deviltry twinkling in his brown eyes.

Mama came over with a tray and said hello.

She was good at interrupting a moment.

"Here you go," she said to Finn and put a big bowl of soup beans and cornbread in front of him. "And here you go." She sat a cup of beans and half a piece of cornbread in front of me. "Enjoy."

She hurried off, not giving me a minute to protest.

"Mama." I got up and stalked after her. "Mama," I called louder.

We made it all the way back to the counter before she turned around.

"What is it, honey?" she asked, resting her hip against the end of the counter. "Are you still mad about the whole Daryl and Gilly thing with the bullhorn?"

"No." Though I would've loved to get into that with her, but Ben's diner wasn't the place. "I asked for a bowl of beans and I'd like a full slice of cornbread."

"Kenni." Mama said my name in the all-knowing mom voice. She leaned in and whispered, "You know my little secret ingredient. I can't have you eating a whole bowl of it since you're on a date."

"I'm not on a date. I'm working." I pursed my lips and jerked away from her whispering lips. "We're work partners and I'm hungry."

"You can eat when you get back to your house. But when you are here, you'll act like a young lady and eat a little. Honey, you ain't getting any younger, and I want grandchildren before I can't pick them up because I'm too old." Mama didn't mince words. She was as serious as could be.

"Mama, get me my bowl of beans and cornbread or I'll tell Jolee your secret ingredient." I knew my words were like a dagger to her ears, but I had no choice but to pull out the big guns. Jolee had been begging me for years for Mama's secret recipe.

After all, I was hungry.

"You wouldn't," Mama gasped, drawing her hand to her chest.

"Try me," I said through gritted teeth and stared her down until she finally gave in and scurried back to the kitchen.

"What was all that about?" Finn asked over his half-eaten bowl of soup.

"Nothing." I shrugged it off and glanced to the back of the diner to make sure Mama was getting my food. "Tell me about the Graves ordeal."

"That Leighann Graves sure is a handful." He swiped a knife full of butter and spread it over the cornbread.

The butter immediately melted and seeped into the airy holes, making my mouth water. I couldn't help but grab a piece off of his plate. He gave a slight grin and pushed it toward me.

"What happened?" I asked and leaned back in my chair to make room for the bowl Mama had Ben bring out and set down in front of me. I mouthed "thank you" to Ben before he moved on to the next table.

"Betty called and said Sean Graves made a trespassing call out on their farm. I headed out there and looked around to make sure everything was secure before I knocked on the door." He took a bite of the cornbread. "They invited me in. In the family room Mrs. Graves offered me an iced tea. There was a girl, a boy, and Mr. Graves sitting in the room."

"Boy?" I asked, knowing Leighann was their only daughter.

"Right." His brows raised. "See, you would question that because you know there isn't a boy in the family, where I don't. And he was the one trespassing. Only he wasn't making any big scene. He was holding the girl's hand."

I leaned in on my elbows to hear better. The diner had gotten a little loud from the customer chatter.

"The boy, Manuel Liberty, had no idea that the father had put a trespassing call on him." He shrugged dismissively. "When the dad told them why I was there, the daughter went off the handle."

"She's known to have a bit of a temper." It wasn't the first time I'd heard this. It also wasn't the first time I'd heard that she and her dad didn't get along.

"Temper? She came off that couch swinging." Finn's head slowly moved side to side, disbelief written on his face. "I couldn't believe it. I grabbed her and the dad scolded me. He said that Manuel was the problem and he needed to be charged with trespassing because he was now eighteen years old and of age to be arrested."

My jaw dropped. I'd take Daryl and Gilly's feud over this call any day.

"Did you arrest him?" I asked.

"No. After I got the mom calmed down and everyone back on the couch, I told Mr. Graves that in order for me to arrest Manuel, he should've been given the common courtesy to have the opportunity to leave on his own recognizance, and if he didn't, then they should've called dispatch." Finn picked up his water and took a few drinks, and I ate a couple spoonfuls of beans. "I escorted Manuel off the property."

"Did he say anything about why Mr. Graves would call on him?" I asked.

"Apparently, he and Leighann have been dating, but she's sneaking out with him at night, which drives the Graves crazy, since her eighteenth birthday is just around the corner. She came home the other night around three a.m. hammered, and it was Manuel who had dropped her off. Mr. Graves had forbidden her to see him, but young love." Finn smiled. "You know the strange thing is that neither Mr. Graves nor Leighann wanted to tell me why he was trespassing. Mr. Graves told me that he wasn't welcome on his property."

"I thought Manuel worked for the Graves' company." Graves Towing was the only tow company in Cottonwood, and the only one the department used. There was one in the neighboring town of Clay's Ferry if Sean couldn't do a pick up. Rarely did we use that one, but it was there just in case.

"He does. Did," he said.

"Now Manuel knows to stay away, and he can get a job over at the towing company in Clay's Ferry."

It was so unfortunate. I really liked both families, even though I'd heard Mr. Graves was a pickle like his daughter. "How did Manuel seem to you?" I asked.

"Calm and cool. Even had a smirk on his face, which I'm sure sent Mr. Graves into a tailspin," Finn said, folding his napkin up into his empty bowl. He leaned back in his chair and took a toothpick from the cup next to the salt and pepper shakers. He looked at the wooden stick and smiled. "You know, I never thought I'd ever be using a toothpick."

"Around here, they are like gold." I loved how he was embracing his new home. "In our homes we keep them on top of the stove."

"Everything good?" Ben asked and picked up our bowls.

"Everything was great," I said. "Where's Mama?"

"She took a couple of bowls home to your daddy, and she even took care of y'all's bill." He nodded and headed off to the kitchen. "She said she had to scatter because she had her church group tonight."

"She didn't need to take care of the bill. That was so nice of her. I'll have to stop by and thank her." Finn got up from the table and Duke stood up with him. I followed them out of the door, which he held for me again.

"You know, Cecily said something about fearing that Beryle was murdered." It was a bit of information that I'd been chewing on since Cecily had mentioned it. "I didn't get into great detail with her because Betty called about the gun slinging."

We laughed.

"But I'll head back over to see Cecily in the morning and take her a coffee. We can discuss why she thinks Beryle was murdered." Duke and I walked up to the Jeep.

"I bet it's because of the supposed tell-all." Finn walked around me and curled his hand around the handle of my driver's door. "It's a cold night." Finn opened the door and snapped his fingers for Duke to jump in. Duke didn't listen, just sat down next to my feet. "But it's beautiful."

"It is beautiful." I looked down Main Street at the carriage lights that dotted the sidewalk on both sides of the street and illuminated the dark that seemed to fall way too early this time of the year. The pops of colors on the hanging baskets filled with burnt orange, yellow, red, and white mums added to the fall feeling. Small banners hung down from the carriage lights' dowel rods. The words on the banners read "Fall Into Cottonwood" with a few embroidered blowing leaves sprinkled around it.

"I have to tell you something." He still had his hand curled on the top of the open door. I stood between the door and the seat with Duke by my side. "When I said that I'd never pictured myself with a toothpick, I wasn't lying." He looked down at his clothes. "I never thought I'd wear this type of uniform for work, and I certainly never would've said that I was going to stop by someone's home to thank them for paying for my meal."

"I guess Cottonwood has a way of making you feel right at home." I gulped when I felt him coming closer.

"I do feel at home," he said, so close that his breath skimmed my cheek, tickling me all the way down to my toes. "You make me feel so welcome."

It was like magic. I leaned a little closer, anticipating what was coming next, forcing myself not to grin.

"Thank you, Kenni," he whispered, leaning even farther and closing his eyes.

Duke jumped up right before our lips met and darted off down the sidewalk in a fit of barking and growling.

Before we could kiss, we had to pull away. I cursed under my breath.

"Duke!" I yelled, wondering what on Earth had possessed him to take off.

Instincts kicked in. Both Finn and I took off running as fast as we could. Duke rounded the corner of Ruby's Antiques and headed to the alley in back. I should have been used to Poppa's ghost by now, but it surprised me when he appeared in the distance, that same look in his eyes that I'd seen when I was leaving the Stone estate.

He lifted his arm without saying a word, pointing in the same direction Duke had run. The sound of something metal hitting pavement echoed into the dark night sky along with Duke's deep bark.

The sound of three pairs of footsteps rang in my ear.

"We aren't alone." I drew my gun and held it straight out in front of me as we rounded the corner to the alley where Duke had stopped. His tail was stuck out stiff behind him and the hairs on his entire body stood up. I could hear footsteps running away from us.

Finn took off the flashlight attached to his officer's belt.

"No, we aren't." Finn's flashlight put a spotlight on someone lying face down next to the back door of Ruby's Antiques. "And it doesn't look like you're going to get any answers out of Cecily Hoover."

We stared down at her lifeless body. I reached down and felt for a pulse. I looked up at Finn and slowly shook my head.

"She's dead." My own words scared the daylights out of me.

Chapter Eight

"I think I found the murder weapon." Finn had grabbed my police bag out of my car after he chased whoever was fleeing the scene.

He'd taken a pair of gloves out and put them on while I looked around for more evidence.

"Ax." He held up an ax, long brown hair hanging off the sharp end of it.

I looked down at Cecily Hoover. Her hair was covered in her deep red blood and rested in the puddle that formed around her head. It was still fresh.

"And her phone." Finn paused and pushed some of the buttons. "Looks like she was trying to dial 911. It's punched in on the phone, but it wasn't dialed."

"When I was with her today," Poppa's voice broke, "I had a bad feeling, so I decided to stay next to her. It wasn't until I overheard you and Lover Boy here about to make out right on Main Street for the entire town to see that I left her side."

Suddenly I felt ashamed for even letting things get so close with Finn. We were partners, and it wouldn't look good during election season if we suddenly started dating, or as the rest of the town would say, "going around making fools of ourselves." Though some citizens, including Mama, would have loved to see us together.

"I'm going to put a call into Max Bogus." I peeled the gloves off my hands and took my phone out, realizing the darkness had really settled around us.

Something crunched under my feet when I stepped away. I shined my phone's built-in flashlight down to the ground and noticed it was glass. I shined the light in front of me and up to the darkened streetlight where it was clear someone had taken something, thrown it at the light, and busted it.

"Look here." I pointed out the light to Finn. "Someone clearly didn't want to be seen."

"Someone knew that she was here, she was going to be here, or they were meeting with her and did it to knock out the light so no one would see." Finn came over and took a sample of the glass for evidence and took some photos. He picked up a rock. "This is probably what they used." He stuck it in a bag for evidence.

"Maybe we can pull some prints off of it." I hoped with all my heart this was going to be solved quickly. "You know the first forty-eight hours after a crime are the most crucial."

It wasn't that I needed to remind Finn of that timeline, because in the academy they drilled that in our heads. It was a reminder for me to keep my head on straight instead of thinking about kissing Finn while we were talking about the case.

I stepped away to make my phone call to Max, our local coroner and owner of the only funeral home in town. It was a one-stop shop for Cottonwood.

"Uh-oh," Max answered the phone. "I know when I see your name pop up on my caller ID this time of the evening, it's not good."

"You're right. I've got a body in the alley behind Ruby's Antiques." I glanced over my shoulder and watched Finn put up the crime scene tape. "It looks like Beryle Stone's assistant has been killed and the weapon was left at the scene. An ax, and there are strands of brown hair that look like the assistant's on the end. Plus, she has a gash in her head." I gave him the basics and we hung up.

When he got to the scene, he'd get the rest. Since this was right in the middle of town, it would take Max close to one minute to get here once he got in his hearse.

"There's no need to call the EMT," I said when I walked back over to Finn and helped him finish taping off the scene. "I guess she was right."

Now I regretted not taking her seriously.

"What are you talking about?" Finn asked.

"She wanted more security for the Stone estate," I reminded him. "Remember, Cecily showed up at the ceremony and said that she needed to talk to me. Since I was busy with Duke and all, I told her I'd be by the Stone estate to talk to her. I went over and she said something about a secret tell-all manuscript that Beryle Stone had written." I bit the inside of my lip and thought about my time at the estate.

"What? You're thinking something." Finn lifted his chin, his eyes drawing down as he looked at me.

"It's not possible." I sucked in a deep breath, not believing what I was about to say. It was something I'd never imagined, and the thought of it made Mama's bean soup creep back up my throat.

"Anything is possible." Finn drew his shoulders back. "What is it?"

"Ruby Smith." I looked at the back door of the antique store that was just a few shops down from the crime scene. Finn directed his flashlight over that way.

The window was busted out.

"The window," I gasped. "Did Cecily break into Ruby's shop, or did someone else break in and Cecily found them?"

"Cecily was here. So maybe she and the killer are, or were, after the same thing. Cecily stumbled upon them, or them upon her, and Cecily threatened to call us, which would explain the last number she was trying to dial on her phone," Finn said.

"And that's when the killer murdered her." My words hung in the air with each step I took, hurrying over to Ruby's shop.

Everything that Finn and I were throwing around was just a theory, and I was sure he'd put it on that big whiteboard he was so fond of that he'd hung in the office, but Cecily's phone was a big piece of evidence. It suggested that she'd felt like her life was in danger. I had to think that I was right about the killer telling her to wait and trying to talk to her before they murdered her in cold blood.

"It looks like our crime scene just got a little bigger." Finn shined his flashlight on the jagged broken window. "What were you saying?"

"I was going to say that when I stopped by the estate earlier, Ruby was there. She and Cecily were having a few unpleasant words. Ruby wanted something and Cecily said over her dead body. That's when I made my presence known. That's not all. Beryle had been living at the estate for some time now. She let the outside look like it was abandoned, but the inside was lived in." My eyes drew up and down the door.

Finn and I took a moment to look at each other when we noticed the door was cracked open. We were in sync. Both of us drew our guns, and with the tip of my toe I pushed the door open enough for us to walk in.

"Cottonwood Sheriff!" I yelled into the storage room.

Finn rushed around me and looked around as I adjusted my stance, pointing my gun to keep him covered. There was a light coming from the main lobby of Ruby's shop.

"Psst." Finn nodded me over to where he was shining his light. He pointed out bloody footprints. We stepped over them and continued to look around.

It looked like someone had brushed everything off of Ruby's desk. Papers were all over the floor.

"Maybe they didn't find what they were looking for and got mad. Really mad, and just threw everything around." I shined the flashlight on the file cabinet drawers that'd been jerked off the rolling hinges, the contents dumped on the floor.

"Cottonwood Sheriff!" Finn yelled from the door between the storage room and the rest of the shop.

No one answered our calls.

"Kenni." Poppa's ghost appeared on the far right of the antique shop. "I think you might want to take a look at this."

"Where are you going?" Finn asked as I broke protocol on how we were supposed to sweep a room and hurried over to where Poppa was standing.

"We have another body." I looked down at Poppa's feet. Yep, the beans were coming up. I gulped for air and tried to say the words. I stopped and took a deep breath.

"And it's Paige Lemar." My voice cracked.

The shoe that I'd been waiting for...it didn't just drop, it was slammed down.

Chapter Nine

"She's alive." My eyes darted up to Finn as my fingertips caught a faint pulse from Paige Lemar's carotid artery.

Finn grabbed the walkie-talkie and called in an ambulance to dispatch. It was past Cottonwood dispatch hours, which meant the service we shared with Clay's Ferry got the call.

There was a quilt in a nearby quilt stand that Ruby had priced unreasonably anyway, so I grabbed it and put it over Paige to keep her body temperature up. She'd already started to turn a faint shade of blue. I continued to check her pulse.

"Paige, you are going to be fine. Just stay with me," I whispered in her ear even though she was unconscious. The gash on her head was dripping fresh blood.

"I don't like one bit of this," Poppa said next to me. "Keep talking to her, Kenni-bug. I feel like she's fading fast."

"Paige, you stay with me." My tone was stern. "It's not an option for you to leave this Earth."

"Remind her of the good times with Lonnie." Poppa fed me things to say. "About the riverbank where we used to cook out and lollygag all day long."

"Remember how you and Lonnie used to go down to the river and be lazy all day." My words weren't exactly what Poppa said. My fingers slipped and I put them back on her neck.

I moved the pad of my finger around to get the pulse back. There wasn't the slightest thump against my finger.

"Paige. Paige!" I called frantically, feeling around both sides of her neck.

"Kenni, CPR!" Poppa yelled. "Remind her of the heart necklace Lonnie gave her and how much she loved it."

Without hesitation, I started to perform CPR and continued until the EMTs got there and took over. Her pulse had come back. When they lifted her up to get on the gurney, I made sure I stayed with her.

"Think about the heart necklace Lonnie gave you. Remember how much you love each other. He needs you. We need you," I whispered in her ear before they put in her into the ambulance.

I stood there outside of the double doors and kept my eyes on her face as they hooked her up to all sorts of lines and wires. Her eyes fluttered open a couple of quick times before she shut them again.

"I swear she looked at me," I told Poppa. He was in the ambulance with her.

"What?" Finn asked.

"Paige." I nodded toward her right before the EMTs shut the doors and they peeled off. The sirens and lights echoed. The black sky enveloped the ambulance as it drove farther and farther down the alley.

"That would be a great sign if she came to." Finn let out a deep sigh.

"I'll go inside and see what I can find, if you don't mind sticking around out here until Max gets here to pick up Cecily's body." My eyes slid across the pavement back over to the body.

The shop had always been a fun place for me to come and take my time to walk around, but now that feeling was gone. I was in a rush to see who or why someone would do this to these two women.

Hopefully Poppa would come back and let me know that Paige is going to be okay. I flipped on all the lights and noticed the clock on the wall was reading close to ten. Ruby would be asleep by now, and it was going to take Finn and me a few hours to process the scene. There was no way we would be able to clear the scene tonight—we really needed daylight to help with that.

"Max is here," Finn called from the back of the shop. I was still measuring the circumference of the area where I'd found Paige.

I left my bag there and headed outside to talk to Max.

"Two victims?" he asked when I came out. He was already standing over Cecily's body, placing a sheet over it.

"I know." The more I thought of it, the heavier my heart got. "I just hope Paige makes it to tell us what went on out here tonight."

"Finn said something about someone running away from the scene?" Max asked.

"I'm hoping Mrs. Kim has her security cameras up and working." I pointed to the outline of the cameras that were barely visible from the working streetlight down the alley. "This light has been broken. Which makes me believe the killer broke it so no one would see. I'm worried that Paige just happened to be in the wrong place at the wrong time. Her car is parked over there."

"My gut feeling is that Cecily was here to meet up with someone who wanted something from the Stone estate and something went wrong." Finn shined his flashlight next to Cecily's body. "I'm pretty sure the ax is the weapon used on both women."

"I'm thinking the beginning of the attacks took place in the shop." I walked toward the shop and inside, both of them following me. "Here is where I found Paige."

Technically, Poppa found her, but they didn't know that.

"Or the killer murdered Cecily out here and went inside to look through the items the Stone estate had put in Ruby's shop for safekeeping," Max threw in his two cents.

"No, the footprints match Cecily's shoes," Finn noted.

There seemed to be a lot of what ifs thrown around, but this was how theories were worked out and crimes were solved. Finn and I were really starting to gel and get to know each other on a professional level. Much different than it was during the last murder we solved, where he waited to see where my head was on the crime. Now he was throwing out the possible details that we needed to catch the killer.

"Maybe Paige walked up on the scene on the way to her car and saw the broken glass in the door and looked in. Out of curiosity, she walked in and found the killer in there going through the items, then the killer knocked her out. Duke started barking and took off, and that's when we followed him. That's when we found the crime scene. We heard footsteps running away from the scene going that way." Finn pointed out the bloody footprints and walked beside them outside to Cecily's body.

"The bloody prints match Cecily's shoes, and there are no other prints going in or out of the shop. That tells me that Cecily was attacked inside, like Finn said, maybe stumbled out because the last few steps closest to her body are smudged like a drag. She lost so much blood that she passed out here, and this is where she died."

Still a little stunned, all three of us stood there looking down at poor Cecily.

"It's almost too dark to do anything now. Why don't you go on home? I'll stay here all night to make sure no one disrupts the scene before we can get a look at it in the sunlight," I suggested to Finn.

It was hard to see the full picture with just the beam of the flashlight. The sun would definitely help us look under the shadows of the night, which could hold evidence we needed to solve the murder and the crime. Not to mention Mrs. Kim's security footage.

"I'm wide awake now. Why don't you go get some rest and bring me a coffee in the morning? You're going to have a busy day answering a lot of questions when this story breaks." Finn was right. Cottonwood would be buzzing with half-truth, half-gossip.

We agreed and Max put Cecily's body up on the church cart before he loaded her into the hearse to take her to the morgue, where he said he'd get started on her autopsy first thing in the morning.

I chewed on the corner of my bottom lip as I watched the taillights of the hearse disappear into the distance. The thoughts that twirled in my head made my gut hurt.

Cecily Hoover knew something. Something that not only someone else wanted, but that got her killed.

Chapter Ten

"Get yourself up out of that bed this instant."

It was way too early to be hearing Mama's voice.

"You are the sheriff." She jerked the covers off me. The cold air was as cold as a tomb and sent chills up along my legs, making me reach down to grab the sheet that had somehow bundled at my feet through the past few hours of shut eye. "If you aren't there to work this case day and night, Lonnie Lemar will win this election hands down. Not that I'm keen on you being elected sheriff again, but I don't like to lose." She tried to jerk the sheet, but I'd curled my fists around it and tucked them under my chin. "So that means we win. Now get up."

"Duke, sic her," I groaned and rolled over to see what time my digital clock on the nightstand read.

Duke lugged his body up to standing, his tail wagging as he gave Mama kisses.

"Bad dog." I blinked. "Does that clock say five thirty?"

"Yes. Now time's a'wasting." Mama patted her leg. "Come on, Duke. I'll let you out. Get up, Kendrick Lowry. Don't make me come back in here."

"Leave your spare key on the counter on your way out!" I yelled, hoping she'd do something I asked for once. "Besides, Finn took the shift to watch so I could get some sleep and take over at seven. And I called in a few of the Kentucky reserve officers to stay at the Stone estate and in the alley behind Ruby's."

"Right now!" Mama screamed back, giving me that tone of voice that had scared the bejesus out of me when I was a kid.

I grabbed my phone to see if there were any texts from Finn. After we'd found Paige Lemar nearly dead and gotten her off to the hospital, it'd gotten up into the wee hours of the morning and Finn and I were so tired, we stumbled over each other. And it was so dark that it was really hard to collect any evidence with the low lighting Ruby had in the shop and the dark night that'd seemed darker than normal.

"You better move your hiney. She's on a roll," Poppa appeared and warned me.

"Fine." I shoved the covers off my body.

There was no sense in trying to please either of them. They were cut from the same cloth. It wasn't that I didn't want to get up, though really, I didn't, but Finn and I'd had a plan. Or it might've been the fact that we almost kissed and in the daylight it seemed much more serious than at night. I was a little nervous to see him.

"I don't hear the shower!" Mama yelled down the hall at the top of her lungs.

"Mama." I grabbed my robe off the chair and put it on. "You're going to have to stop yelling or you'll wake up all of Free Row."

Free Row was what I lovingly called the neighborhood I lived in on the south end of town right off Main Street. The house was actually Poppa's, and he left it to me in his will. It was natural for me to live here. It probably wouldn't sell if I tried. Free Row was where most of the people who lived off food stamps and commodity cheese lived sprinkled in with a few drug dealers and petty criminals. Of course, Mama hated it and said that after Poppa died all the bad people moved in since there was no longer the law watching over them. I'd never had a problem and enjoyed every minute living here.

Mama groaned and complained under her breath as I made my way down the hall to the bathroom. The smell of the freshly brewed coffee she'd made did perk me up a little. I started the shower and got in.

"Now, I was thinking." Mama had no boundaries. She came right on into the bathroom while I was in the shower and sat on the closed toilet seat. She curled the shower curtain back with her finger, her legs crossed and her top leg bouncing up and down. "If you play your cards right, this will seal your election."

"Mama!" I jerked the shower curtain closed and quickly washed my hair, skipping shaving my legs. "You stay out of this. There is a woman dead and another woman barely hanging on. This is a real crime and I don't have time to talk about elections."

"You've got to be kidding me. Paige Lemar is too damn mean to pass on." Mama's words actually shocked me.

I turned the water off and reached out to grab my towel off the rack, wrapping it around me and tucking the edges underneath my armpits.

"What do you mean?" I was so stunned by what Mama had just said that I was almost speechless.

I stepped out of the shower. Mama's leg continued to swing up and down and she picked at her nails.

"Paige Lemar used to be Beryle Stone's housekeeper and she just thought her you-know-what didn't stink. I remember my daddy talking about it," she said. "Paige was always so la-dee-da."

I took a deep inhale through my nose. This was a bit of information Poppa had completely left out, and that was concerning to me.

"What did Poppa say?" I asked Mama.

She jumped up and stood facing me. "Now what I've got to say is important?"

"Mama." She was good at playing the guilt card with me. Issues I chalked up to being an only child. "Tell me what you know."

"All I know is that..." Mama was talking with her back to me as we walked down the hall into the kitchen, but I couldn't hear her due to Poppa talking behind me.

"Paige Lemar had been Beryle's housekeeper for years. Lonnie always complained about how much time Paige spent over there and that she was more of Beryle's best friend than employee. Beryle took Paige all over this country when she first hit it big. When

Beryle moved to New York, she didn't need a housekeeper anymore. Luckily for Paige, the Inn opened up and she went to work there. Lonnie told her she could stay home, but she refused and started working for Darby." Poppa and Mama's words were practically in stereo as they told the same tale.

"And if Paige knew something..." I curled my bottom lip in once I realized I'd said those words out loud. "*And* Cecily knew something, then the killer might've tried to get them both in one place."

"You don't say?" Mama gasped and poured a big cup of coffee, setting it down in front of me.

"Have you happened to check on Paige this morning?" I asked Mama, knowing that the henny-hens were on top of things concerning gossip.

"I did." Mama eased down in the kitchen chair next to me. Her hands were curled around the mug. "All I know is that Lulu said that Stella said that Lonnie called the pastor to come and pray over her for a full recovery because she hasn't woken up yet, but her vitals are good. She took a nice blow to the head."

I needed to get ready and get going so I could find out exactly what Paige did know when she did wake up.

"They said she might not wake up for days." Mama nodded her head. "I'd like to sleep for days, but not like that."

"I was trying to sleep before you broke into my house." I took another drink of the coffee hoping it would kick in.

Mama took my mug. "You can sleep after the election. I can tell you another thing. Lonnie also told the pastor who told Stella who told Lulu that he wanted the Sweet Adelines to keep a vigil over Paige because he was going to hunt down whoever tried to kill his wife."

"That wouldn't be good." I was going to have to make my first stop be Lonnie's house to make sure he remembered just how investigations went and that he didn't cross the line and interfere. "Did you happen to go to church group last night?"

"I did." Mama refilled my mug and handed it back to me. "It

was a doozy. Preacher Bing was up in arms about the finances and Stella was tight lipped. It was what I'd call tense."

"Did you see Paige and Ruby there?" I asked.

"I did." Mama's eyes popped open, her mouth forming a big O. "They didn't talk, but you know," she wagged her finger, "Paige left early."

"Did she say why? And what time was that?" I asked, now thankful that Mama had used her extra key to wake me up.

"I don't know what time it was. And no," she said, as though it was completely out of line that I even asked if she knew why Paige left. "I don't know." She tilted her chin up to the left and shifted her eyes to the right and looked at me. "But I do know she got a phone call that she left the room to take." She wagged her finger at me. "Which is good manners. Anyways, it was shortly thereafter that she left. And she didn't tell anyone she was leaving. She slipped out." Mama tapped her nose. "But I noticed." She swung her finger from her nose to pointing at me. "You know you get your keen sense of intuition from my side of the family. Just like my daddy."

"She's right, ya know." Poppa appeared. I glared at him. He should've told me long before Mama had that he knew Paige had a connection to Beryle Stone.

Mama shooed me. "Go on and get ready," she instructed me. "And put on some lipstick. It'll make the dark circles under your eyes not stand out so much."

I could've said a few choice words to Mama, but that was another fire that I'd have to put out, and I had bigger issues. There was a killer among us, and it seemed that Beryle Stone's estate lay at the center of the crimes.

Chapter Eleven

"You could've told me about Paige's history with Beryle." I was a tad bit irritated with Poppa.

He sat in the passenger side of the Wagoneer and Duke was in the backseat with his head hung out of the window and ears flopping in the cold air. Overnight the temperature had plunged and the first frost of the season had practically covered the entire town.

The defrost in the Wagoneer was on full blast, and it was taking forever to clear the windshield, even with the wipers on full speed.

"Shoot the juice to it," Poppa pointed to the washer fluid, "and keep doing it."

"Poppa." I rolled down my window so I could see to make a left onto Main Street from Free Row, heading downtown to Ruby's Antiques. I'd wait a couple of hours and let the sun come up before I went to see Lonnie.

"The windshield wiper fluid will just harden as soon as I use it because it's so cold." I took a left out of Chestnut and headed north on Main Street.

"I'd forgotten about Paige working for Beryle," Poppa said. "That was a long time ago, and I'd thought Beryle lived out of town until we showed up yesterday." Poppa's arm was resting across the front seat, and his fingers drummed on the edge of it.

"Don't you have some connections up there?" I pointed to the sky.

"It doesn't work that way. Just like my memory." He took his arm off the seat and pointed to his temple. "Every memory is kinda foggy, but as soon as something triggers it, it becomes clear. Just like the fact that Paige worked for Beryle."

"I can't wait for Paige to wake up so I can question her, but it has to be before Lonnie gets to her." There was some urgency in my gut about this whole situation. One problem—there were only two of us. Finn and me.

I turned right on Walnut Street and took a right behind the alley behind Cowboy's Catfish, parking the Wagoneer behind the department. It was easier to park there instead of behind Ruby's. I hooked my bag in the crook of my arm and grabbed the two to-go cups of coffee Mama had made for Finn and me before I'd left the house.

"Too bad you can't help me carry something," I joked with Poppa who had ghosted himself next to my open door.

He smiled. "I can help with Duke." He patted his leg. "Come on, boy."

Duke wagged his tail and happily jumped out of the Jeep.

"This way," Poppa called after Duke, who had trotted to the back door of the department.

On our walk across the street and down the alley behind Ruby's, I called Max Bogus. Poppa and Duke walked ahead of me.

"Good morning, Max," I said when he answered.

"Hey, Kenni. I've been waiting for your call," Max replied. "Our victim was definitely killed by blunt force trauma to the head. I'm confident to say that it was the ax that was found at the crime scene. I'd taken a picture of the weapon, and when I looked at the blow to her skull and the hair follicles that are gone from her skull, it completely matches up."

"I just wanted to double check what we really knew," I said with a pang to my gut.

What a terrible way to die.

"I'm just now getting to the fingernails and swabbing them for any sort of material underneath the nails. I'll let you know as I progress," Max said.

We said our goodbyes just as I turned the corner of the alley where Finn's Charger was still parked behind Paige's car. Finn got out of his car once he saw Duke.

Our eyes met and we smiled at each other. It'd been a long time since we'd spent some real alone time together. We were due.

"Be sure to tell Finn I made that" were Mama's parting words when I left. Mama would've gone down to the Bridal Carriage on the south side of town and picked out a mother-of-the-bride dress if I'd even mentioned to her that Finn and I almost kissed.

"Aww, Kenni-bug. You've got a thing for him. I can see it." Poppa shook his head and shuffled his feet, walking away until he faded into the cool early morning air. "I'm going to check on Paige." His voice lingered in the brisk air.

"You're early." Finn's deep voice sounded tired and brought me out of my stare at where Poppa had just been. He bent down and gave Duke a brisk rub behind the ears. "Hey, buddy."

I held out a coffee for him. "Compliments of Mama." I wiggled my eyebrows. "She literally dragged me out of bed because she said this was a make-or-break moment in the election."

"Lonnie versus you?" he asked.

"I guess. I don't care about all that. I just want to bring the killer to justice." I took a sip. "Anything happen around here after I left?"

"Lonnie came by and was all crazy saying he was going to do someone in for trying to kill his wife, but it's been real quiet after I sent him off. He also wanted to get her car towed, but I told him that it's part of the crime scene and to leave it." Finn pulled the cup up to his lips. He stared at me over the lid. "I guess before it gets crazy this morning I should probably apologize for last night before all this took place."

"Apologize?" I played stupid, but he cocked his head to the side with a you-know-what-I'm-talking-about face. "Oh, you mean?" I gestured between the two of us and let out a nervous giggle. "Pfft." I waved my hand at him. "No apology necessary."

"Yeah, it's my fault and ridiculous that you and I..." He

shrugged. "I mean, election season is coming up. It might sway people's vote."

"Exactly," I said.

"Good. Now that we got that out of the way." He let out a sigh of relief. "What's our plan?"

"I've been thinking about that." *And you*, I wanted to add, but the discussion was now dropped, so it was time to put it out of my head. Cecily's words were stuck in my head, and no matter how hard I tried, I couldn't un-hear them. "Two times I heard Cecily say 'over my dead body' to two different people."

"Who did she say it to?" Finn asked. He folded his arms across his chest and leaned against my Jeep.

"Darby Gray, the owner of the Inn, and Ruby Smith, the executor of the estate." I gazed at him, giving him a fake smile. "I just can't imagine what could be in that manuscript that would cause someone to kill."

"Yeah. I know we have to find that manuscript. Even if it is contracted to go to a publisher. If there are secrets in there about people here in Cottonwood and they know about it, those could be more suspects for us to look into." He looked toward the antique shop.

"Plus, I know why someone wanted to kill Paige," I said. "She worked for Beryle as her housekeeper when Beryle lived here. I can't help but wonder if the killer thinks she knows something and wanted to keep her silent."

"That would be a good reason." He pushed off the Jeep when Ruby's DeVille sedan pulled up behind us. "And another reason to find the manuscript."

"I'm going to head over to the library at some point and see if I can get some more information on Beryle Stone and her life. All I'm going on right now is what everyone is saying about how nice she was. If there's a tell-all, then maybe she wasn't so nice." I spoke quickly before Ruby got to us. "Then I'm heading to the hospital to see if Paige is awake and give Lonnie a shoulder of support and a fair warning to leave this investigation up to us." My chest lifted with a deep breath to prepare myself for the wrath of Ruby Smith.

I was glad to see her because it saved me a trip to track her down. I looked at my watch. It was still a little early for her to be here. The doors said the shop opened at nine a.m. but that meant ten or eleven a.m. on Ruby time.

"What in blue blazes is going on around here?" Ruby asked as she got out of her car, a cardboard coffee cup in her hand.

"I was hoping you could tell me." I stepped up, Finn taking a stand behind me and Duke next to me.

"Kenni Lowry, you've done gone and lost your marbles. I don't know what you are talking about." She pointed to the police tape. "What is all this?"

"Last night someone killed Cecily Hoover over there next to your shop, and Paige Lemar was found nearly dead inside," I said in a stern voice.

Ruby's face froze, her jaw clenched and eyes fixed. She charged toward her shop.

"Where are you going?" I rushed next to her.

"I'm going inside my shop to see if anything was stolen." She threw her cup on the ground, the lid popped off and spilled steaming coffee on the concrete. Her arms pumped.

"You can't go in there right now." I hurried in front of her and tried to beat her to the door, but her spry nature beat me.

But she didn't beat Poppa.

Poppa ghosted himself at the back door of Ruby's Antiques and hollered for Duke. Duke stood between the door and Ruby. He was a big softy, but by the way he ran over to Poppa, Ruby pulled back.

"Paige isn't awake, but the doctors were saying her vitals look like she's going to be okay and they will try to start waking her up." Poppa gave me some news I could be excited about.

"Did you train him to be a police dog?" Ruby jerked around. "You better sic him off me."

"I never sicced him on you. Yet." My eyes drew down on her.

"Kenni Lowry, don't you make me call your mama," she

warned and shook her finger at me.

"This is a murder investigation out here that either ended in your shop or started in your shop. You aren't going in there for a few hours. Do you understand?" I didn't give her the opportunity to answer. "Did you hear what I said about Paige Lemar?"

"How is Paige?" She cleared her throat and lifted her chin in the air.

"I'm not sure," I said and noticed her arms at her sides, her thumbs rubbing her forefinger on each hand.

"I've got to go see her." She twisted around to go back to her car.

"Not so fast." I stopped her. "I'd like to know exactly where you were last night."

"Do you think I tried to kill Paige?" she asked.

"You haven't even mentioned Cecily Hoover," Finn said to her. She looked between Finn and me.

"I have nothing to say about Cecily Hoover. I don't know her. I just met her a day or so ago. Besides, I was at my church group meeting last night, and if you don't believe me, you can ask Stella or anyone else there." She clasped her hands in front of her. "Now, may I go, Sheriff?"

"I have a few more questions I'd like you to answer," I said.

"Are you arresting me for something I didn't do?" she asked. "Because that's what they do in the movies."

"I'm not arresting you. I'm simply asking you questions," I stated.

"I have a question for you. When can I open my shop?" she asked. "As you know, there are a lot of visitors interested in Beryle's things."

She was dancing around my questions.

"Why do you think Paige was here with Cecily last night?" I asked.

"I have no idea. So either arrest me so I can call my lawyer, or let me go so I can go visit with Paige before I have to open up." Her brows cocked.

The fall morning sun was starting to rise above the shop's roof. Ruby's red hair glistened from the early rays.

"I'm going to go in and look around your shop one more time before I let you in." I looked at my watch. "You usually aren't here this early."

"I had things to do." Her words were clear, concise, and to the point. "May I go see Paige now?"

"You may, but I will need you to come to the station to answer a few questions." I didn't want her to think she was off the hook, because in my book Ruby Smith was a suspect. I just didn't have the evidence I needed to keep her.

"Fine." She shook her head. "I'll call Betty."

She shuffled back to her car. Her car jumped when she threw it in reverse. After she got the car turned around, she sped off.

"Good boy." I walked over and rubbed Duke's head.

"You're welcome." Poppa tugged on the top of his pants and rocked back on the heels of his shoes.

"Why didn't you insist on her answering some questions now?" Finn asked.

"First off, she's in a bit of a shock. I've known Ruby all my life and she's never at a loss of words. I know she needs to process what's happened if she didn't do it, though I'm not sure she didn't. But I know we have to go with the evidence. Secondly, that's not how we do things here. I don't have the evidence to keep her because Cecily wasn't found in the shop. She's going to see Paige. I don't think she'd go see Paige if she was the one who tried to kill her." I chewed on the inside of my cheek. "And Ruby Smith ain't skipping town."

"What do you mean it's not the way you do things?" He wasn't satisfied with my answer.

"I don't jump on someone right away unless I know for sure. That's what I mean." I didn't like how he questioned me about my tactics, but he was still pretty new and we were just starting to get our groove. "Did you find any more evidence other than the ax?"

He shook his head. "I did find the inventory sheet from the

estate sale on Ruby's desk, and I went off and checked the items. I tagged them with an evidence marker so you could go in and take a look. I opened the drawers and felt around for any sort of secret compartment that would be able to hide something like a manuscript, but I found nothing. Maybe you can find something. I also bagged up some stray hairs. I took some blood samples from the splatter, dusted for fingerprints and shoe prints, and took a lot of pictures. I also walked around the front of the shop, but there wasn't anything there."

"I didn't think there would be since we were standing out there last night and didn't see anything." I swallowed back the images of Finn and me in front of Ben's last night. "Do you believe that Paige was attacked and Cecily was killed over this supposed manuscript?" I asked.

"I think that Beryle Stone knew something like Cecily said. That something has to be so telling that someone really didn't want it to come out." Finn confirmed what I already knew.

"That someone also knew that Paige Lemar had worked for Beryle all those years and probably figured Beryle had confided in her. So the killer got Cecily and Paige in the same place. When we heard Duke barking, we came running, and the killer had yet to kill Paige and that's who we ran off." I glanced up at the building now that the light of day had come and looked for a security camera I'd not noticed last night.

"There is a security camera here." I pointed to it and started to walk back down. I dragged my finger alongside of me and pointed off in the direction of Kim's Buffet. "The person running away from the scene went that way, so if we have some luck we'll be able to get a good picture of them."

"I'll get right on that," Finn said.

"No, you go home and get some sleep. Mrs. Kim isn't there yet, and she won't be until ten. I'll look around in Ruby's Antiques and hopefully clear it for her to open, but I'll keep the alley roped off since it's still an active case," I said.

"I don't need sleep. I need to catch the killer." Finn bounced on his toes as if adrenaline was coursing through his veins. "We need to find the killer. Besides, I'm too pumped to try to close my eyes."

"Are you sure?" I asked.

"Positive." He nodded. "Do you want me to go visit the hospital while you stay here and check out the shop and wait for Kim's Buffet to open?"

"That'd be great." It was a relief to have his help. "Can you stress to Lonnie how important it is that he doesn't do anything to hurt the investigation?"

"Absolutely, but he was out of his mind this morning." Finn pulled his keys out of his pocket. "My car is still parked in front of Ben's. I'll let you know if Paige is awake."

"Sounds good. I'll keep you posted too," I said.

"Is there anyone else you want me to go see? Like Darby?" he asked.

"No. I need to go talk to her. Say," I stopped him as he was walking away, "do you know anything about macaw birds?"

"Nope. Why?" His brows bent in a v shape.

"Kiwi said something about Beryle being dead and being glad of it." That made me wonder if Kiwi was repeating something Darby had said, but how do you take a bird's word for it?

"Who is Kiwi? And why aren't they on the suspect list?" he asked.

"I'm not sure I can question a bird." My gentle laughter pierced the cold air.

Finn's face was so serious that I couldn't help laughing louder at his confusion.

"Kiwi is a macaw that lives at the Inn. He repeats a lot, and he just so happened to repeat to me that he was glad Beryle was dead. I did try to question Kiwi, but he couldn't repeat it again." I shrugged. "I can't help but think he'd heard it from Darby, especially since she had that little spat with Cecily at the ceremony yesterday."

"Looks like we need to question everyone at the Inn and see if they overheard something." Finn had good suggestions.

"That's a great idea. I'll get Betty to get a list of Inn guests for us to interview, and I'll also go see Mrs. Kim about the security camera," I said.

"Okay." Finn faced me. The sun's morning rays streamed from behind me and made a spotlight on him. "I went through Paige's car. The only thing I found was her purse."

"No cell phone?" I asked.

"No. And her wallet and cash were still in there," he said. "That car over there had been here all night so I decided to look through it. It's a rental from the airport. Paige rented it a couple of weeks ago. There's a rental agreement and her purse. Nothing missing. I put her personal items in an evidence bag for you to look through, but I didn't see anything."

I nodded. "Good job." I smiled. I continued to tell him about what mama had said about Paige leaving the meeting, "Mama told me that Paige received a phone call while they were at the church meeting last night and that's when Paige left. We need to get our hands on her cell." I bit the edge of my lip.

"Or her phone records." He cocked a brow. "I'll work on that."

"Great." I smiled a huge smile and then blushed.

He peered intently at me as if he was about to say something. My smile melted.

"What?" I asked and I looked around to see if I'd missed something—his vibe had suddenly turned odd. "Is there something else?"

"I was just wondering what would've happened last night if this didn't happen." He laughed out a puff of air through his nose. "Thanks for the coffee."

"Nothing would've happened. I would've made sure." Poppa drew his fist in the air. I ignored him.

Finn walked off, leaving me with a tingling pit in the bottom of my stomach.

Chapter Twelve

The streaming sun was very deceptive, warming the inside of Ruby's Antiques even though it was cold outside. Sort of like the store. The outside showed a cute antique shop, but the inside looked like a crime scene.

Duke wandered around the shop and sniffed all the old furniture like he did every other time we'd been there.

"Well, anything?" Poppa ghosted next to an old-timey gumball machine. He propped himself up with his elbow on the top of the glass ball that held the gumballs.

"Not yet." I continued to not only look at the items Finn had tagged but the items around them. I'd taken a couple of evidence baggies out of my bag and put them in my pocket just in case I found something Finn didn't. "Have you ever wondered about antiques and their history?"

"It's just old furniture to me," Poppa said. "I was never into old stuff."

"Just think about that old dresser over there." I pointed to a flame Mahoney dresser that had a sign on the top that boasted its credentials. I read, "Civil War era. Entirely handmade furniture, the drawers are hand dovetailed, and the paneled back is rough sawn and hand planed." I ran my hand along the top of it. "Just think of all the things this piece of furniture has seen. The Civil War."

"Too bad it can't talk like me." Poppa winked. "Come on, Kenni-bug. What's going on? You're getting all sentimental on me."

"I don't know. I just want something to get me on track with who did this. Not to mention this mysterious tell-all manuscript. I wonder if that is really the reason Cecily was murdered or something else." I looked around and walked back over to one of the items that Finn had tagged.

It was a double-door tall chest that was lined with cedar. There was a drawer at the bottom of the chest. I pulled it open. There was nothing there. For the next forty minutes I looked at every single piece of furniture that Finn had labeled as evidence from the Beryle estate. I ran my hand along all the seams, nooks, crannies, bolts, and nails to double check there weren't any hidden compartments, even though Finn had already tried to find something. There wasn't anything wrong with making sure, especially when there was a murder involved.

I bent down and looked at the spot where we'd found Paige. There was an evidence marker next to the blood drops where she'd lain. The interesting thing was that she wasn't even near any of the antiques from the Stone estate. She was clear across the room, up near the front door.

"The front door is locked," Poppa noted. "The alarm wasn't tripped." He pointed to the small wire.

I walked the length of the wire that ran up the side the door, over to the corner of the wall, and across the ceiling over to the checkout counter.

"It looks like Ruby only has an alarm system that's attached to the front door." I rubbed my head. "The killer could have called Paige and Cecily just like Finn and I had thought. Paige had to be the first one in, because if she'd seen Cecily outside dead, she wouldn't've come in here."

At least I wouldn't think so.

"Of course she wouldn't've." Lonnie Lemar stood in the back of the store in the doorway of the storage room. "Who are you talking to?"

"Lonnie." I threw my hands in the air. "I'm talking to myself. I'm sorry to hear about Paige. I'm just glad I found her when I did. How is she?" I asked.

Though Lonnie and I were currently on opposite sides of the

election, he'd still been my deputy for a few years, and I really did love him and Paige. Not that I knew them all that well outside of the job.

Duke trotted over and shoved himself against Lonnie. He'd always loved having Lonnie at the department because Lonnie didn't do anything but sit there and pet Duke all day.

"She's clinging on to life. But I didn't come here to discuss her health status." He put his paper-thin elderly hands in his front pockets. The bags under his eyes spoke of his stress and lack of sleep. He stalked over and stopped when he saw the evidence marker where she'd lain. He spoke in a husky voice. "If you think you are going to send your goon to the hospital to make sure I keep my head on straight, you have another thing coming to you, Kendrick Lowry."

"Lonnie," I said in a calm and reasonable voice, "I'm not going to sugarcoat anything. You know how this works."

"I have the mind to beat the living crap out of you right here."

Poppa put up his fists and danced around on his toes like he was going to knock Lonnie out. "You think you're gonna come in here and corner my Kenni, you got another thing comin', buddy," Poppa warned.

I cocked a brow and rolled my eyes at Poppa.

"I gave you that deputy job when you needed a job." Poppa cussed and mussed and danced around Lonnie. "You forget that you came to me begging for a job. Enough money to pay the bills. I gave you that job. And now you repay me by trying to take Kenni-bug's job."

Duke danced around with Poppa and Lonnie gave him a cross look. I tried to ignore them both.

"You and I both know that I'm waiting for Paige to wake up. I sent Finn over there to see if there was any change in her status and to make sure that you didn't interfere with the investigation," I stated so he couldn't leave here saying I said something else.

I did my best to ignore Poppa, who'd taken a swing at Lonnie and must've hurt himself because he was rubbing his shoulder and cursing under his breath.

"I didn't think it was fittin' for me to stop by since you and I are running against each other," I continued. "But I am very sorry, and it's my number one priority to find out who did this. And you need to stay out of it. From what Finn said, you came in there guns blazing and hell bent on catching the killer yourself. You and I both know that's not the way to go about things."

"You can't keep our town safe." There was hate in Lonnie's eyes. "We have less than five thousand people in this town and there's been two murders and Paige..."

"Whoa, back up." My eyes narrowed and my brows crushed together. "Two murders?"

"Almost two murders," Lonnie corrected himself. "Paige was as close to death as you could get." His voice cracked. "If it weren't for you..." He hesitated and a wall of tears formed on his eyelids. "If it weren't for you and Finn playing kissy face out there for the town to see, then I guess no one would've found her until it was too late."

Kissy face? I closed my eyes and wondered who on Earth had seen Finn and me. It had been late and dark. Regardless, I was the sheriff and there was no time to get into a pissing match when he clearly was taking his feelings about his wife and her attacker out on me.

"I'm sorry that Paige has become an innocent victim in this, but I'm going to have to ask you to stay away from the crime scenes and let me do my job while I'm in office." I kept my voice calm to let him know that I meant business. "The more information you give me, the quicker we can solve who did this to Paige."

He jerked his shoulder back and away from me, causing my hand to drop back down to my side. His eyes slid from my face to the blood spots next to us.

"What do you want to know?" he asked, giving control of the situation to me.

"What was Paige doing down here so late?" I asked, trying to determine where she'd gone from the time Mama said Paige had left the church to the time she was attacked.

He said in a quiet voice, "She called to tell me that she was going to be a little late because the Inn was full, and it'd taken her all day to get the rooms cleaned since she was used to cleaning one to two rooms every few days." His eyes looked hollow. "She just doesn't have the stamina to get all those rooms cleaned as fast as she used to." He shook his head. "She'd called earlier asking if I knew of any other antique shops in the towns surrounding us because the guests had asked her."

"So she was talking to the guests about different attractions?" I asked, and he nodded.

It made me more sure than ever that I needed to interview all the guests at the Inn. If she'd overheard someone or someone had said something to her and she even mentioned that she worked for Beryle years ago, they might've thought she knew something.

"She also had her weekly church group meeting, so she was going to go there after she left the Inn. Which means she was at the church until late," he said.

"That would be a good reason for her to be over this way," I said. The church was just a block or so down the street. I still wanted to follow up with Preacher Bing on what he knew about Beryle and the whole cremating thing since Cecily had mentioned something about her being murdered. Not to mention the small memorial service she'd brought up.

"I heard that she left the church meeting after she got a phone call. Do you know where her cell phone could be? Finn looked in her car last night, but there wasn't anything in there but her purse. Nothing missing. Her wallet and money were still in there." I decided to tell him everything Finn had found. It was best going in with all the information when it came to Lonnie because he'd ask me anyway.

"I have no idea where her cell phone would be. The hospital gave me all her belongings and it was only her clothes." He shrugged.

"All those years ago when Paige worked for Beryle—"

"How did you know about that?" he asked with force,

interrupting me. His eyes shot up at me and bore into my soul.

Duke looked over at us. He ran over to my side as if he didn't like Lonnie's tone.

"Is it a secret?" I asked.

"How did you know?" he demanded me to answer, standing a little taller. Duke walked between Lonnie and me. "Only four people in this town knew that Paige worked for Beryle. Beryle, me, Paige, and your poppa."

His demeanor had turned odd and alarming.

"Who told you?" This time his voice made me tremble and made the hair on Duke's back stand up.

"I'm not telling you, but one thing I can tell you is that more than four people knew she worked for her. Why is it such a secret?" I asked.

"Beryle was a private person. She didn't like anyone knowing her business." Lonnie's shoulders softened. His eyes shifted down to Duke. He reached his fingertips out for Duke to smell and when Duke wagged his tail, Lonnie patted his head. "She paid Paige good money, and as you know, being a deputy isn't the best-paying job, but we do it for the love of the work."

A knowing look passed between us, and I couldn't help but give a sympathetic smile.

"I guess it don't matter now. I do want this solved." His chest puffed out as some of his anger started to subside. "Beryle didn't want anyone to know her business. Paige had to bring Beryle's garbage to our house because Beryle said that she feared someone would go through it."

"Did you know anything about a tell-all book that Beryle had written about her life? In particular, a tell-all about someone in Cottonwood that they wouldn't want to get out?" I asked.

"Not that I know of." The edges of his eyes dipped with sadness. "She was a real nice woman, and she took care of Paige. She took care of a lot of people."

"People?" I asked wondering, who he meant.

"You know, her charities and all. When Ruby came to see Paige this morning, she said that all Beryle's money was going to charities, which didn't surprise me a bit since she didn't have kids or anything," Lonnie said.

The front door lock clicked and the door flew open. The fall breeze blew in. I looked down and felt a tickle across my pant leg. Next to my shoe was a feather. A big long stiff green feather.

Chapter Thirteen

"Kenni, did you hear me?" Ruby Smith asked over the loud beeping alarm sound.

She rushed past Lonnie and me to the counter and jabbed at the alarm keypad on the wall next to the phone. Lonnie followed her.

"If I'd only had a camera, right?" she said.

"Yes, then I wouldn't be in this predicament." Lonnie sighed deeply. "I can't promise that I won't stop looking into this."

"Kenni?" Ruby called my name. "Are you listening to us?"

"I do wish you'd had some cameras," I muttered and waved my hand for Duke to move.

He'd taken just as much of an interest in the feather as I had. Only he wanted to play with it, and I wanted to see if there was any DNA on it because it definitely came from Kiwi.

I tried to hide the feather from Lonnie and Ruby. I needed to get it into an evidence bag, but I didn't want Lonnie or Ruby to know since it had blown out from underneath the piece of furniture next to where Paige was found. They didn't need to know what evidence I had, and this seemed like a key piece.

"Do you have any furniture from the Inn or Darby here?" I asked, just in case Darby had brought in the feather on a piece of furniture. Kiwi did have the run of the Inn.

I shooed Duke away and moved my foot over top of the feather and let it hover over it so I wouldn't touch it.

"No. She's such a tightwad that if you shoved a piece of coal up her keister, within an hour you'd have a diamond." Ruby's nose curled as though she smelled something awful.

Lonnie and I laughed. It was good she confirmed that the feather probably hadn't been brought in by a piece of furniture.

"Thanks for making me smile," he said.

Ruby called Lonnie over, leaving me standing there with Duke next to me.

"I'll be darned." Poppa had ghosted himself over and stood next to me. "Does that belong to Kiwi?"

"I think so," I muttered under my breath just loud enough for Poppa to hear me.

I bent down, dragging an evidence bag out of my pocket and swiftly picking up the feather and placing the bag back in my pocket.

I grabbed my flashlight off my belt and laid on the floor to get a good look up under the piece of furniture. There wasn't another feather, only jagged edges, which made me wonder if the killer was someone from the Inn and a feather had been on their shoe or clothing. Possibly when Paige tried to fight back, the feather was knocked off the killer and swept under the piece of furniture and caught on the jagged edge.

Incomplete thoughts of the feather swirled as I stood up. And the only way to narrow down who'd come to Ruby's was to go to the Inn and talk to every single guest, along with Darby. I headed back over to Ruby and Lonnie.

"Lonnie, I think it's best for you to stay by Paige's side, and let me know as soon as she wakes up because we both know that her memory is crucial." My right eyebrow rose. "I need to hear it from her lips and not yours."

"I'd tell you everything she said." Lines creased his forehead as his brows dipped. "But I do understand that you can't use what I say as evidence. I don't want to leave her side, but I don't want the first forty-eight hours to go by without a single soul in custody."

"Let me do my job." I ran my hand over the outside of my pocket.

I had a feeling Kiwi had seen more and the feather wasn't just a coincidence.

"Can I have my shop back or not?" Ruby asked. "And I called my lawyer about all your questions. We'll be down at Cowboy's sometime this afternoon. He said he'd call Betty with a time."

"Wally Lamb?" I asked.

"Yep," Ruby snapped and strutted past me turning the CLOSED sign to OPEN. "I'm assuming it's okay to open?"

"Finn did a good job sweeping the place and taking photos. I was just here to go over the evidence and make sure he got it all." I put my hands on my hips and took one more look around.

I walked around and picked up all the evidence markers. The bell over the front door signaled someone had come in.

"Are you open?" A tall lanky woman with brown hair coiled up in a bun on the top of her head walked in. She had on a long black turtleneck dress and a pair of sensible black shoes.

"Am I?" Ruby grunted. Her brows arched in a triangle. Lonnie stood next to her, anticipating my answer.

"Yes, but don't sell anything of Beryle Stone's." I grabbed my bag and put the evidence markers in it.

I took another glance around the shop, feeling sure we'd gotten all the evidence that was there.

"Don't go behind the alley." I looked at my watch and knew that the reserve officer should be back there by now to stand guard so no one would disturb the crime scene. "It's still an active crime scene."

Lonnie's cell phone rang and he scurried away to answer it.

"Don't go doing anything," I warned and pointed at Lonnie before he disappeared and I headed out the front door. I stopped with my hand on the handle and turned around. "Ruby, I'm assuming a lot of guests staying at the Inn have come in here the last twenty-four hours. Did you happen to get any of their names?"

Her lips thinned across her face and she shook her head.

"If you do remember something, please let me know." I pushed the door open and Duke followed.

Even though Finn had looked around the front of the building, I thought I'd take another quick look to satisfy any worry of missing something important.

The activity on the sidewalk on both sides of Main Street was already picking up. The shops had tented their chalkboard signs with their sales and daily specials. The city workers were busy watering the mums hanging from the carriage lights, and the sun was trying hard to warm the chilly morning.

I stood in front of Ruby's store and looked in to see what I could see from the outside. Had someone seen Paige in the shop? How did Paige get in the shop? My eyes focused on Ruby, who was talking to the customer. Had Ruby let Paige in?

I pushed my walkie-talkie.

"Betty," I said into the mic.

"Go ahead, Sheriff," Betty answered.

"Wally Lamb is going to call to set up a meeting with him and Ruby. If you don't hear from him in an hour or so, can you call him?" I wanted to make sure I got the answers I needed from Ruby.

"Got it, Sheriff." Betty was quick to answer. "I've also confirmed the reserve officers have taken their posts, including outside of Paige's hospital room."

"Thanks, Betty," I answered back. "And can you keep me posted if Paige wakes up?"

"I heard she took a turn for the worse a half hour ago," Betty said. I didn't want to know how she'd heard. If I had to guess, it was probably one of the Sweet Adelines talking gossip. No wonder Lonnie ran out of the store.

I had resisted telling Lonnie that I'd asked for an officer to be placed at Paige's door for the simple fact that I didn't want to hear him grumble and complain that he could keep her safe himself. If she'd taken a turn for the worse and he was on his way back to the hospital, he'd know soon enough.

"Can you call Darby at the Inn and get a list of guests that have been checked in for the last week?" I added, "And a list of where they live?"

"I sure can," Betty said.

I clicked off and squatted. My eyes scanned the pavement and every nook and cranny of the front of Ruby's store.

"Out of the way." Mrs. Kim nearly knocked me over. "Oh, Kenni. Duke."

I looked up, catching an unexpected look of concern on Mrs. Kim's face.

"Another dead body. Might be two." Her voice was tight as she spoke. "I thought moving here keep me safe. Not dead."

Duke sat in front of Mrs. Kim as though he was trying to understand her thick accent.

"You are just the person I was waiting to see." I pushed myself up to stand. "I see that you have a security system in the alleyway. I'm going to need to see your feed."

"I know my rights. You need subpoena. But I like Cottonwood, so I give it to you." Mrs. Kim pulled her purse closer to her. "I vote for you, but I don't know now." She shook her head. "It take Gina a couple hours to get film. You come by before dinner."

"Great. I'd like to catch up with Gina." I was glad Mrs. Kim didn't fight me on getting a warrant. Not that I couldn't, but the time it would have taken might've held up the investigation.

Unfortunately, Lonnie was right. The first forty-eight hours was crucial to a murder investigation, and I didn't have time to wait for Paige Lemar to wake up to tell me what happened. If she did wake up.

"Morning, Bartleby," I greeted Bartleby Fry, the cowboy of Cowboy's Catfish and the landlord of the sheriff's department. Duke rushed past me and sat at Bartleby's feet with his big brown eyes fixed on Bartleby's hands.

"Mornin', Sheriff. You like a cup of coffee? I've got a fresh pot brewing." He wiped his hands down the front of what used to be a white apron. He pulled a dog treat out of the front pocket and tossed it up. Duke stood up on his hind legs and snatched it right out of the air. "He's such a good dog."

"He is, and I'd love a cup," I said, standing by the door that led back to the department. I opened the door and let Duke in the office. It was about time for his nap, and he'd stay in his dog bed for as long as I'd let him.

"It'll be done in a sec." He held up his finger and went back to taking someone else's order.

"Any news on who killed that woman?" someone at a booth next to me asked.

"We don't have anyone in custody, but we've got some good leads." I smiled. "Won't be long."

In the corner booth in the back of the restaurant, Leighann Graves was all snuggled up with Manuel Liberty. I moseyed on over.

"Hi, Leighann. Aren't you supposed to be in school?" I asked. "You too, Manuel."

Leighann jerked out of Manuel's loving arms and both of their faces reddened.

"I don't think your daddy would like this." I pointed between the two of them. "Skipping school. Didn't I get a call about some sort of trespassing?"

"We ain't trespassing here." Leighann pulled her long red hair around her shoulder.

"No, but you are skipping school and going against your dad's wishes from what I see." I nodded toward Manuel.

"This here is none of your business, Sheriff." Manuel stood up. He was about an inch taller than me, and you could tell he was a football player with his stocky build and muscular neck. The mustache on his upper lip quivered. "Me and Leighann are having breakfast before we go to school."

"Here you go, Sheriff." Bartleby walked up with a to-go cup of coffee and two plates of pancakes. He put the pancakes in front of Leighann and Manuel.

"See." Leighann pointed. "We've got a right to eat. No wonder my daddy is voting for Lonnie Lemar," she said in a smart-aleck tone.

"I'll see to it that your daddy knows you are here eating

breakfast right now." I clicked on my walkie-talkie. "Betty, can you call Sean Graves and let him know that his daughter is at Cowboy's eating breakfast with Manuel?"

The girl glared at me with hatred in her eyes.

"You are a bitch, Kenni Lowry!" Leighann grabbed her light jacket and backpack before she slid out of the booth and stormed out of the restaurant.

"Never mind, Betty." I pushed the walkie-talkie again. Little did they realize, I really didn't call Betty. It was all pretend.

I eased down into the booth next to Manuel. I curled my hands around my coffee cup and rested my forearms on the edge of the booth's table. Taking a breath, I turned toward Manuel and said, "You listen to me. Sean Graves is not a man to mess with. If I were you, I'd cut my losses. Focus on football, get an education, and go off to college. You don't need the hassle of Sean calling the cops and having you arrested. You don't need a record."

"Yes, ma'am." Manuel looked down. "But she calls me and I lose my mind. I love her so much."

"I understand," I lied. I didn't understand. Mama was right. All I ever did was spend my time being sheriff and not having a life. "But you are young and have a wonderful football career ahead of you. That's what's important to you and your family. I heard your folks are real proud of you, and that the University of Kentucky is looking to give you a scholarship."

"Yes, ma'am, they are." He nodded again.

I slid back out of the booth and held my coffee.

"Now, you get on out of here and go to school. I don't want you fooling around with that Graves girl again. You hear me?" I asked for good measure.

"Yes, ma'am." He grabbed his book bag and stood up. "I'm sorry about what Leighann said about not voting for you, but my parents are. They even have a sign in the yard."

"You thank your parents for me." I offered him a smile.

At least that was one vote for me besides my mama's.

Chapter Fourteen

The day was slipping away fast and I'd felt like I'd gotten nothing accomplished on the murder of Cecily Hoover or the assault on Paige Lemar. After I scared the ever-living you-know-what-out of Leighann Graves, I walked into the department, where Betty was on the phone and writing things down on a pad of paper.

Her head tilted up to see me when I walked in the door. The phone was jammed between her ear and her shoulder. She put her finger up in the air for me to wait.

"Okay, thank you so much," Betty said into the phone. "I appreciate all of your help."

Betty hung up and grabbed the edge of the piece of yellow paper. She jerked the corner and ripped it off the top of the pad. She waved it in the air.

"Here's the list you asked for." She smiled. "I called immediately and Darby answered. When I told her what I needed, she said something about privacy and all that and hung up. But I knew that she had a meeting with your mama to get Derby Pies delivered. I called your parents' house and your dad said that your mama was out at the Inn dropping off pies to Darby. So I called back, knowing that flighty girl Darby just hired would answer the Inn desk phone and she'd flap her lips."

"Good job," I said, loving the enthusiasm Betty showed. I took the paper and looked at the list of twelve people before I looked over at Duke, whose snoring had caught my attention. "Who is the new girl working for Darby?"

"I don't know." Betty rolled her eyes. "Said she was just

coming through town and liked it, so she stayed."

"Really?" I asked, looking at her. "That's odd."

"You're telling me, but Darby trusts everyone." Betty cocked a brow.

"I didn't see the new girl when I was there yesterday." I wondered how I'd missed that. I noticed most everything, and I distinctly remembered when Finn and I walked down from Hattie's room after the critter catching that no one was at the desk. "How long has the new girl been there?"

"Oh, I don't know." Betty scratched her noggin. "I reckon a few days."

"What's her background?" I asked.

"Kenni, I don't know." Betty seemed annoyed. "Why don't you ask her when you go over there?"

"I just might. Did you get her name?" I asked, looking down the list.

"No, I didn't. Why? Is she a suspect?" Betty suddenly became interested.

"Everyone's a suspect." I waved the paper in the air on my way over to my desk.

"Oh, Gina Kim is going to drop the security footage off at some point today. She called earlier. Wally Lamb called too. He said that he was bringing Ruby by this afternoon." She looked at me over her glasses.

"Did Gina say what time?" It would be great if there was something on the video that would tell me who was running away from the scene, and doubly great if Ruby had some solid answers to my questions.

"No. I told her I'd be here until 5 p.m. Quitin' time," Betty said, needlessly reminding me that her quitting time was five p.m. on the dot. That was when she moved all dispatch calls over to Clay's Ferry dispatch. Clay's Ferry was the town next to us, and since we were both small, it wasn't in either of our budgets to have a full-time dispatch service all night long. Especially when we rarely had a call.

Over the next few hours as I waited on Ruby and Wally to

show up, I sat down at my desk and tidied up my reports on both Cecily and Paige. I added what little evidence I'd collected to be sent to the lab, including the feather I'd found at Ruby's Antiques. I even filled in Finn's dry-erase board with all the information since he liked to see everything in black and white.

"Well, if it ain't Low-down Lamb." I winked, referring to his high school nickname he'd gotten from doing anything to be elected as class president.

"And you are looking as fine as ever, Kenni." He winked in his own smarmy way.

"New haircut?" I noticed his blond slicked-back hair filled with gel was a bit shorter on the sides.

Smoothly, he ran a hand alongside his head. "Tina said I should take it a little shorter. I love that you noticed." He smiled that bright white gleam.

"Enough, you two." Ruby smacked his arm. "We are here to discuss my shop and how Kenni thinks I had something to do with these crimes."

"I never said you had anything to do with it. I'm simply gathering information. It's not unusual for me to ask you, as the owner, your whereabouts, and exactly what could be in your shop that someone would not only kill someone outside your shop for, but also try to kill someone who was inside." I gestured for them to sit in the chairs in front of my desk.

Wally nodded for Ruby to go ahead and sit. After she took her spot, he sat down, and I got out my pad of paper and pen. I also took my mini tape recorder out of my desk drawer and set it on the edge of the desk closest to them.

Into the running tape recorder, I stated the day, date, and time as I always did. "This interview is conducted between me, Sheriff Kendrick Lowry, Ruby Smith, owner of Ruby's Antiques, where the first victim was found outside the shop, as well as a second living victim inside the shop. Wally Lamb, lawyer for Ruby Smith, is also present." I looked between them to see if there were any objections so far. Neither said anything, so I began my line of questioning.

"Ruby, can you please tell me where you were the night of the murder and break-in of your shop?" I asked.

"I was at the church for church group. You can ask Preacher Bing and Stella." She nodded at the definitiveness of her answer. "Let me tell you that Beryle Stone was the topic of the night. Now, we did pray for her too, but all this scuttlebutt about a secret tell-all manuscript has everyone talking."

"How did you know about the novel Beryle was working on?" I asked since I'd not made it public knowledge.

"Kenni, you know somehow word gets around town. Secrets buried don't stay secrets for long." Her painted on brows wiggled up and down. "Everybody knows."

By everyone, I was one hundred percent positive she was talking about the henny-hens.

"Just stick to answering the questions about your whereabouts. Don't give information the sheriff isn't looking for," Wally advised. I glared at him.

"Have you ever met Cecily Hoover before this week?" I asked.

"No," she stated with a definitive nod. She looked over at Wally and smiled. "Like that?"

He reached over and patted her hand like she was a good girl.

"Tell me about the argument you and Cecily were having at the estate when I showed up," I said.

"What fight?" Wally asked.

Ruby leaned over and whispered into his ear. While she did that, I texted Finn to let him know that Ruby and Wally were at the department giving her statement, and I'd give him a call after they left to get an update on Paige and the hospital situation. He'd been sticking close to Paige's room.

"My client is ready to answer your question." Wally adjusted himself in his seat and tugged on the edges of his suit coat.

"I'm the executor of Beryle's estate, which took me by surprise since I never really knew her. Maybe we saw each other at a family function when we were children, but other than that, never." Her eyes grew big, and she shrugged. "There was a painting missing off the list that was supposed to come to the store. When I asked her about it, Cecily claimed she didn't know anything about it and was just there to make sure the charities got their money and, in the meantime, try to find this tell-all book. She's in Beryle's will, which states she's to stay in the home until the sale of the estate and all items are out."

"Did you question Cecily Hoover?" Wally Lamb asked in a condescending voice.

"Let me get on that, Wally. I'll just mosey on over to the morgue and hold a séance in hopes that she'll come through and maybe even tell me who killed her." My brows rose.

Wally let out a big sigh, crossing his legs. He clasped his hands and set them in his lap.

"Such an idiotic question does deserve that answer." Ruby cackled and picked at the edges of her red hair.

"I'm sorry," I said. "Yes. I did talk to her before she died, but she was vague about the whole situation and seemed very adamant about not letting that supposed tell-all get into the wrong hands."

"If Beryle did have a tell-all, all the proceeds are going to a private fund that Beryle had set up on her own," Wally said. "She only left me the numbers of the account, and I'm not giving you those until you subpoena me. And honestly, I don't know. I'm not interested in where her money goes, I'm only interested in my client, Ruby Smith, and the allegations that you made against her today." Wally Lamb had decided to play hard ball.

"I didn't allege anything against Ruby. I was simply doing my job." I sucked in a deep breath. "So you went over to see Cecily to find the missing piece of art?"

"Yes," Ruby said. "Things escalated, and the next thing I know the poor girl was found dead in the alley behind my store, along with one of my best friends nearly dead inside my shop. I don't know what I'd have done if she died too."

Ruby put her hands over her face. Wally reached over and rubbed her back for comfort.

"Take your time," I said. My heart broke for Ruby as she, along with the rest of us, struggled to see why this had happened in our small community.

"And the only thing I can figure is that Beryle has something that someone else wants. Only the furniture I have isn't worth killing anyone over." She looked up, her eyes red from tears.

That was my fear. Whether there really was a tell-all manuscript or not, Beryle had let the cat out of the bag that she was writing one or wanted someone to believe she had one. But who?

"I found this feather at your shop." I pulled the evidence bag out of my jacket that hung on the back of my chair. "It seems to me that this is from Kiwi over at the Inn."

"You know, I did see Cecily and Darby arguing at Duke's ceremony." Ruby's eyes bugged out.

"Has Darby been to your shop lately?" I asked, wondering if Darby's fight and the crime scene were related, making Darby a strong suspect.

"Not that I can recall. Not recently." She shook her head. "Is that why you asked me about the tourists that were staying at the Inn coming to the shop?"

"It is. Someone came in there with the feather attached to them." I smiled and set the bag on the desk. After the interview, I'd lock it up in the evidence room. "Unfortunately, with the traffic coming in and out of your shop, and most of them staying at the Inn, it could make anyone there the killer."

After a few more questions and signatures to Ruby's statement, she and Wally left.

"That was interesting." Betty busied herself at her desk.

"Isn't it past five o'clock?" I let Betty know that I knew she'd only stayed after quitting time so she could eavesdrop.

"See you in the morning." She grabbed her purse and waddled out of the office.

It was soon after that that Duke and I were on my way over to the estate. I gave Finn a call.

"Hey, Kenni. Um, Sheriff," Finn corrected himself.

"You can call me Kenni. It's not like everyone else in town

doesn't," I said. A smile crossed my lips. "How was the hospital?" I asked.

"They put Paige in an induced coma because they said she has some swelling on her brain around the wound. They are hoping to give her some medication for it and then slowly take her out of the coma by tomorrow morning. I also heard from the lab about the quick analysis of the ax. There was only two set of prints on it. Cecily's, and someone who's not in the system," he said with a resigned voice. "Cecily Hoover had prints on file from one of those kid ID kits that parents used to fill out just in case their kid went missing."

"Smart." I was impressed by his forward thinking. "No others on there?"

It made sense Cecily's prints were on there. I was sure she was trying to defend herself by grabbing it.

"No," he said. "But when I was at the hospital, I sort of sweet talked a nurse into letting me curl Paige's hand around a cup."

"You sort of sweet talked a nurse?" I chuckled. "You know what, I don't want to know how you got it. I'm just glad you got her prints so we can narrow it down."

"Where are you?" he asked.

"I'm headed over to the estate to look around and try to find the manuscript. I've got the Inn's guest list from Betty and am hoping to stop by there at some point, but I'm running out of day." It was already almost suppertime, not that I had to look at the clock. My stomach told me. "Gina was supposed to drop the security tape off, but she didn't. I'll give her a call in the morning."

"I have to run by and look at a house, but afterward do you want me to run out there?" he asked. "Or check on the tape with Gina?"

"A house?" I questioned what wild goose chase Betty had sent him on.

"Yeah. Lulu isn't all that happy with Cosmo," he said.

"Oh, you mean a house to live in," I said.

Finn had been renting a room over Lulu's Boutique and

recently he'd adopted Cosmo, a cat formerly owned by one of the people we'd just stuck in prison. His sister was actually going to take Cosmo, but found out real fast that her roommate was allergic to cats, and Cosmo came back to live with Finn.

"She said that she can't have cat dander and fur flying in the duct work since the shop is underneath and some clients might be allergic to cats. It's a shame too, because it's a perfect place for me to live," he said. "Not too big or too small. But I guess since I'm officially a paid employee of Cottonwood, I might as well start putting down some roots."

"Finn Vincent." My jaw dropped. "I never ever thought I'd hear you say that."

"This town has grown on me." While he was talking I got another call. I pulled the phone away from my ear and saw that it was Max.

"Listen, Max is calling. I need to take it. Just come by the estate when you're done looking at the house. Don't worry about Gina. She'll bring it." I didn't have time to ask him where the house was. I didn't even bother telling him goodbye. I just clicked over. "Hey, Max."

"Well, you aren't going to believe what I found." Max always had a way of keeping things suspenseful.

"What?" I asked, taking a right onto the estate drive.

"While I was harvesting Cecily's organs and doing the autopsy on them, I got to her esophagus." He hesitated. "I found the normal contents in her stomach. When I got to her esophagus..." There was a pause. "I found a small key," he finished, as if he was in disbelief.

"A key?" I asked and put the Wagoneer in park after I pulled up to the house.

"In her esophagus." He could've knocked me over with a feather. "Did you hear me?"

"Like she had swallowed a key?" I asked.

"Yes. She definitely swallowed this key right before she died, because I found it in the space below the end of the tongue muscle where it meets the esophagus," he said. "I'm just as shocked as you.

Never in my life have I seen a murder victim with a key in their esophagus. And it's not a normal key. It's small and gold."

"Was she wearing a necklace with a key dangling from it?" I asked.

"Not when I brought her to the morgue," he said. "I've inventoried all the items on her person and there's no key. Why?"

"When I saw her at Duke's ceremony, I remember she had a key on a necklace. An old key like the one you described."

"Do you think it has anything to do with the investigation?" He asked.

"Initially I though the key was a decoration like most young kids wear nowadays, but now I'm more sure than ever that she was keeping that key safe around her neck and somehow it has to do with her murder."

"Like I said," he paused in an uneasy way, "I've never seen anything like this ever."

"I'm here at the estate now. I'm going to have Finn swing by and get that key," I said.

"Sounds good. I'll have it waiting for him." Max clicked off the phone.

Immediately I dialed Finn back and told him exactly what Max had found.

"I'll go right over there after I meet with the realtor," he said.

"I bet if we can find out what that key opens, we'll be able to find what the murderer's looking for." My mind swirled with crazy thoughts. "Someone wanted that key."

"Someone still wants it. And I'm not sure if I believe the killer is done." Finn's words crept into my soul and sent a fright right through me.

Chapter Fifteen

The reserve officers that'd been acting as security at the estate said that a few people had stopped by and tried to get an early look at auction items, but no one seemed suspicious or linked to the murder. Of course, the officers didn't let them look around, instead rightfully sending them away.

Cecily had said that Beryle had died in her sleep. That she'd made all the necessary arrangements that Beryle had asked her to upon her death. Had Beryle been sick? Was she threatened and felt like she was in danger? Did she really just die in her sleep?

I pulled on a pair of gloves and thought about these questions as I sifted through Beryle's things in her bedroom. If she was sick, I was hoping to find anything with a doctor's name or number. The bed was made, so if Beryle did die there, someone had cleaned it up. The room was spotless. There was no hint that Beryle was a writer or had been writing. There wasn't a pen, pencil, paper, or laptop around.

Everything was neat and tidy. Too neat and tidy, I thought as I looked around. I checked every bedroom to see if I could find anything that needed a key to open. Especially if there was something that would fit the key that Max had described.

After I took a good look upstairs and didn't see anything, I headed down to the kitchen.

"Kenni?" Finn's voice echoed through the house.

Like me, Duke jumped to attention. Only Duke ran in the direction of Finn's voice, and I held myself back. Lucky dog, I thought when I stepped into the hallway from the kitchen and saw

Finn bent down next to Duke. Duke had keeled over on his back, his legs up in the air, ears flailed to the sides along with his tongue.

"He never refuses a good belly rub." I smiled. "So how was the house hunting?"

"It was fine. I'm not sure what I'm going to do. It's actually two houses down from you." He looked up at me. "Away from Main Street."

"I didn't know there was a house for sale there." My brows furrowed. I thought I knew everything going on along Free Row, but apparently I didn't, or the fact that my entire mind was caught up in this investigation meant I missed it.

"There's not a sign in the yard." He shoved his hands in his pocket. "Lonnie Lemar actually owns it, and after I got him calmed down this morning, I mentioned something about needing a place to live."

"I bet he thought that was a good one since he's running against us." I chuckled. "He'll use it in his campaign that he's doing the best for the community and even giving the current deputy a deal on this house."

"Uh-oh." Poppa's voice gave a warning.

"And he owns the house and is willing to sell it to me." Finn's voice broke off like a piece of chalk breaking in half.

"That Lonnie Lemar is a dirty old dog," Poppa griped. "How do you like them apples?"

"That's kinda what I wanted to talk to you about." Finn seemed to beat around the bush. He hemmed and hawed. There was no way he'd be able to shove his fists down in his pockets any deeper.

"Go on," I encouraged him. "Cat got your tongue?"

"Lonnie said that he planned on keeping me around if he won," Finn said.

"All hell's about to break loose." Poppa patted his leg. "Come on, Duke."

I rubbed my hands in front of me. I rocked back on the heels of my shoes. "You mean to tell me that you are not loyal to me?"

Those were fighting words around these parts. And loyalty was as rooted as God in Cottonwood.

"Yes, I am. God, yes," he said. "But I don't want to invest in buying a house if I don't have a job. I love it here, and I want to be a deputy. And with all that's going on..."

I stopped him.

"By all that, you mean murders? Crime? Everything under my watch?" I asked. "You don't think I'm going to win the election?"

"I...I..." He hesitated like he needed a minute to contemplate. Heck, a second was too long.

"Well, if this isn't a humdinger then I don't know what is." Poppa stomped around. "And I was beginning to like this boy." Poppa stood next to me. He eyeballed me good. "Kenni? Kenni-bug, don't be flying off the handle," he warned.

The more I thought about Finn Vincent and Lonnie Lemar conspiring against me while Paige was laid up in that hospital bed, the madder I got.

"Bullshit!" I yelled at Finn. I didn't have a short temper, but I sure did have a quick reaction to bullshit. "You!" I was so mad I was shaking. "You don't know what loyalty is."

"Kenni, now, Kenni." Poppa's ghost stood between Finn and me. "I understand this man doesn't understand the loyalties of the South, but there is no need for you to pitch a hissy fit right here in the middle of an investigation and during election season."

The election might be just under two years away, but that was close enough to call it election season.

"Let me tell you something, Finn Vincent." I stepped up and got nose to nose with him. "When the going gets rough, that's when we stand beside each other and dig our boot heels in. We don't waiver. Our loyalties lie deeper than the Mississippi River. If you can't stand by me in good times and bad, then maybe you aren't the deputy for me. Or the deputy I thought you were."

I shoved past him, but not without looking up to see Edna Easterly, the town reporter, and her big fat camera lens in my face, clicking away. The flash was so bright, I had to throw my hand up to shield my eyes.

"New flash," Edna boasted.

"I'm not going to run with Lonnie. I wished I'd never said anything!" Finn shouted at my back.

I turned around and glared at the both of them.

"You," I pointed to Edna. "Get out of this crime scene. You can stick that new flash you know where," I said through my gritted teeth.

"Lettin' the cat out of the bag is a whole lot easier than puttin' it back in." Edna's lips curled, her eyebrow cocked. I continued to walk down the hall. Behind me I heard Edna say, "Aw, honey, southern women will rip your heart out, fry it up, and put it on a biscuit while washing it down with some sweet iced tea. She'll come around."

"Come around my hiney," I grunted as the Wagoneer bounced up and down the curvy road that led back into town. "If Finn Vincent thinks he's going to undermine me, he's got another thing coming to him."

I talked to Duke like he was a person. If Poppa was here and not disappearing to God knows where, I'd be complaining to him. On second thought, maybe he knew that and that was why he wasn't here.

The library was going to be my last stop of the day. Spending time on some research would keep my brain from thinking about Finn.

The three-roomed library was located in a white colonial house next to the courthouse on Main Street. Marcy Carver had been the librarian for as far back as I could remember. She never aged. Her milk-chocolate skin was smooth, and her black hair was always pulled up in a thick knot on the back of her head. She claimed that if she let her hair down, it'd take up the entire space in the children's room.

"What in tarnation are y'all doing in here so late?" Marcy called from the reference desk. She grabbed a book from the returned book shelf and used the scanner to scan the barcode

"Duke and I have a little work we need to do on Beryle Stone," I said.

"Aw." Marcy lifted her chin. "Our local celebrity seems to be in high demand after her death." Her brows rose. "A lot of people have been coming in here asking for one of her books."

She walked over to another desk behind the counter, pulled out a treat for Duke, and picked up a book before she walked over to us. She handed Duke the treat and me the book.

"Here is one of her romance novels. *Crimson Hearts.*" She winked. "Don't tell your mama I gave it to you directly. She'll have a conniption fit."

I smiled and looked at the cover with a half-naked man that looked to be man-handling a woman into submission as her boobs practically spilled out of her brassiere.

"Seriously, this is the stuff she wrote?" My ick factor went off.

Marcy tapped the hard cover with her nail. "That's her name, isn't it? Deceit, lies, and cheating make for a good book."

"Ugh." I felt all icky and held it out to her. "I'm not interested in reading it. I'm interested in Beryle Stone's life outside of Cottonwood."

"Interesting you'd ask. Edna Easterly has been in and out of here the past couple of days doing the same thing. You wouldn't believe what people in Cottonwood look up." She flashed a sly grin. "Sometimes when they leave," she curled her nose, "I go over to the computer and look up the history. They never erase it."

She nodded her head to the right towards the computer.

"In fact, Edna was the last one to use it earlier this morning." She nodded again.

"Is that right?" I pointed to the computer knowing Marcy was telling me without seeming gossipy.

Slowly Marcy nodded. "Uh-huh."

"You're a gem." I patted her on her arm. "I guess I'll check out this book."

"I'll take care of it for you." She took the book, and over her shoulder she said, "You know that if you read between the lines and change a few names, you might recognize some people in her books."

"Really?" I drew back.

Was this a motive for murder? Did sweet Beryle Stone use real-life people in Cottonwood as characters in her books? Did someone figure it out? Was the tell-all where she was going to reveal who everyone was?

"You let me know how you like it." The computer beeped when she scanned it, and she handed me the novel. "I'm going to go lock the doors and do some paperwork in the back. You take your time. If you need to print, just holler."

"I will. Thanks, Marcy," I called on my way over to the computer station.

When the screen lit up, I put in my library ID, which was my birthdate. All the hacking experts always told you to never use your birthday, but who in the world would hack someone in Cottonwood?

I scrolled the mouse to the right of the screen and clicked on the three lines and then clicked on the history. Marcy was right. Edna had looked up about thirty different things, mostly interviews.

"I love the smell of books." Poppa stood over me with his hands on his hips.

"Where have you been?" I asked Poppa.

"Here and there. Reminiscing about old times with Beryle." He stood over my shoulder.

As he gabbed on about old times, I scanned articles about Beryle and her interviews. There was a court document where Beryle had put out a restraining order that caught my attention. But thanks to Edna, the next website listed was the obituary of the person who had the restraining order against them. A dead end.

The photos of Beryle weren't any more interesting. She was under the Eiffel tower, in museums, a lot of her holding her books, and not even one with her fans. There were a lot of reviews about the book that'd been turned into a movie, but not much about the novel itself.

It seemed that the old saying "don't judge a book by the movie" held true in Beryle's case.

"Don't you find it odd that she never married or even had a boyfriend?" I asked Poppa.

"She said she never wanted to have kids." Poppa's eyes scanned the computer screen. "Have you noticed there was one question that every person who interviewed her asked?"

"No. What?" I asked.

"They all asked her if any of her characters were based on anyone she knew." He pointed to one of the open tabs and I clicked on it. "Right there, and there, and there." He continued to point to the tabs and I'd reopen them.

One after the other the question seemed to pop up, and she answered it exactly the same way every time. *Every character of mine has a little bit of someone I know, and every plot line has a little bit of truth.*

I clicked on the tab that had a list of all of her novels. All fifty-five of them. The same shirtless guy and a different woman were in various positions on all of them.

"Who on earth figured out Beryle Stone was writing about them? And which book do you think it was?" Poppa asked.

"There's no way I can read fifty-five of these kinds of novels." My ick factor went off again.

"No, but your mama sure did devour them." He smiled, a twinkle in his eye.

"You know Mama. If there's an underlying message in one of these, I bet she's already got a list of who Beryle Stone was talking about." I sucked in a deep breath. "Marcy?"

"Yes, honey?" She came out of the room where she'd disappeared.

"Can I get a list of Beryle's book titles?" I asked.

"I've already printed some of those out for the library." She pointed to the far side of the counter where there was other literature for people to take.

"Thanks." I took one and turned back to her. "Do you think Beryle Stone wrote about anyone in Cottonwood?"

"Every author I've ever talked to has said that there is some truth to their fiction." Her face stilled. "Do you think Beryle wrote about someone in Cottonwood and it's in that tell-all book I keep hearing about?" She gasped. "And someone came to Cottonwood to find it and killed that girl?"

"Oh, Marcy." I played it off. "You've been reading too many of those mystery novels."

"She ain't too far off." Poppa noted exactly what I was thinking.

"Thanks, Marcy. You're a gem!" I called as I walked to the door and unlocked it. "Let's go, Duke!" I yelled for my treat-begging dog.

Chapter Sixteen

"Pink is your color."

Mama's voice wasn't the sound I wanted to hear first thing in the morning. But whenever my phone rang at five a.m. and her name scrolled across the screen, I had to answer it.

Call it the guilt in me, but if she or Daddy had a heart attack and I didn't answer, I'd never forgive myself.

"Mama, I'm tired. I didn't get a wink's sleep last night." My mind immediately went from the crime scene to my fight with Finn.

"Because of Finn Vincent?" she asked.

"You heard about me and Finn?" I groaned, knowing Edna Easterly had probably used the telephone chain from church to spread the word about the disloyal officer I'd insisted become my deputy.

Finn wasn't the reason for my lack of sleep. I'd stayed up all night reading Beryle's book. There was enough backstabbing, disloyalty, and affairs in the one book to keep me from reading any more of her novels.

"I'm not gonna lie." Mama sounded a bit sad. "I was hurt. Hurt that you didn't come to me, your mama, and tell me the news, that I had to hear it from Ruby Smith. How on earth am I going to face the women at our Sweet Adelines meeting?" she whined.

"So Ruby is over you in the telephone chain?" I asked, knowing I was getting Mama's goat, knowing the more prominent in the community you were, the higher up on the chain.

"What does this have to do with the church chain?" Mama asked.

Pink? It was like my mind had just woken up. I remembered the first words out of her mouth after I answered.

"Wait. Pink? What does pink have to do with loyalty?" I questioned.

"Loyalty?" Mama threw the question back at me.

"Mama." I sat up in bed and ran my hand down Duke's warm body that took up over three-fourths of the bed. "Let's start over. Good morning, Mama. Is there something wrong? There'd better be something wrong if you are calling me at five in the morning."

"Yes. There is something wrong. How on Earth do you think I feel that I had to find out from Ruby Smith that my daughter has been seen around town lip-locking with Finn Vincent, which by the way is fine with me, but you didn't bother telling your own mother who has busted and broke her perfectly manicured fingernails pinning pins on crazy people for you, kissing babies and smudging my lipstick across my face, and ruining my heels when I go into a yard and drive a campaign sign into the dirt?" Mama sucked in a breath, but I couldn't even think fast enough to interrupt before she ranted some more. "I am your mama and I've been waiting for you to date Finn Vincent, and this is how you repay me?"

"You've got to be kidding me." I flung the covers off me. I shivered from the cold air hitting my bare legs. "Come on, Duke," I called for my lazy hound to get him to go outside.

"A wedding is nothing to be kidding about. You know that a wedding is just as important as a funeral around here," Mama whined on the other end of the line.

I let out a long deep sigh.

"Pink?" It suddenly clicked. "Even if the accusations you are throwing at me were true, which they aren't, then I'd never pick pink as a wedding color, so you might as well get that out of your thick head."

I flipped on the coffee pot switch, ever so grateful that I'd prepared the coffee the night before, and opened the door for Duke to go outside and potty.

Duke darted out the door and into the fenced-in yard, barking his head off at a poor squirrel trying to grab one of the big green walnuts that'd recently fallen from the tree. The squirrel lost out, and Duke grabbed the big round walnut like it was a ball and tossed it up in the air a couple of times before he got bored and decided to sniff around for a spot to use the bathroom.

I shut the door behind Duke to shield my legs from frostbite and dragged a quilt off the quilt box Poppa had left there since my granny died. I pulled the quilt around my shoulders and watched Duke out the kitchen window.

"So you and Finn aren't a couple?" Mama asked.

"No, Mama. Ruby Smith is wrong." Especially now, was what I wanted to say. But I kept his disloyalty issues a secret.

If Mama knew about Finn and Lonnie's conversation, she'd form an all-out ban on him with all the Sweet Adelines despite the fact they all thought he was a hunk. Not that their thinking was wrong. His priorities were.

"She said that Lonnie said that you and Finn were out front of Ben's the night I saw you and you too were awfully chummy." Mama's voice suddenly sounded disappointed.

"That's impossible. We walked out of Ben's, and that's when we heard Duke bark and we found the body." I watched Duke dart to the back of the fence and bark his head off. I opened the door and stepped out. "Duke, shh."

It'd be something else if dispatch called about a disturbance on Free Row and it was Duke.

"Duke," I called to no avail.

"So no budding romance?" Mama just didn't believe it.

"Mama." I'd about had it with her. What did she not understand? "Finn Vincent and I are not dating." My voice escalated. "In fact, he probably won't be around much longer."

I snapped my lips together in regret that I'd just said those words. But that was what Mama was good at. She could get people to talk when they didn't want to. I'd say she was good at sending people over the edge.

Duke darted along the fence line in a dead sprint toward the front of the house. Abruptly, he stopped at the gate with his head in the air and tail wagging. An arm reached over the fence and my eyes followed it up to its owner.

"I won't?" Finn asked. His stare made my heart hammer.

Chapter Seventeen

"Mama, why don't we meet up after your Sweet Adelines meeting at Kim's?" I knew I had to ask Mama about the novels Beryle had written because if Poppa was right about Mama reading all of them, I might be able to narrow down who Beryle was writing about and put them on the suspect list.

"Fine." Mama hung up on her end.

I clicked the phone off and ran my hand through my hair before I turned to face Finn. "What are you doing here so early?"

He opened the gate and stepped in, but not without stopping to squat down because Duke wasn't going to let him get any farther unless he was given the good ear scratch he knew Finn could give.

He didn't bother asking to be invited in, not that we did that type of thing around here. We pretty much never invited anyone over; it was acceptable to show up without calling ahead of time, and usually that was good by me. I loved drop-in company, but not Finn dropping in before I'd even brushed my teeth.

"I couldn't sleep after our little scuffle last night, so I went into the office and used the whiteboard that I'm so fond of. I saw where you filled in some new information too." The corner of his lips tilted up. "I got a fax about the ax and the fingerprint results, plus some of the DNA back. I thought I'd come share it with you. And this." He held a small evidence bag with that key Max Bogus had fished out of Cecily Hoover's throat in one hand, leaving the other on Duke.

The freshly brewed coffee's scent fluttered out the crack of the back door. The light morning breeze caused a few leaves to fall off the trees and carry the awaking aroma along with it.

"I'd like a cup of coffee." Finn stood up and put the key in my hand. Duke darted a couple of times between Finn and me.

"We are partners. Not loyal ones, but I have to at least work with you, so you might as well tell me so I don't have to go to the office yet." I jerked my head toward the house and curled the quilt in my fists, bringing the edges of the blanket tighter to my neck.

I turned around and walked back into the house. I could hear Finn's footsteps stalk toward me.

"You know what?" His words had bite. "You are so hard-headed. Did you ever stop to think that I'd never take Lonnie's offer, and that I just told you so you wouldn't hear it from someone else? Because God knows this town runs on coffee and gossip."

"You're gonna have to help yourself to the coffee while I get dressed," I said and walked into the bathroom.

There was no way around it. I needed Finn's help to get the murder solved. And I hated to admit it, but he was right. I was hard-headed. Always had been. You didn't become sheriff by being soft.

I stared at myself in the mirror after I splashed water on my face. I dragged the towel down my face and grabbed my toothbrush to brush my teeth. I didn't bother putting on makeup. I was on a mission to get the murder solved, and my appearance had nothing to do with it. My skills to put pieces of a puzzle together and tie evidence to Cecily and the crime scene were what was important. I brushed my long honey-blonde hair back into a ponytail and headed to my bedroom where I grabbed a fresh uniform out of my closet.

"Reading smut now?" Finn's voice trailed down the hall. "*Crimson Hearts?*"

"Research." So maybe a time or two I'd pictured the scantily clad couple on the front as me and Finn. He didn't have to know that. "On Beryle Stone."

"Oh yeah?" He snickered.

"I went to the library and did some research. In all of Beryle's interviews she said the same thing about her characters. They were based on people she knew." I might've paraphrased, but I didn't have time to tell him everything. "I decided to read the novel and see if I recognized anyone. Thank God I didn't, because Beryle has a dirty mind." I shivered just wondering who Beryle had in mind when she wrote *Crimson Hearts*.

I left my room and walked down the hall with my belt tucked under my armpit.

"Did you figure anything out?" He suddenly got interested.

"No, but my mama has not only read all of them, she also knows all the gossip around Cottonwood, and I'm going to take her to lunch today and pick her brain." I stopped in the doorway of the kitchen. "Listen, about last night..." I tugged on my belt and buckled it. "We are coworkers, and what or how you keep your job after an election is your business. But while you are deputy for me, then you will do what I need you to do."

"Kenni, I didn't take his offer. You didn't want to hear anything—" he said before there was a light rap at the door. "Besides, I always do my best, regardless of my boss."

Mrs. Brown, my elderly neighbor, was knocking at the back door, her hair tucked up under her nightcap. She had on an overcoat, and I wasn't sure what was under it. She had on a pair of yellow house slippers. I could see that she needed to go to Tiny Tina's for a pedicure and get her heels pumiced.

"Mrs. Brown," I greeted her and opened the door wide. "Come in for some coffee."

"No. I'm here to get answers." She looked at me and then at Finn. "That's what I thought." She nodded, as sure as shinola, and held out the *Cottonwood Chronicle*, our town paper. "It's just like Edna Easterly to print something not true just to sell paper."

Duke ran over to Mrs. Brown. He loved her. She always helped me out with him when I was at work all day and he was at home. Come to think of it, everyone not only helped out with Duke, but with everything. Just like this. Mrs. Brown had come over to make sure that Finn was loyal. Finn might be right that Cottonwood ran on coffee and gossip, but we also looked after one another.

I took the paper and read the headline. "Turmoil in Sheriff's Office." I turned the paper toward Finn and showed him the photo Edna decided to use. It was the one where I was nose to nose with him and the look on my face was one that shouldn't be seen...ever.

"I look good," Finn joked, causing me to smile.

"Shut up," I murmured to Finn, feeling my anger toward him softening. Darn him for being so cute at five in the morning. I folded the paper and handed it back to Mrs. Brown. "It's just a bit of gossip taken a bit too far," I said to her.

"Deputy." Mrs. Brown gave Finn a firm look. "I hope you know that we are loyal to each other, and if there is any truth in this story, you might as hightail it out of town."

"I can assure you, Mrs. Brown, that I'm loyal to Sheriff Lowry, the Sheriff's Department, and the fine citizens of Cottonwood." Finn used his finger to criss-cross his heart. "Edna did capture a moment where the sheriff and I weren't seeing eye to eye. I should've known that the sheriff was right."

"She is a smart one, ya know." Mrs. Brown's brow lifted. She looked down at Duke. "You want to come home with me?"

He wagged his tail and jumped around as if he knew what she was saying.

"I don't mind. I could use the company." Her small brown eyes looked up at me. "It's getting a little lonely over there now that my garden has died and most of the birds I feed left for warmer weather."

"Duke," I called. "You want to go with Mrs. Brown?"

He barked.

"Why don't you fill us up a couple of cups of coffee to go while I get some kibble for Duke," I said to Finn.

"You two are like a fine-tuned automobile." A smile curved on Mrs. Brown's face and traveled up to her eyes, making them sparkle. "Definitely work well together. That Edna..." Mrs. Brown tsked, showing her disapproval for how Edna had acted.

Mrs. Brown was right. Finn and I worked around each other

with ease. He made his way around my kitchen as if he knew exactly where everything was while I got Duke's food ready for the day.

"You be a good boy." I patted him on the head and gave the bag of kibble to Mrs. Brown.

"You be a good girl." She winked and walked out the door with Duke next to her.

I headed back to the bedroom to grab my badge, phone, and bag. My heart hammered in my chest. I was going to have to find a way to get this excitement I felt being around Finn under control.

It hit me that I was more upset about Finn's loyalty to me as a person than as a deputy with regard to the job. Truth be told, if I did lose, which I didn't anticipate, but if I did, there was no one I'd rather have in that office with Lonnie than Finn Vincent.

My cell phone rang.

"Mama," I whispered when I saw her name scroll across. "Now what?"

"And you said that you two aren't an item," she cried through the phone.

"What?" I asked.

"Kendrick Lowry. I'm ashamed that I had to hear that Finn Vincent spent the night at your house and Mrs. Brown saw him!"

Yep. There were some things in a small town that I just wished didn't happen. Gossip was one of them.

After I assured Mama that there was nothing between Finn and me and that he was here to bring me up to date on some evidence, I finally headed back into the kitchen to find Finn with the cups ready to go.

"I'll meet you at the office?" I opened the back door for him.

"Sure." He looked confused. "Aren't you coming?"

"I have to do something first, but I'm going to be right behind you." I pointed toward the hall, vague about what I needed to do.

When I heard him start his Charger and pull out of the driveway, I walked back down the hall to my bathroom and quickly put on a little bit of makeup.

It wouldn't hurt to look decent while I was working alongside Finn.

"You're as limp as a dishrag when it comes to that boy." Poppa ghosted himself in the front seat of the Wagoneer when I got in.

"Oh, stop it." I gripped the wheel and took a left onto Main Street, heading toward town and the department.

"So what do we know?" Poppa was ready to get to work.

"I know that we have a key Cecily swallowed, and that key has to open something," I said. "I have to go to the Inn today and interview all the guests because I have to figure out what Kiwi heard and who went to Ruby's Antiques and dragged that feather along with them. Finn said some DNA results came through, but he didn't say more, so I'm assuming it's nothing to point to a killer." I sucked in a deep breath. "I'm guessing Paige still isn't awake because I haven't gotten a call."

"It would be good if she did wake up so she could tell us what's going on." Poppa's eyes were hollow. "Maybe you need to go to the Inn and focus on that today instead of that key. Not that the key isn't important. It might unlock answers." Poppa smacked his knee. "Get it. Key will unlock?"

"Yeah. Ha ha." I rolled my eyes. "But you're right," I confirmed as we entered the downtown area. "I'll go see what Finn has and send him on the goose chase with the key." I smiled at Poppa.

The answer had to be at the Inn, but it was too early to head over there now. I wondered if the killer was still in town. Who had made Cecily scared enough to swallow the key?

Chapter Eighteen

The carriage lights that dotted each side of the downtown area were still on. There were a few stragglers parking. Probably going to grab a bite to eat before they went to work and got their day started.

I pulled down the alley behind the department and parked the Wagoneer in the sheriff's spot right beside Finn's Charger.

I grabbed my coffee and got out of the Jeep.

"Let's see what's been reported." Poppa suggested heading straight to the fax machine in hopes there'd been some evidence reported over the night.

"Good morning," I greeted Finn and Betty.

Both of them were looking at different papers. Finn hovered over the fax machine and Betty hovered over the *Cottonwood Chronicle*.

"Oh, Kenni." Betty tsked and smacked the paper on her desk. "Does Edna Easterly have no shame?"

"What?" I asked.

"You aren't going to be happy," Betty muttered, looking at me from under furrowed brows.

"What?" I asked again and walked over to see the newspaper.

Finn cleared his throat. "We didn't read what Mrs. Brown showed us. We only looked at the photo."

I picked up the paper. "I guess we'll read it now." I snapped the pages taut.

"The Sheriff and her deputy are at odds over the Stone Mysteries," I read. I continued, "Is there or isn't there a tell-all novel out there that Beryle Stone wrote before she died? That's the hubbub around the mysterious death of Beryle Stone's assistant,

Cecily Hoover, and the attack on Cottonwood citizen Paige Lemar. Paige is the wife of Lonnie Lemar, the rival and opponent facing Sheriff Kendrick Lowry in next year's election. Things are heating up not only in the election, where campaign signs are tearing our community apart, but also internally in the sheriff's department. 'Yes, I asked Finn Vincent to be my deputy when I get elected back to the sheriff's office,' Lonnie Lemar stated when asked about the blowup between the sheriff and her deputy. 'He is a good officer. He has a good head on his shoulders and is certainly qualified to one day become the sheriff once I'm out of my term. We have to look to the future and the safety of our community. By the looks of your photos, Sheriff Lowry is not only having a hard time keeping the peace in our community, but within her own office.'"

With one swift move, I slammed the paper into the wastebasket next to Betty's desk.

"No wonder Mrs. Brown rushed over." I'd thought it was a little strange. On second thought...she'd probably seen Finn's car there and hurried over to get the real scoop about him and me.

"Aw, sugar." Betty stood up and put a hand on my back. "Don't you worry about this silly paper. I don't know what you and Deputy Finn were doing, but I know y'all are a good team. Now, you hold your head high and get out there and solve this murder. Prove them wrong."

"I know, Betty. And I appreciate your kind words, but you know how the media tries to turn the truth and make it worse than it is." I shook my head.

"Edna Easterly don't have nothin' better to do," Betty said. "You can give an update at the council meeting tomorrow night and dismiss any rumors Edna has started."

"Oh, gosh." I groaned. "I forgot all about the council meeting."

"I can go and represent us," Finn suggested.

"No way. Not with that crap published. We," I pointed between us, "will go together and be a cohesive unit. And we can always be honest and ask for anyone to come forward with information."

"Or you can go to Edna and ask her to do an exclusive and ask the community for help and to report anything they might've seen. Nothing is unimportant," Betty suggested.

"You know," I nodded my head, "that's not a bad idea. And Edna will be there tomorrow night."

"She needs to get on our side." Finn looked down at the fax machine that was beeping and spitting out papers. "This isn't good." I detected disappointment in his voice. "The tape Gina Kim dropped off yesterday was analyzed and the person seen running away was too shadowy. They are seen in only one frame looking back. They can't determine whether the shadow alongside the face is long hair or just a shadow, which means they can't determine the sex of the person."

I walked over and took the paper when he offered it to me. I quickly read through what he'd said and groaned.

"When did she drop off the tape?" I was at the department most of yesterday, and she didn't show up when I was there.

"She left it with Bartleby. The Kims had eaten supper at Cowboys and you'd already gone for the night. Bartleby gave it to me this morning," Finn said.

"Kenni." Betty got my attention. "Darby has something to tell you." Betty had the phone hooked to her ear. "I'm getting the messages off the machine, and she called saying she needed to talk to you."

"Did she reference the case?" I asked, wondering if Darby was going to come clean about her little run-in with Cecily Hoover at Duke's ceremony and admit there was really something between her and Cecily that she'd been keeping a secret.

"No, just asked if you had a minute to stop by. Nothing urgent." Betty shrugged.

"Any more messages?" I asked.

"Nope." Betty tapped her ear. "I've got my ear to the gossip channels though. Maybe somebody will say somethin'."

"I was going to give the guests at the Inn a little more time to wake up, but maybe right now isn't too early." I wanted to make sure that when I went over that they'd be there.

"Nah, it's not too early. Antiquers love to get up and go, plus she serves breakfast starting at eight." Betty eyes darted toward the clock on the wall.

I grabbed a few business cards off my desk along with my pen and little pad of paper and stuck them in the front pocket of my uniform shirt.

"Good thing, because I'm hungry." I headed out the door.

The oranges, reds, purples, greens, and yellows of the fall trees nestled around the blue-painted clapboard Inn created the coziest feeling. It was picture perfect. Darby had decorated the front of the Inn with hay bales and fodder shocks with pumpkins and gourds. A few scarecrows were even sprinkled around the front.

There were a few carved pumpkins on each step up to the wrap-around front porch. The rocking chairs were empty. Quilts were draped over the back of the chairs for the guests to snuggle up in. The heaters that hung from the ceiling were turned on. I'd guess Darby had them on timers to coincide with breakfast. She made it a very nice place to stay.

She'd even set out an old bourbon barrel from one of the Kentucky bourbon facilities in the corner where Kiwi was a couple of days ago. A steaming Crock-pot filled with warm apple cider along with a glass-covered dome of pastries sat on top of the barrel for guests to enjoy while they sat in one of the rocking chairs and enjoyed the amazing view.

The screen door of the Inn creaked, catching my attention. A young girl came over with a stack of napkins and put them next to the pastries.

"Good morning," I said. "You must be the new girl."

"Yes, ma'am." She looked up and down my uniform. "Sheriff."

"You can call me Kenni," I said.

She nodded with a tight closed-lip smile and turned to walk back into the Inn.

"What's your name?" I asked.

"Jenny Rose Neil," she said. "Jenny." She shrugged one shoulder.

"Welcome to Cottonwood, Jenny." I held the screen door open for her and followed her inside.

"Thank you," she called over her shoulder.

I got the funny feeling she was trying to rush off, but I had a few questions.

"How long have you been in Cottonwood?" I asked and leaned up against the counter on the left where the guests checked in.

"A couple of days." She pinched her lips together and avoided eye contact. Her long dishwater blonde hair fell in front of her face as she looked down at the desk behind the counter as though she were looking for something to keep her busy.

"What brought you to Cottonwood?" I asked.

It wasn't a question anyone else in Cottonwood wouldn't ask; the only difference was that when it came from my mouth in this uniform, it seemed more official than nosy.

"I've been here all my life." I offered a warm smile to help break the shield Jenny had up.

"Passing through." She ran a finger down the guest sign-in sheet.

"Good morning, Kenni." Darby walked down the stairs with a wooden tray in her hands.

"Good morning." I turned my attention to her for a split second and when I turned back to talk to Jenny, she'd taken the opportunity to slip away.

"I expected to see your mama this early, but not you." Her brows twitched. "I'm assuming you got my message."

"I did, and I'm here to talk to your guests about the Stone estate sale that's taking place tomorrow." I looked around, noticing Darby didn't have a lot of antiques and wondered what her conversation with our victim had been about. "I need to get a list of items they wanted to check out and how they found out so fast after Beryle's death this was going to happen." I pulled the list out of my bag and snapped it open with a good fling.

"Sure. We can cooperate since you have a list. I was hoping that talking to me was enough." Darby lifted her chin and her eyes drew down her nose as she tried to look at the list. "How did you get my guest list?"

"I've been here talking to people." I didn't necessarily lie. I just hadn't talked to the people on the list.

"Let me go put this tray in the kitchen and give Jenny some morning jobs. She's new and I'm still training her." She turned and walked down the hall past the stairs and through the swinging doors that lead into the kitchen.

I moseyed into what used to be a large dining room of the old house that Darby had turned into a small dining room with a couple of cozy café tables. Each table had a small pumpkin centerpiece.

"Lawdy be." Poppa appeared and stuck his nose in the air. "It smells so good in here."

"Hi there." Ignoring Poppa as he went around and stuck his nose in all the guests' food, I walked up to two women who appeared to be in their sixties. "Y'all in town for the Stone estate sale?"

"We are." The lady aggressively nodded and smiled.

"I'm Sheriff Lowry. If you need anything at all, please call us anytime." I took a business card out of my pocket and put it on the table for them.

"Hope and Bea. We're sisters." Hope pointed between them. She had short blonde hair with big green eyes that stood out with the green turtleneck she had on. "We heard there was an original painting by Ms. Stone that we'd love to get our hands on. We loved her books. Anything she created with her hands is exactly what we want."

That reminded me that Ruby had said there was a painting missing from the inventory list. Where was that painting? Had Beryle painted it?

"I'd forgotten all about Beryle and her paintings." The memory put a twinkle in Poppa's eyes. "She did love to paint. We'd jump in her little red MG and park down by the lake. I'd swim, and she'd paint." His face stilled. His mouth frowned. "The last time we went was when I last saw her paint. The next day was when her sister was gone. It was the saddest thing."

Poppa needed me to discuss his sadness, but it wasn't like I could do it here, right now. I tried to give him a sympathetic look without people noticing me staring out into space.

The woman's companion nodded while stuffing her face with some eggs that looked and smelled good. My stomach growled.

"How did you hear about the sale?" I asked.

"The internet." Bea's brows lifted. Like Hope, she had blonde hair and green eyes, only her hair was pulled back into a high ponytail and she had on a black turtleneck. "We have Beryle's name set on Google alerts. Anytime someone posts about her, we get an alert. Plus, with her books," the woman's face hardened, "though she hasn't put out a new book in years, those online bookstores have a feature where you can follow your favorite authors." She rubbed her hands together. "When I get one of those emails, I silently beg for it to be about Beryle. But I guess we won't be getting any more novels from her."

"I hope you get that painting." I did a double tap on their table with my fingertips before I walked over to the next table. "Good morning." I greeted a couple who were enjoying a couple of pastries and coffee. "Those doughnuts look so good."

"They are." The man nodded. "We have really enjoyed your town since we got here."

"Today we are heading down to Main Street where we heard you had a lot of small boutiques," the woman said.

"And the antique shop," the man said.

"Oh, yes." Her eyes bugged out and she smiled. "Definitely the antique store."

"Ruby's?" I asked.

"Yes. We are very excited to see what Beryle Stone has down there," she said giving me to opportunity to ask more questions.

"I'm Sheriff Lowry, and if you need anything while you are here, be sure to holler." I plucked a couple more business cards from my pocket and handed it to them.

"We're the Ganders. From Minnesota." They nodded.

"Wow, that's a long way. We are proud of Beryle here in Cottonwood. How did you hear about the sale?" I asked.

"On eBay, and there are estate sale newspapers and magazines. Though it's not on there yet, but they put up a photo that says coming soon." She looked at her husband and gestured between them. "I Googled and saw where Beryle had died." She drew her hand to her lips that took a sudden downward dip. She curled her lips inward, closed her eyes, and slowly shook her head. "Awful she died. Just awful."

"Instead of waiting to see what the sellers on eBay are going to buy, we decided to come and get our own stuff," the man said. "They jack all those prices up. Especially with a celebrity who's passed."

"Good luck." I offered a friendly smile. "Be sure to head on over to Ben's for lunch. They have the best beans and cornbread."

"I heard that's a must," another woman's voice said next to me. She was sitting alone in a wing-backed chair next to the large stone fireplace, which I'd heard nearly cost Darby her entire budget when she was redoing the old house.

It was well worth the money; the workers built it by hand and cut each stone to fit. I was sure Darby has recovered ten times the cost since she opened the Inn. A much-needed place for our town since it was one of the only places to stay. The Inn and Tattered Cover Books were the only offerings in Cottonwood for our out-of-town guests.

"Hi there." I walked over to her. "You're here for the sale?"

"I'm here to see what sells and what doesn't. I'm a photographer. And now that there's been a murder, of Beryle Stone's assistant no less, I've taken an active interest in the case and hope to turn that into the magazine article instead of lousy photos." She leaned back into the chair, resting her elbows on the arms and intertwining her fingers in her lap.

"I'm sorry. I'm Sheriff Lowry." I put my hand out for her to shake.

"Jetter. Everyone at work calls me Jetter. I work for a tabloid magazine out of California. And I'm here to get the details on the estate." A slow and steady smile crossed her lips. "I was just reading about the turmoil in the sheriff's office. Makes for an interesting story." She tapped a copy of the *Cottonwood Chronicle* with her finger. "And I must be on my way, since I have a meeting with the editor-in-chief. Edna Easterly?"

Jetter stood up and grabbed the *Chronicle* off the table, folding it in half and sticking it up under her armpit.

"Have a good day, Sheriff." Jetter nodded.

Poppa stuck his foot out in front of Jetter. Something happened. She stumbled but didn't fall completely down. Her torso flailed as her feet tried to keep up with her. She jerked around once she had her footing and glared at me.

I didn't say anything to her. It was better to keep my mouth shut. Now she'd definitely write an article. There was sure to be some blow-up about it, and I didn't want to waste my time with it. At least not until I got this murder solved.

"You shouldn't have done that," I whispered out of the corner of my mouth. "I really think she felt your foot."

"Nah. She's just clumsy." Poppa tilted his head to the side, peeking around to see where Jetter had gone.

I pulled the list of guests out of my pocket and checked off the Ganders, Jetter, Bea, and Hope. I didn't get a sense that they'd said the words Kiwi had repeated to me. I'd just knocked out half of my list.

Jetter had stopped at the front desk and was saying something to Darby. Darby gave me a look that told me she wasn't too happy.

There was a shuffle down the steps. I looked up and saw Hattie Hankle taking each step carefully. Kiwi was propped up on her shoulder.

"Hi, Hattie." I walked over to the stairs and up to help her down the rest. "How are you today?"

"I'm okay." Her brows were furrowed. "I'm not sure where my sister is." Her eyes popped open wide and she swung them at me.

"Do you think a critter got her?"

"Hattie, I didn't know you had a sister," I said, trying to play along. I'd found it was much easier to just go with what Hattie said.

"Where's my seester? Seester?" Kiwi tried to imitate Hattie's southern accent. "Tag, you're it. Tag!" Kiwi squawked.

"What did he say?" Poppa asked and stood next to Kiwi.

"Tag, you're it." Hattie tapped me on the head and giggled.

"Tag, you're it." I tagged her back.

"No, Kenni. That's not right." Hattie stomped and Kiwi's claws dug into her shoulder as though he were holding on for dear life.

"Not right, not right." Kiwi's feathers waved up on his neck as he repeated Hattie. "Freeze!" Kiwi squawked.

"Evie said you have to freeze." Hattie started to sit on the floor, but she was really trying to get on all fours and crawl.

"That's enough." Darby rushed around and grabbed Hattie by the elbow. "It's not time to play tag."

"Not just any tag." Poppa smacked his hands together and did a jig, kicking his hip up to the side along with his elbow. "Beryle Evie Stone. Her sister used to call her Evie."

"Wait." I put my hand out for Darby to leave Hattie alone. "Hattie, did you and your sister play freeze tag?"

"All the time." Her face lit up in delight. "She hasn't been here in a while. Paige tries, but she isn't as fun as Evie."

"That's what I had to talk to you about." Darby let out a long deep sigh. "Hattie Hankle is Beryle Stone's sister."

"Smile!" Jetter yelled.

We all turned around with shock and awe on our faces. All but Hattie Hankle. She was grinning as big as a possum eating a sweet potato.

Click. The flash of Jetter's camera blinded me.

Chapter Nineteen

"You knew all this time that Hattie Hankle was Beryle Stone's sister, and you didn't think to tell me?" I asked after I'd dragged Darby into the Inn's kitchen and planted her in the chair at the table.

"It wasn't that I wasn't going to tell you." She put her head into her hands and shook it. "That's one reason I called Betty. I knew I had some information that you might find helpful."

"What was it?" I asked.

"Son of a biscuit." Poppa's jaw dropped. I'd never thought I'd see a ghost at a loss for words. "Beryle told me that her sister tried to follow us to the river that day I told you about and they found her dead."

"I was trying to keep a family secret, well...secret. They'd gone to great lengths, using Hattie's middle name as her last after Beryle moved her here." Darby's eyes dipped. "Beryle came to me after I bought the Inn. Her father had just died, and she told me how this adult-care facility had called her about payment for her sister. Hattie." Tears filled Darby's eyes. "She was so shocked to find out her sister was still alive because she'd spent all these years thinking she'd died. Come to find out, her parents were hiding that they'd put Hattie in a facility so Beryle could live a normal life. So she wouldn't have to stop her dreams of being an author, traveling the world to stay in Cottonwood to take care of her sister. Beryle was distraught. Instead of taking her in due to her crazy traveling schedule, she asked, practically begged, me to rent her a room at the Inn on an ongoing basis."

"Go on." I took out my notebook and began to write down everything she was saying.

"This is on the record?" Her eyes popped open. "I can't have it on the record."

"This is a major development in the current investigation of the murder of Cecily Hoover and attempted murder of Paige Lemar," I said. "What did Hattie mean about Paige trying to play tag?"

"Kenni, I want to help, I do, but I..." She hesitated. "I promised Beryle that I'd keep Hattie a secret, and if I did, then Beryle would continue to pay for Hattie. I just can't let her live here for free. I mean, I love Hattie, but this is my business and my life."

"I understand that, and maybe we can talk to Wally about some of the charity money going to her sister, but you have to tell me what you know. This could be a major break in the case." I wasn't sure how, but somehow I knew this was a piece of the puzzle.

"Kenni." Darby looked up and her eyes were wet. "I don't know. What if I say something and end up like Paige, or even Cecily?"

"What if you don't and still end up that way? Because your guest, Jetter, she's with a national newspaper. You know they publish gossip and half-truths." I left out the fact that it was a celebrity tabloid and most of the articles had to be taken with a grain of salt. "I can't protect you if you don't give me a reason to."

"You're telling me that if I tell you everything I know, you will put Finn here to keep us safe?" she asked.

"I'd get a reserve officer here for sure. And right now," I said, putting my hand on the walkie-talkie.

"Fine," she said. "Let me put a pot of coffee on."

"You do that and I'll call in an officer." I pushed in the button on my radio. "Betty."

"Yes, Sheriff," Betty immediately answered back. "Over."

"I need you to call over to the Stone estate and get one of the reserve officers over to the Inn. I need a twenty-four-hour officer on duty. Meals included." I looked over at Darby and lifted a brow. She nodded her head.

"Will do, Kenni." She corrected herself, "Sheriff."

While the coffee brewed, Darby sat back down across from me at the table.

"I told you how she got here. I make sure Hattie gets to all of her doctor appointments," Darby said.

"Who is her doctor?" I asked.

"Dr. Camille Shively," Darby said. Camille was the only doctor in Cottonwood. "Once a month I have Camille here for a lunch and at that time she sits with Hattie and makes sure everything is good. Beryle had it set up like a finely tuned machine. Hattie has a special diet and plays different games. And Paige Lemar takes care of her like her sister would."

"Yes. I want to talk about her." I flipped the notebook to a fresh page and wrote "Paige Lemar" at the top.

"Paige had worked for Beryle for years as her housekeeper. When Beryle was moving was also when I was turning the old house into the Inn. Beryle said she had to leave in order for her to fire," she put air quotes around the word fire, "Paige and then make it look like I gave Paige a job. I do pay Paige to clean the other rooms, but Beryle pays her to take care of Hattie. She said she needed to move out of town in order to care for her sister and keep writing to make money so her sister could live the same way when she was dead and gone. I think it literally killed her inside to leave her sister and her home, but Beryle was so selfless that she only wanted what was best for Hattie because she carried the burden of her parents putting Hattie in a home."

"How long has Beryle known about her sister?" I asked.

"After her father passed, there was a letter he'd left her in his will. He told her about Hattie and how they'd faked her death back when Beryle was in high school." Darby's chest heaved up when she sucked in a deep breath.

"They obviously knew then that Beryle was going to try to pursue a writing career after college and didn't want to hold her back with a lifelong burden." It was all coming together.

"Right. Her parents were getting older and they knew Hattie would be a lifetime commitment, and Beryle was so kind-hearted that she would give up her dreams to care for Hattie," Darby confirmed. "Beryle said that she'd made so many career commitments for books that it wasn't fair to take Hattie. That's when Beryle moved Hattie from the home her parents had placed her in to the Inn. And like I said, only a handful of people knew about it."

"Did Paige know about all this?" My mind swirled.

"She did. She knew that Beryle didn't fire her. But she couldn't tell anyone, not even Lonnie. He thinks that Beryle fired Paige and I hired her." Darby's voice faded. "Beryle put money in an account, and I pay Paige out of that account. So when I saw Cecily at the ceremony the other day, I asked her about the account, because nothing's been put in for the care of Hattie or for Paige's wages. She told me that I was going to have to figure it out. That's when I told her I'd heard about the manuscript and I could only imagine the story about Hattie is in there."

The front bell rang at the desk, signaling someone was up front and needed help.

"Jenny must be cleaning rooms." Darby stood up. "She was God sent. I had to hire her quick since Paige was put in the hospital." She held up a finger. "I'll be right back."

After the door swung shut, I stood up and started to pace.

"This is big," I said to Poppa. "Not only that Hattie is Beryle's sister, but Paige, along with Darby, knew it. Somehow someone knows or thinks they know what's in the tell-all manuscript." I bit my lip. "If we only knew where it was. Where did Beryle hide it?"

"The only way to find out is to tear the estate apart. She always said there were so many hiding places and after the death—" Poppa stopped himself. "After Hattie was taken away, Beryle said she'd hid for hours in those secret places. But she never told me where." He wisped across the floor and looked out of the small round window of the pass-through door. "Hattie doesn't look like the girl I remember. But you know she still acts the same. I can't believe Beryle never told me."

"Maybe she didn't know until she was older," I suggested.

"Whoever killed Cecily and nearly killed Paige knows about something. Hopefully that person doesn't know about Hattie, or she could be in danger of being the next victim." Just as Poppa finished his sentence, Jenny Rose Neil walked into the kitchen with Kiwi on her shoulder.

Chapter Twenty

There were many things about Darby's story that bothered me, and Jenny was one of them. Not only did she just so happen to show up on the day of the murder and attack, but she'd fit in all too well with Hattie and kept Kiwi close to her.

There was a person at the guest counter dinging the bell as I caught up with the reserve officer that was sent over. I'd given him instructions to stick close to Hattie. Play games with her, stay at her side twenty-four seven. I also gave him a quick rundown on my suspicions about Jenny, but told him to keep undercover until I could get some background and solid evidence on her. Darby said she was a good worker and nothing on her application made her think Jenny wasn't telling the truth. To me, it was a little too convenient.

"Betty," I called for her, pushing the radio button as I was getting into the Jeep.

Poppa sat in the passenger seat. It was great to have him with me. If I wasn't on the right track, he had no problem telling me.

"Go ahead," Betty confirmed.

"Can you get me a background check on Jenny Rose Neil? I don't have any more information than that. Where is Finn right now?" I asked and steered the Wagoneer back to town. I had to meet Mama for lunch, and after that I wanted to go see Preacher Bing. It was time I saw him and Stella to see what they knew about this and about the charities Beryle wanted to benefit from her estate.

"He's gone to the hospital to check on Paige Lemar. I heard that she was rousing." Betty gave me the best news of the day.

"Thanks, Betty. Let me know if any new developments come in." I clicked off the radio and picked up my phone. I dialed Finn.

"What's up?" His voice was a welcome warmth.

"I hear you're headed over to the hospital." I turned off the country road and headed into town. "Are you there yet?"

"No. After you left the office this morning, Betty got a call from one of the henny-hens saying they'd heard Paige had moved around her bed all night like she was having some bad dreams. I thought it'd be a good idea to be there in case she was waking up. You know," he paused, "so Lonnie couldn't get to her first."

"Good." I smiled, not only because it was so nice that he could think and act on his own without me telling him what to do like I had to do with Lonnie, but also how he was now referring to the gossipy women as the henny-hens when just a few short months ago he was so businesslike. "I have a major development."

I turned onto Main Street.

"Hattie Hankle is Beryle Stone's sister." I still couldn't completely wrap my head around it.

As much as I tried, I couldn't remember just when I'd had my first memory of Hattie. I was able to recall Poppa's stories, and sometimes Mama and Daddy would take me to the Inn for supper or special occasions like Easter brunch and I'd see Hattie there, but other than that, nothing.

"What?" Finn asked with quite an emphasis.

"Yep. Apparently, she didn't die like her parents told the community. According to Darby, Beryle came to see her after Darby bought the old house and was renovating it into the Inn. Beryle's paid for everything for Hattie."

"Do you think there's something about Hattie that someone wouldn't want to be known and that she's in the tell-all?" he asked.

"I don't know. But I do know that the new girl, Jenny, the one on the list of the Inn guests, seems a little suspicious to me. She showed up on the day of the attacks."

There was a parking spot right in front of Kim's Buffet on Main Street. I maneuvered the Wagoneer in the spot and parked.

"It would completely be possible that Jenny showed up in town to get the manuscript, because we have no idea who Beryle met along the way when she didn't live in Cottonwood. Jenny could have known Cecily and somehow got Cecily to meet her in town or even at Ruby's where she unknowingly brought the feather along with her. She could have killed Cecily and broken into Ruby's to see if the manuscript was in one of the estate antiques. When Paige walked down to get in her car, she noticed the door was broken in her friend's shop, so she went in there, and that's when she happened upon Jenny, who then took the ax and struck her. That's when we heard all the commotion, only we scared her off, and she's just young and fast enough to get away in the darkness," Finn said.

"Possible." I looked into the restaurant window. All the Sweet Adelines were in pink pillbox hats and matching suits. Some of them had on gloves. Even Edna Easterly had changed out the feather on her fedora to a big pink one. The writing on the notecard glued to the feather read "PRESS" in pink Sharpie. "I guess at this point, Paige holds all the answers." As I spoke, little puffs of my breath hitting the cold air floated out of my mouth.

"Did you get to talk to any of the guests?" he asked.

I turned the knob to turn on the heat in the Wagoneer. As the morning turned into afternoon, the sky was actually getting a little more gray, like it was about to snow. The temperature had dropped.

"I talked to half of them. I only really learned about them hearing about the sale through estate-based newspapers, eBay, and Craigslist. It's interesting that not only was Beryle an author, she was also a painter, and a good one from what I hear. Ruby said there was a painting missing from the inventory list." I reached in the back of the Wagoneer and grabbed my coat. "I don't recall seeing any paintings in the house, but I'll take a better look around. I'm on a mission to find out where that key goes and if there is a manuscript, just in case Paige can't tell us anything."

"How did you find out about the paintings?" he asked.

I could hear some beeps and voices over an intercom as well as some background noises.

"One of the guests knew that Beryle painted and was hoping to get a piece of her artwork." I glared over at the door of the Buffet—a few of the women were leaving.

"Listen, I've got to go. Let me know if Paige is awake." I clicked off the phone and turned the Jeep off. I tugged my coat on and zipped it up. I grabbed *Crimson Hearts* and got out.

"Good afternoon," I greeted some of the women.

"You're so sweet to meet your mama for lunch." Viola White peeled her gloves off her perfectly manicured hands, one finger at a time. She picked at the edges of her gray hair and then pushed her big black-rimmed glasses up on her nose.

"Thank you, Viola." I held the door as Ruby Smith came out.

"You got the person who broke into my shop in custody yet?" Ruby's bright orange lipstick sure did add color to the gray day.

"Working on it. Have you heard anything about Paige?" I thought I'd ask.

"No." Her lips pressed together. "I just don't know why someone would want to hurt her."

"Me either." I patted her on the back and walked into the restaurant.

"Kenni, how you?" Mrs. Kim asked in her broken English. "How criminal going?"

"I'm good. Investigation is going well." Maybe the "fake it till I make it" attitude would help me get these clues together and solve the murder. "I'm meeting my mama for lunch. Is Gina here today?"

"You just missed. She go to the store." She waved.

Mrs. Kim plucked off her pink pillbox hat and walked off. She darted from table to table taking the pink polka dot tablecloths off. Pink glitter fluttered all over the floor. Mama was sitting at a table with a water for her and a Diet Coke for me.

"Mama." I greeted her with a kiss and sat down.

"What do you want?" Mama's southern charm was more sarcastic than endearing. "I know you want something if you wanted to take me to lunch."

"Take you to lunch?" I smiled. "I'd love to pay for your lunch.

But you're right, I have a few questions to ask you about this."

I put the book on the table in front of her.

"I can't wait to hear what your mama's take is on these novels." Poppa showed up. "She knows her gossip."

"*Crimson Hearts.*" Mama's face lit up. "You know," she tapped the cover, "they don't write 'em like they used to." She winked.

"Mama, that's gross." The ick factor rushed through me again. "I've come into some interesting facts about Beryle. Apparently, she based all of her characters on people she knew. I'm wondering if she wrote about someone in Cottonwood. Then maybe when they found out she was writing this tell-all book, they went looking for it and killed Cecily, Beryle's assistant."

"Honey, *Crimson Hearts* was about a woman painter who had an affair with her best friend's husband. There aren't any women in Cottonwood who paint." Mama twisted in her seat. "And then there was *Cuff Me*, which was about a local jeweler who was having a secret love affair with the town sheriff." Mama leaned in. "He loved to be cuffed with jeweled handcuffs."

My eyes slid over to Poppa. He was rubbing his wrists.

"Ew." I frowned. "Did Poppa ever date Viola White?"

"Now, Kenni, that's none of your business." Poppa's eyes popped open. "We are here to talk about the murder."

"What you want?" Mrs. Kim stood next to the table with her pen and tablet.

"We aren't sure yet." I smiled and picked up the menu as if I was interested in ordering.

"I be back," Mrs. Kim said and rushed off to the next table.

"You know..." Mama eased back into the seat. "They did go to some movies after my mama died, but I don't think—" She slowly shook her head then suddenly stopped. "Viola better not be the woman in *Cuff Me*." Mama huffed.

"Okay, that's enough. I'm out." Poppa disappeared. All this told me was that I was on the right track.

"If I find out that Viola and Daddy had a thing, I'll jerk her bald." Mama downed her glass of water. She was shaking her leg, making the entire table wiggle back and forth.

"Calm down and focus. Tell me about her other novels."

"They all had the same sort of story, just told in a different way. There was a girl who either dated a married man or had someone else's baby, and their love was so great it was hard not to root for them to get together." Mama's wheels were turning.

"Now that you think back on her novels, do you see anyone from Cottonwood disguised in them?" I asked.

"*Cuff Me* could be your Poppa!" she cried out, plunging her head in her hands. "I'm disgusted. Do you think Viola White killed that girl?"

"No, Mama. Why on earth would Viola White kill someone because she and Poppa had a fling?" There was no reason for it. "Who cares? She and Poppa enjoyed a little company. I'm just not sure how Beryle would know any gossip if she didn't live here."

"What you want?" Mrs. Kim came back. She looked between me and Mama. "No loitering. You want eat, you order."

"I've lost my appetite." Mama stood up. She tugged on the edges of her pink suit coat and ran her hands down her pink pants. "I'm suddenly sick to my stomach."

"Mama," I called after her. "Mama, please don't go saying anything to Viola White." I stood, running alongside her.

"Then she shouldn't have done such dirty things for Beryle Stone to write about!" Mama smacked the front door of the restaurant and ran out.

"That didn't go so well." Poppa was sitting in the car when I got back in.

"Would you want to know about your parent's affairs?" I asked him and then decided to drop the *Cuff Me* plot. "We know that one plot could possibly be about you. What about the others? Mama was so upset about you that she didn't answer any more of my questions. But at least your little tryst with Viola was a possible plot, which means that she might've written about someone else in Cottonwood."

I started the Wagoneer up and did a U-turn on Main to head

south a couple of blocks down, where the church was located on the right.

"Let's face it," Poppa paused, "I'm fine with people knowing Viola and I had some fun, but others might not be so open to Beryle knowing their story. Now at the end of her life she decided to come clean and let everyone in on who was who in the novels."

"Plus, most of her plots aren't really morally acceptable." I shrugged and parked in the parking lot across from the church.

"We need to write down all the plots and make your mama focus." Poppa suggested something that no one could do: make Mama do anything.

Preacher Bing crossed the street behind the Wagoneer and stopped in view of my rearview. He bent down and looked into the window and waved. It looked like there was a light on in the office area, which meant someone was there, and I hoped it was Stella. I was pretty good at getting information from her since she got nervous around me in the uniform.

Poppa had already ghosted out of the car and stood next to Preacher Bing.

"His sermons sure could get your heart pumping back in the day." Poppa referred to Preacher Bing's young preaching days.

Unfortunately, he didn't exude so much excitement in his later years. But there was no way the church committee was going to get rid of him. It was the whole loyalty thing.

"Hi, Kenni." Preacher Bing stood six feet four inches tall. His coal black hair made his pasty white skin and dark eyes stand out.

He'd always scared me, reminding me of Lurch from *The Addams Family*, and he was just as scary now as when I was a child. There was no way I dared move when I was in church.

"Been a long time since I've seen you here." He clasped his hands, and his deep voice rang out.

"I was just here for the wonderful reception after Duke's ceremony," I reminded him.

"I mean for this." He pointed to his heart. "I do think there has been a lot of stress in your life over the past year with all the crime we've been having. I've had to do a lot of stress counseling for some of our members."

There went the Baptist guilt Mama was so good at, but coming from Preacher Bing, it was slapped on thick.

"I understand that with growth in town, there's more crime, and all of these crimes have been isolated incidents." I shoved my fists into my coat.

"Is Paige Lemar an isolated incident, or a victim of being in the wrong place at the wrong time?" His thick scary brows lifted up under his strange bangs.

He'd definitely make a good Lurch on Halloween. My thoughts brought back the fear I had of him when I was a kid.

"I guess we'll have to see when she wakes up." I sucked in a deep breath.

It sure was hard to get up confidence when a figure of authority your whole life seemed to be taking control of the conversation.

"And that's why I'm here, sort of." I tried to offer a nice smile, but he didn't buy it. He was stone faced.

"Your mama does good work around here. I'd like to see the sheriff's department contribute." He wasn't going to let it go.

"Betty Murphy does a lot for you, I hear." In fact, Betty contributed her time to count the Sunday collection money and deposit it on Mondays.

"All of the department." He pointed his open palm toward the church. "Shall we discuss matters inside where it's warm?"

"That's great. Because I really need to talk to you about Beryle Stone and what the church has to do with her last wishes." I walked next to him. "Stella mentioned that some of Beryle's money was going to charities and the church knew about it."

"Did she?" His brows dipped and formed a perfect hairy V.

He held the big glass door open for me. I stepped in. There was nothing wrong with the church's heating system. The heat took my breath away. I peeled off my coat and stuck it up under my arm. I couldn't help but notice Preacher Bing's eyes draw down to my gun.

Apparently not a fan.

We walked down the hall and entered the door where there was a small plaque on the wall that said "Office."

Stella was sitting behind the desk filing her fingernails. She quickly shoved the file in her desk and stood up.

"Kenni." There was surprise on her face.

"Hi, Stella. How are you?" I asked.

"Fine," she said, stone faced.

"I guess you've recovered since the Euchre game?" I asked.

"I'm just fine." She grabbed some papers off the desk. "Here're your messages." She handed them to Preacher Bing.

"Our Euchre night sure could use a good prayer," I suggested to Preacher Bing. "Some of them women, all who come here, sometimes flat-out lose their religion over a silly little card game. Ain't that right, Stella?"

"I wouldn't know." She shifted uncomfortably. I was getting her goat, since she was the main one who gossiped, and she'd never want Preacher Bing to know. "I don't participate in such activity."

"Is that right?" I asked. "Huh."

Her lips pursed, her nose curled, and her eyes grew big as if she were signaling me to hush.

"Hold all my calls, please." Preacher Bing walked into the other room in the office that boasted a sign with his name on it. "Kenni." He stood at the door.

"Good to see you, Stella." I smiled and walked into Preacher Bing's office.

He shut the door.

"Can you tell me about those funds? We're following up on some leads that are confidential, of course." I gave the aw-shucks look so he wouldn't question me.

He took his eyes off my sheriff's uniform. I was glad he saw this was a business call and not a come-to-Jesus meeting.

"You can ask Wally Lamb, but she stated in her will that she wanted only me to be privy to where her money was going since I was her clergy." He pulled off his black overcoat and hung it on the coat tree next to the door.

"Can you tell me about those funds?" I asked again.

"Yes. There was a private fund." He walked over to his desk and sat down. He motioned for me to sit in the chair in front of his desk. He clasped his hands and rested them on the desk. "I know you're going to walk out of here and get a warrant from the judge so I'm going to tell you. She had some art foundations where she was on the board. She was on a lot of boards outside of her life in Cottonwood. And the private fund goes to Hattie. I'm sure you've already found out about her."

I nodded.

"I'm not even sure Darby knows about the funds yet because Wally is still finishing up all the paperwork."

On the board. Inwardly, I groaned. Art foundations outside of Cottonwood? My mind whirled back to the sex scene with the artist in *Crimson Hearts*. Did the killer live outside of Cottonwood, hear about the tell-all manuscript, come to look for it, and kill Cecily? That would make finding the killer harder and a lot longer to solve. At least there was a fund for Hattie to be taken care of. Darby will be happy about that.

"You're thinking what I'm thinking." Poppa appeared next to Preacher Bing, looking at me. "The list of suspects could be ever so long if Beryle was on all these boards. She could've made anyone mad or written about anyone."

"Did Beryle leave any money to the church?" I asked. "Mama said finances were discussed at the meeting Paige was at before she was attacked."

"You think that Paige was attacked by someone here?" Preacher Bing asked.

"I'm just covering all the bases," I stated, not wanting to alarm him. Was he avoiding my question? "Did she leave any money to the church?" I asked again.

"She didn't." He looked down at the messages Stella had given him and shuffled through them.

"Are you surprised?" I asked.

"No. She didn't attend church here for a long time. She was simply comfortable with me handling her death because I was her clergy while she was in Cottonwood," he said.

I believed him, putting Stella's idle gossip down to her wanting people to think she knew more than she really did.

"She simply asked me to be in charge of the funds for Hattie in case something ever happened to her." He continued,

"Beryle came to me years ago with a heavy heart about what had gone on with Hattie. We prayed, and I helped her cope. It was then that I agreed to take the money she'd send in an envelope and deposit it into the fund she set up at the bank. Stella thinks it's Beryle's tithe and should only be handled by me." His chest rose with each deep breath." He looked at me. "Now, if you don't mind, I need to get these messages returned." He put the messages on his desk next to his phone. "Is there anything else I can help you with?"

"Thank you, but I think I have all I need. I appreciate you letting me know." I walked back to the door. "Bye."

"Kenni, it sure would be nice to see you in the front row with your mama." He had to go there.

"Thank you." I waved and shut the door behind me.

Stella was hunched over a grocery-store crossword puzzle.

"See ya, Kenni," she said after she looked up.

"Have a good day," I said and found my way outside of the church right before my cell rang.

It was Finn.

"Hey, Finn." I pinned the phone between my ear and shoulder, digging in my pocket for the keys to the Wagoneer.

"She's awake," he whispered.

"Huh?" I grabbed the phone and held it tight to my ears.

"Paige Lemar is awake and she's talking. Lonnie won't let me in." He said the words I'd feared.

"On my way." I hit the off button and jumped into the Jeep.

I grabbed the beacon with one hand and rolled the window down with the other. I licked the suction cup, flipped on the switch, slapped it on the roof, and threw the Jeep in gear.

Chapter Twenty-One

"Kenni, she's sensitive." Lonnie tried to stop me at the door when he saw me walking into the Intensive Care Unit. He had his palms flat out to me. "She's tired."

"Tired?" I asked, knowing it sounded insensitive. "She's been sleeping for a couple of days. I'm sure she can answer some simple questions. You know I have that right."

Myrna Savage must've been the Sweet Adeline chosen to stand vigil for this particular time. She was patting Paige's hand when I looked into the room.

"I want her to rest. I almost lost her." Lonnie's voice cracked. He looked down and shook his head. His finger lifted. He pointed at me. "You upset her and you're gone," he warned.

There was no way I was going to give him a chance to change his mind; I pushed past him. The reserve officer and Finn stood at the sliding glass door to Paige's room. The curtains on both sides were pulled back. There were a couple of nurses next to her bed.

"Kenni." Paige's voice was soft. "I don't know what to say."

One nurse had Paige sitting forward while the other nurse was behind her fluffing her pillows. Dr. Camille Shively was sitting next to Paige on the hospital bed and talking to her. Paige's color in her cheeks looked good, though there were dark half-moon shapes under her eyes. Her hair was covered by white bandages.

"Kenni, really?" Camille asked with a bit of disgust in her voice.

"You don't have to say anything, Paige." I walked over and patted her hand, ignoring Camille. "Can you tell me what you remember?" I asked. "Anything? Anyone? Why you were there?"

Paige looked at Camille.

"If you want to answer the questions, you can, but you don't have to," Camille told her. "I don't want you to have a setback."

She squinted her eyes as though she was trying to process what Camille was saying.

"I'll try." Paige's voice was weak and it cracked.

"Take your time. You were hit over the head with an ax," I said, trying to comfort her. I really wanted her to trust me and tell me what she remembered.

"Cecily?" She gulped.

"She died." There was no sense in sugar-coating it. Paige was going to have to face it eventually. "Finn and I heard Duke barking at the killer and rushed over to the shop, and that's when we found you."

"Killer?" she asked, bringing her hands to her face. She began to sob. "Oh my gosh."

Lonnie rushed to her side and sat down on the bed. He put his hands on top of hers. He turned his head toward me.

"That's enough, Kenni." Displeasure showed on his face. "She can't take anymore today."

"It's okay." Paige brought her hands down. Tears flowed down her face. "I'd gotten a call from Cecily; she asked me to meet her at the shop. I'd been working all day at the Inn and I had my church meeting. I left early because Cecily had called me frantic."

"What did she say?" I asked.

"Something about a tell-all book, and she thought it was in the shop and that she had to get it or lives would be changed forever." She looked down at her fingertips. "I remember walking down there because I'd parked my car in that area. When I got there, she was inside the storage room. Then..." Her jaw dropped, her eyes darting around the room. "I can't remember."

"That must've been the time of the attack." Lonnie rubbed her arm. "You did good, honey. You need to rest. You might remember more later."

"We found Cecily outside the shop and you inside next to a piece of furniture." I wasn't going to just leave my questioning, I was going to try to get everything I could out of her. "Did you know Cecily before she came here?"

"No. Well, I knew of her from Beryle. I guess I should tell you that Beryle and I were friends." More tears streamed down her face. Lonnie wiped them from her cheek.

"Shh." He encouraged her to stop talking.

"That's probably enough for one day," Camille said in a stern voice.

"Have you found Cecily's killer?" Paige asked, looking around Camille.

"No." I wanted to make up excuses. "There aren't a lot of leads, but Cecily's hair was found on the ax."

Paige's eyes popped open. There was a deep-rooted fear in them.

"What?" Lonnie asked. "Are you okay?"

"I remember something." She put her hand palm down on the top of the bandage on her head. "When we were in the storage room, I told Cecily that I didn't think there was a tell-all and tried to calm her down because Beryle never said a word to me about it." She hesitated and looked off into the distance as though the memory was playing in her head. "I glanced over Cecily's shoulder, and I remember seeing a man. Tall. Dirty." She dragged her eyes to mine. Her mouth opened, her eyes dipped, and tears poured down her face. She gulped. "Sterling Stinnett."

Paige fell back on her pillow, sobbing. Lonnie wrapped his arms around her and rested his head on her chest. He took one arm from around her and stuck it out to me.

Myrna jumped to her feet and grabbed a wet washrag. Lonnie backed away and Myrna rubbed the cloth down Paige's face.

"Enough for today." His stern voice told me that I'd overstayed my welcome.

I nodded. Sterling Stinnett. He was tall. He was mysterious. And he liked to stay in the shadows. Now that I thought about it, he fit the description of the shadowy figure in the video from Kim's Buffet security tape. But a killer? Had he been a character in one of Beryle's novels?

Camille and I headed out into the hallway. Just as I was sliding the glass doors shut, Lonnie pushed back.

He pointed for me to go over to the nurses' station, and both Finn and I followed.

"If you don't find Sterling Stinnett before I get my hands on that S.O.B., I'll kill him," Lonnie said through his gritted teeth.

"Listen, Lonnie. You and I both know Sterling. He'd never hurt a fly." I couldn't imagine the Sterling doing anything to hurt a soul. In fact, Sterling always kept a good eye out and reported anything fishy. "But I'll go find him and see what he knows."

"He worked for Beryle too." Lonnie's brows shot up. "He did all of their family's landscaping and," his voice was joined by Poppa's, "when Beryle left town, he didn't have a job anymore and became a bum." Poppa and Lonnie spoke the exact same words at the same time.

"I'll let you know." I put a hand on Lonnie's arm. "You take care of her and yourself. Now that she's awake, you go down to the cafeteria for some food."

Lonnie had lost a few pounds over the past couple of days. I could tell by how gaunt his face looked.

"Let me know," he said, his words stern. "Kenni, I appreciate it."

It was the first time that he'd actually given me a vote of confidence since Paige had been attacked.

"Thank you. Take care. I'll be back." I curled my lips together in a tight smile.

"Kenni, seriously." Camille lifted her elbow and rested it on the counter of the nurses' station. "Paige is weak. She's got a major contusion on her head. Her brain is no longer swollen, but her state of mind is definitely fragile. I can't under any circumstances give you full permission to question her. It has to be on her time, at least not until I release her to go home."

I put my hands in the air.

"Fine, but I've got a murder to solve, and she's a key witness." I waved over the reserve officer. "Be sure you or another officer stays here all the time."

He nodded.

To Camille, I said, "Please let dispatch know when you decide to release Paige, because I can't guarantee that whoever tried to kill her won't come back to finish the job." I tried to maintain curtness, but I needed Camille to know the severity of the situation. "While I have you here, can you tell me if you've seen Beryle Stone while she was in town?"

"I did. But not in the capacity you think," she said.

"You went to give her an update on Hattie?" I asked.

"How did you know?" She tugged me by the elbow and dragged me into one of the family consult rooms. She shut the door behind us.

"I know that Hattie is her sister and that you go to the Inn regularly to make sure she's doing okay." I took my notebook out of my pocket along with my pen. "When did Beryle contact you about her sister?"

"When Doc Walton was killed." She reminded me of my first murder investigation as sheriff of Cottonwood.

I'd like to say that was a bad memory, but it wasn't all bad. Yes, it was terrible that Cottonwood's beloved doctor, Doc Walton, had been murdered, but it was when Poppa's ghost first showed up.

Camille Shively and I were long-time acquaintances. I wouldn't say friends, because we didn't hang around in the same circles, but we were friendly. She tucked a strand of her black hair behind her ear, and then pushed her hands into her white lab coat. Her black eyes stared at me as she talked.

"Darby called me and asked if I'd come to the Inn to see a patient. We all know that Doc Walton drove all over creation to see patients." She laughed, bringing back many memories of him.

If I had a fever, Mama called Doc Walton right away, and within minutes he was there. He did this with all of his patients, until I had to take his driver's license away after he'd committed a hit and run, though he saw it differently.

Apparently, he was still going to see Hattie Hankle at the Inn up until his death.

"When Darby gave the cash payment, it was up front yearly. And that's without insurance, so it's a lot of money. Darby had asked me not to tell anyone, which I couldn't anyway because of patient confidentiality. Still, I used it to my advantage because I had to know ethically where the money was coming from and wouldn't treat her until Darby told me Beryle Stone was funding the account." Her phone beeped and she took it out of her pocket. She hit a button and put it back in. "I've got to go." She took a step toward the door. "Long story short, Beryle's dad lived a very long time, and it wasn't until his death that she found out that her sister was still alive. She had a hard time understanding how her parents could just lock Hattie away. She said that loyalty is the number one priority with her, and she felt betrayed by her parents. That's when she brought Hattie here until she could complete her commitments to her career and move back, which to my understanding she was in the process of doing the past couple of months."

"One quick question before you go." I stopped her as she took a step out of the door.

She turned around and let out a long sigh.

"Was Beryle sick?" I asked.

"Yes." Camille shook her head. "She had stage four brain cancer. It was just a matter of time." She turned to head down the hallway. She stopped and snapped her fingers. "You know, they didn't call me to pronounce her dead or anything. She made sure I didn't tell anyone she was sick. Not even her assistant."

"Really?" I looked at her in disbelief. She shrugged and walked down the hallway, disappearing into another patient room.

"What was that about?" Finn asked over my shoulder as we walked down the hall of the hospital.

We got into the elevator.

After the doors shut, I asked, "Paige or Dr. Shively?"

"Both," he said.

"Paige said that she saw Sterling Stinnett at the shop the night she was attacked. That's all she remembers. Which would make sense, because she probably lost all memory right before and after the attack. The security footage from Kim's Buffet showed a tall shadowy figure running away. Those are probably the footsteps we heard. Sterling Stinnett."

"Lonnie said that he worked for Beryle too." Finn leaned against the wall of the elevator and we stared at each other. "You know him much better than I do. Do you really think that he's capable of this?"

"I think anyone is capable of anything when secrets might leak." The tell-all book still seemed to be the root of the attacks. "Even an even-tempered man like Sterling Stinnett."

"I didn't see him at his regular places this morning. So it looks like I'm going be spending the rest of my afternoon looking for Sterling," Finn said just as the door of the elevator opened. He pushed his hands in the pocket of his sheriff's jacket. He pulled out an evidence baggie. "Here is that key."

"Thanks." I took it. "I'll head out to the estate at some point and see if I can find what it goes to."

I ran the baggie between my finger and thumb, wondering what on Earth the key had to do with the murder of Cecily Hoover. Images of her holding the key, fighting with someone, and being frightened enough to swallow it swirled around my mind.

And Sterling Stinnett had been there? Was he really the killer? What would be his motive?

"I just can't believe that Sterling Stinnett could kill someone." The words hurt my heart as they came out of my mouth.

"You've said it before, and we both know it. People do uncharacteristic things in times of desperation. Maybe he knew something and wanted to get his hands on the tell-all?" Finn questioned.

"Maybe." I chewed on his question. "We won't know what he knows until we pick him up. Be sure to check all his usual places like Cowboy's Catfish, Ben's, and Cole's on the river."

Cole's was a gambling joint where the men loved to go drink beer and play cards.

I continued to rub that key between my finger and thumb. The plastic bag had grown warm under my fingertips. I couldn't shake the feeling that if I found out where the key went, our killer would be exposed.

"I agree with you, Kenni-bug." Poppa appeared next to me. "That key holds the truth." He hesitated. "I've seen it before. At Beryle's house."

Chapter Twenty-Two

Beep, beep. The walkie-talkie signaled Betty from my end.

"Kenni, I was just about to call you," Betty answered.

"I'm on my way to the Stone estate to take another look around. Can you make a few phone calls before you leave for the day to see if you can locate Sterling Stinnett, or find out if anyone has seen him? If you find him, call Finn and let him know." I asked, "Why were you going to call me?"

"Myrna Savage just called and asked me what I knew about Sterling. Apparently Lonnie wants to find him, and Paige is telling everyone that Sterling has to be the killer and the one who attacked her," Betty said.

"Well, it's all hearsay until we talk to Sterling." I knew it was probably all over town by now. Which could be a good thing if someone would tell us where he was so we didn't have to hunt him down. But nothing was easy in this investigation.

"I'll call around," Betty said. "What about the estate sale? Are you going to have to cancel?"

"I haven't made a final decision yet, but I'll be sure everyone knows." We said our goodbyes.

I hated to think that I might need to cancel the estate sale since I hadn't cleared the house from the investigation. Granted, no crime had been committed on the property, but there were still so many out-of-town visitors here just for the sale. Cottonwood itself was benefiting from all the extra tourists and the money they were bringing into the town.

"I know you hate to disappoint people, Kenni-bug, but sometimes as the law, we have to do what's best for our town." Poppa and I stood on the front steps of the Stone estate that overlooked the vast acreage.

I gripped my bag, the feeling that I was missing something very important that was right in front of my face welling up inside me. Clear-cut lines of Poppa's stern face told me that he too knew there was something here.

The gray clouds off in the distance were rolling over the river and would soon be hovering over us. The wind whipped around us, curling around the old trees, knocking off what little leaves were left. The dried leaves tumbled and twirled across the land. A storm was brewing.

"Where is that manuscript?" I was so sure the Beryle had hid it on the estate somewhere.

"Have you looked in the barn yet?" Poppa asked. He turned to face it.

"No." My nose wrinkled. "I'm not sure if it looks stable enough."

"The roof looks a little caved in on the one side, but the walls look good," he said. "No stone—"

"Unturned," I interrupted him, finishing his motto. "No stone unturned." I pointed to the dilapidated old barn. "Why don't you use those fancy ghost powers you have and look around before suggesting I put myself in danger."

He laughed.

"I'm not ready to join you on that other side, so I'm not doing it," I said.

"Chicken," Poppa taunted me.

"Really? I can hear the scary music playing and people yelling, 'don't go in there.' Like in those scary movies." I got the shivers thinking about it.

I suddenly wondered what movies Luke Jones was going to have playing in the next month. He loved hosting scary movies during September and October in anticipation of Halloween.

"We haven't had any luck in the house," he said. And just like that, Poppa had whispered away, and I was sure he was already in the barn.

My stomach knotted. He was right. And no matter how much I wanted to throw a girly fit and protest, to be just his little granddaughter and not the sheriff since no one was around to see me, I knew I couldn't.

"Fine." My eyes drew up to the sky where the gray clouds hung. Why was it that gray cloudy days never represented the curl-up-and-read-a-book or binge-watch-movies kind of days for me?

In fact, when I thought about it, cloudy and rainy days generally brought memories of sadness. Like the day Poppa died and was buried. Or the day that Doc Walton was found dead in his home.

With each step I took toward the barn, I sucked in a deep breath of the fresh country air and let it fill my lungs. The smell of impending rain floated into my nose, lingering. I prayed the rain would hold off until I took a good look around the barn. The last thing I needed was a rainstorm—the darn thing really would come down around me.

There was a broken-off broomstick jammed in the handles across the two large barn doors. It wasn't a tight fit. Any critter could've gotten in the open space. Like Hattie Hankle, I didn't like critters either. I set my bag on the ground and unzipped it, taking out the camera. Everything had to be documented whether it was evidence or not. I snapped pictures of the door handle and the broken broomstick from every angle before I retrieved my flashlight from my duty belt and pushed the button on the side to turn it on.

Slowly I dragged the beam of light up and down the open crack before I decided to slip the broken broomstick out of the handles.

"I'm looking!" Poppa's voice echoed out of the crack.

"Do I honestly need to come in there?" I questioned, feeling a little silly that I was relying on a ghost. Not that I didn't believe in Poppa.

"Everything looks stable. There's a loft that separates the roof from the interior. I wouldn't go up there without having an engineer look at the structure to make sure it's sound, but the rest of the barn looks good. The loft floor is still intact too." He gave me the reassurance I needed to proceed.

The broom handle must've been in there a long time. The wood was splintered and weathered on both ends. What was left of the chipping paint on the handle gave a hint that it was once green. It was pretty tightly wedged through the handles and tilted diagonally.

Bam, bam, bam. The butt of my flashlight knocked the broomstick loose enough that I could tug a little and push it toward the ground, letting the stick fall. I knocked it out of the way with my shoe. The doors of the barn opened slightly.

"You in here?" I curled my hand around one of the handles and cautiously opened the door, just in case something was going to jump out or fall on me.

"Yep, no critters. Come on in." Poppa appeared at the front of the barn. "There doesn't seem to be any lighting in here."

"It's not been a working barn for years." I swung the light up, down, and around to get my bearings. It was a typical abandoned barn, like I'd seen on a lot of properties around Cottonwood. Most serious farmers now used prefab and steel barns that were already constructed and came in pieces. Not the good old sturdy barns that lasted years, like this once was.

The camera's flash lit up the barn with each click of the shutter.

"Look at all of these old tools," Poppa said and pointed to a joint wooden plane. "I wonder why they didn't come in here to get stuff for the sale."

"It's probably included in the sale of the house." I shrugged and walked around, snapping photos of everything I was seeing.

The inside was a typical barn, a center aisle and stalls on each side. In the back there were two big doors, just like the front. I walked down the right side and stuck my flashlight in each stall as I walked by. There were a few old bridles and what looked like some shoeing tools, but other than that, it was musty and just plain old and dirty.

The back right was where the tools were kept. Once I made it back there, Poppa had already started to look on the other side of the barn.

"Did you see anything up in the loft?" I dragged the flashlight up the wooden stairs that led to it.

"Nothing. It's empty up there. I'll be," Poppa gasped with a giddy tone.

"What?" I hurried down his way, skipping the first few stalls on the left side of the barn.

"I think this is Beryle's old car." He pointed to something in the stall.

"Toy car?" I asked on my way over.

I curled up on my tiptoes and noticed the stall was a little bigger than the others, but not by much. There was an old brown cloth tarp that covered something fairly large.

"Man, oh man." Poppa rubbed his hands together. "I haven't been in this car since that last day I told you about me and Beryle riding down to the river so she could paint."

I opened the stall door and walked in and around the tarp while taking photos from the front, sides, and back.

"Well, let's take a look." I pulled the tarp off with one jerk. Dust flew everywhere.

"Smart," Poppa joked about me jerking off the tarp. I smiled. I loved that his ghost had a sense of humor.

"Wow." My jaw dropped at the sight of the old convertible MG car. "This is really cool."

"And I bet no one knows it's in here, because it would bring a lot of money to the sale." Poppa nodded. "Beryle loved this car. Back in the day, she'd take a scarf and put it over her head, knot it under her chin, and put a pair of big black sunglasses on. She looked like a famous person before she became famous." Poppa grinned. "She was one of those women that when you looked at her, you knew she was going to be someone."

"This sure is pretty." I dragged my hand down the side. The paint was still immaculate, and though I was no car expert, it made me do a double take. "I bet you're right. This will fetch a lot of money. I need to tell Ruby about this."

The photos I had taken weren't doing the old car justice. It was in amazing condition. Obviously, it wasn't used much.

My phone rang deep in my pocket. When I pulled it out, the baggie with the mystery key in it came out too.

"Kenni," Poppa whispered with a hint of disbelief. "I can't believe I didn't think of this. Beryle loved this car. Maybe Cecily saw Beryle keeping this key close to her side, and she knew it was the key to where Beryle hid the tell-all."

"And maybe Cecily didn't know that the key belonged to this car. That's why she couldn't find the manuscript." It was possible that Beryle would've hidden something in the car. Cecily did say that Beryle would escape for a couple of hours outside and she didn't know where she went. "Well, let's see if the key fits."

The phone continued to ring in my hand. The baggie warmed under my grip.

"I'm telling you, it belongs to this car," Poppa said with confidence. "Back in the day, the keys were tiny. None of them fancy key fob thingies. Try it."

I didn't hesitate. I opened the baggie and took out the key. I held it up to my face. There weren't any sort of markings on it. Just a small gold tarnished key with a round top and a half-moon hole in the middle.

I stuck the key in the driver's side door and turned.

My eyes slid across the black convertible soft-top and stared at Poppa, who stood on the other side of the car.

It worked. The smell of leather pushed out of the open door. I turned my flashlight and looked inside. The bucket seats were black with a tan stripe on each side. There was a small backseat with something under a cloth.

"I wonder what that is." I shined the light on the cloth. Poppa shrugged.

I ran my hand down the side of the old leather driver's seat and found the small lever that moved the seat forward. I bent down and reached into the backseat to pull out the draped item.

I had to put my flashlight down on the barn floor so I could get both hands on it.

"I could use some muscle here," I teased Poppa about his ghostly inabilities to help me with any physical stuff.

"Listen, I told you it was safe to come in," he joked back.

"This is fancy," I said about the red drape.

I leaned it up against the car and picked my flashlight back up.

"Pull that cloth off." Poppa had ghosted next to me and squatted down next to me.

I stood the flashlight on its end so the light shined up to the ceiling. My phone started to ring again, but I ignored it. If it was important, dispatch would call me over the walkie-talkie.

"It's a canvas." I slipped the drape off.

"It's one of her paintings." Poppa leaned in and took a closer look.

Boom! A clap of thunder rolled through the sky and I felt it in the ground, giving me a shimmy shake. I shook it off and picked up the flashlight and shined it on the canvas.

"Imposter," I read the word that was written across the top in red, dripping down as though Beryle had tried to make it look like blood.

"What's it of?" Poppa's eye squinted, and his nose curled up like something smelled really bad.

"I can't tell." Both of our heads tilted to the left and the right trying to figure out just what was on the canvas beside the word "imposter" and Beryle's signature on the bottom left corner.

"It's some sort of billowy wave." Poppa's head was nearly sideways, his ear stuck on his shoulder. "This isn't anything like what she painted before."

"What did she paint before?" I asked, standing up. Maybe a different angle would make something come into focus.

"Flowers. Fields. Happy faces." Poppa pushed himself up to

standing. "Nothing this disturbing."

The flowy-looking thing was wispy, with deep black and maroon as the focus colors. The top of it was a light brown and shaped in curlicues as it hung down the flowy image. In the middle of the flowy design were two identical oval green shapes a couple of inches apart and a black round hole underneath them. The flowy design ended about three inches above the bottom of the painting, which had been faded into what looked like abstract book covers, which would make sense since she was a writer.

"I get the books, but the shapes? Is it a figure?" I took a step back and looked harder, deeper.

"Maybe it's a character from one of her books and that's why people are trying to get their hands on it." Poppa posed a really good point.

"Okay, maybe. But what is so important about this car that would make Cecily swallow the key?"

My phone rang again.

"I better see who's trying to get in touch with me." I reached in my pocket and took out my phone. It was Finn. "Hey." I couldn't wait to tell him about the key.

"You aren't going to believe this." He sounded out of breath. "Someone took Paige Lemar right out of the hospital."

"What?" I gulped. "What?" I asked again.

"Paige Lemar is missing. I'm not sure what happened, but I'm in the process of getting the hospital video. All I know is that the reserve officer called and told me. I figured he was mistaken, so I rushed back over there. The nursing staff can't find her, and Lonnie is gone too." He talked so fast my head was spinning. The beeps of equipment and voices in the background told me he was near the nurses' station.

"Did Camille discharge her?" I took my phone from my ear and hit the speaker button. Maybe one of the calls I'd missed was from Camille, since she said she'd call me when she was about to discharge Paige. But no, all three were from Finn.

"No. The nurses said that Dr. Shively had said that she was

going to start the discharge paperwork tonight, but not this early because they were going to get some blood results back from the lab to make sure she was still stable. Listen, once I'm done here I'll head to their house to see what's going on. Lonnie's car isn't here."

"Then he probably broke her out. But before you go, I found out the key goes to an old model MG car I found in Beryle's barn," I said.

"You found?" Poppa's jaw dropped. He jabbed his chest. "I found it."

"I'm going to finish going through the car to see if there's anything in it that'd make Cecily Hoover want to swallow the key." I looked back down at the painting, not telling him about it since it didn't seem important. "Any news on Sterling Stinnett?"

"Nothing. It's like he vanished." Finn's voice faded off. "Let me get out there and I'll call you back."

"Okay. Bye." I clicked off the speaker and hit the end button before I put the phone back in my pocket.

"Why would Lonnie take Paige out of the hospital?" Poppa asked. As if I knew the answer.

I shined the flashlight all over the inside of the car and patted my hands under the seats.

"I have no idea. More importantly, why would Cecily swallow this key?" I asked and dragged my eyes down the car. "What secrets are you hiding?" I patted the car. "And where did Sterling vanish to?"

The same key opened the tiny trunk. There was nothing in it. I felt around to see if there was a secret compartment where a tire was kept, but there wasn't anything. I made my way over to the passenger side of the car and did the same routine. The glovebox had the owner's manual in it but nothing else.

The rain that accompanied the thunder and lightning began to beat down on the old barn. Trickles of water were coming from the loft where the rain was getting in the sunken roof. The sky had completely given into the dark gray afternoon storm, making it even harder for me to see.

"I think we've looked through the car as much as we can in the darkness. I'll give Mr. Graves a call and see if he can get his tow company over here so we can get a good look at it in the daylight. I'm marking it as evidence, along with all the photos I've taken."

Chapter Twenty-Three

The rain beat down on the pavement so hard, I could see the raindrops explode.

"Where are we going?" Poppa asked.

"I'm going to head on over to Graves Towing to see if I can get him over to the Stone estate quick."

"I thought you were going to call them?" Poppa asked.

"I'd rather drive. It helps me think." I kept my eyes on the road and my hands on the wheel.

"It also gives us time to talk some things through without being disturbed." Poppa rubbed his hands together.

This was one of our favorite things to do together when he was among the living. I had fond memories of us discussing his cases, sitting at the kitchen table in the house I lived in now. He'd have a steamy cup of coffee, and I would have a big mug of hot chocolate with a pile of marshmallows on top. It was like a game to me, a puzzle of sorts. Throwing out ideas of what could've happened sometimes turned into great leads. As I got older, I began to take our clue games more serious, and eventually, I decided to go into law enforcement, which sent Mama straight over the edge without a rope to cling to.

In fact, Mama took to the bed. The Sweet Adelines took turns visiting her and enticing her with her favorite dishes, but she insisted nothing was going to help her come to terms with the fact that her only daughter was out to sabotage her dreams of me taking over the ladies groups, sitting around doing our nails, and god knew whatever else the women in Cottonwood did with their time.

"Here is what we know." I gripped the wheel, careful not to take the curvy turns back into town too sharply because the fallen leaves got slippery when they were wet. And today had turned out to be a gully washer. "Which isn't much." I let out a long unhappy sigh. "Okay, Beryle Stone's assistant claimed there was a tell-all manuscript already contracted with a publisher. Apparently, Beryle had many secrets."

"One, Hattie is her sister, and she's been paying for her this whole time." Poppa held up his finger. "Two, Paige Lemar worked for Beryle all those years as her housekeeper, and when Beryle moved after her fame took off, she made a deal with Darby to keep Paige on at the Inn, but in charge of Hattie and her needs."

"Don't forget Darby, though I'm not entirely certain that I think she's the murderer. But I did see her arguing with Cecily, and she'd have an inherent reason to make sure the money kept coming in." I hated to bring up the fact that maybe Darby's good deed of keeping Hattie in the Inn all these years turned into a misunderstanding, leading to a fight, and then to death. "Which is what Preacher Bing was in charge of."

"Yes, he was in charge of Hattie's fund. There has to be more to it. Beryle wouldn't have been so embarrassed about her sister being alive. There has to be more to this than keeping Hattie a secret." Poppa looked out the window of the Jeep as we headed into town. Graves Towing was on the north side, past Lulu's Boutique. "I have a suspicious feeling that Beryle knew something was about to go down."

"Why do you say that?" I questioned, driving straight down Main Street.

The downpour of rain didn't seem to hinder tourists from visiting the shops along Main Street. I'd also noticed the store owners had put out some specials, using the estate sale to their benefit.

"I find it interesting that there's this tell-all that no one can find. Beryle wasn't one to hide things. She was very open and free-spirited." Poppa craned his neck as we passed through town, looking at all the people.

"She wasn't open about Hattie. Maybe it was because she had a busy schedule. Then she came down with cancer, so maybe she figured why let it out now," I said. "That's a huge secret. It might taint her squeaky-clean image. Still, why would someone kill Cecily?"

"There has to be more about Hattie. Something that doesn't make sense, because you're right. She did keep it a secret for a long time, since she found out right after her father died." He pointed across my body and out the window. "Isn't that the Jenny girl from the Inn?"

My foot let up off the gas pedal and I coasted by, looking at Jenny. She was standing on the porch of Lulu's Boutique with Lulu McClain. They were gabbing away, and it piqued my curiosity.

Enough so that I jerked the wheel to the left and decided to stop. I pulled up behind Jolee's On The Run food truck, which would make for a good cover to stop and check out the scene.

"Have you heard back from Betty yet about Jenny's background?" Poppa asked.

"Not a word." I pushed in the button of the walkie-talkie and noticed they'd watched me pull up. "Betty?"

"Go ahead, Sheriff," Betty answered back.

"Have you gotten the background check on Jenny?" I asked.

"I got something back a couple of minutes ago and was just going over it. She's just a kid from Kentucky. Graduated high school. Worked at the dental office. That's about it. There's no arrest record, no record of her living any other place than the foothills of Kentucky." Betty clicked off the radio.

"So that seems to clear her of anything out of the ordinary. Unless we do some kind of intensive background check with her and Beryle." Doubt that Jenny had anything to do with Cecily and Beryle Stone set in. "She just seems like a young girl trying to find her way."

"I knew a girl like that once." Poppa gave me a sympathetic smile. "Look at her now."

"Thanks, Poppa." A lump formed in my throat. Though I loved being with the ghost of my poppa, it wasn't exactly like having the living Poppa.

I got out of the car and gave a wave before I knocked on the side door of On The Run. It seemed like the thing to do since I didn't want it to be so obvious that I'd just stalked a probably innocent girl.

"Kenni," Jolee greeted me and waved me in. "Get out of that rain. I was cleaning up and getting ready to pull on out."

The truck was so cute. She'd done such a great job. The inside was just like a kitchen you'd see in a restaurant, only Jolee used pink pans. The motif was light green and pink, and when she rolled out the awning, it was striped in the same colors and had a picture of her truck on it with the name.

She wiped her hands down her food-covered apron.

"I've got some leftover stew. How about a bowl?" she asked.

"That'd be great." I rubbed my hands together realizing that I was hungry. I sat down on a stool and realized just how much of a toll this investigation had on my mental health and how much I missed my girlfriends. It wasn't like they needed to know all the clues or even any clues; it was the sounding board that I missed. The interactions with just girl things during investigations.

"This case has really got me stumped," I said.

"Oh, yeah." She took the lid off the steaming pot and used the ladle to scoop and pour the stew into a bowl. "I think it's some crazy fan of Beryle's. Maybe Cecily was rude to the fan and now that Beryle's dead, they are seeking revenge. Or they thought Cecily killed Beryle."

"And that's why you're a chef and I'm the sheriff." I laughed out loud at Jolee's crazy idea. I wished it was that easy to solve. "I needed that."

"Good. I'm glad to see you smile." She set the bowl down in front of me. "You're going to love it." She pushed a piece of French bread across the counter.

"What are you doing tonight?" I asked. "Maybe we can go to

Luke's and see a movie. He loves playing those scary ones. Right now, I could use some fattening popcorn and a Diet Coke."

"I'm working." She stood over the sink and washed the dishes up.

"Working?" I asked. "Party on a weeknight?"

It wasn't unusual for people to hire Jolee to bring her truck to their homes or businesses for parties. The bridal parties had really gotten big.

"Mmm-hmm," she sing-songed above the running water.

I looked at her. She glanced up at me and quickly looked away.

"What is it?" I asked. "I've known you all my life. We're closer than sisters. Something is going on."

"No," she tsk'd and slowly shook her head with a scrunched-up nose.

"Yes." I nodded. "What is it?" I asked as her cell phone rang right next to me.

"I got it!" she yelled and leapt across the tiny interior of the truck with her hand jutted out, covered in soap suds.

I grabbed the phone when I noticed Ben's smiling photo pop up and held it over my head.

"Ben Harrison?" I asked with a smile.

She jumped for the phone and grabbed it out of my hands.

"You have a date tonight with Ben!" I gasped. My eyes popped open. "You weren't going to tell me?" I pointed at her.

"Shhh." She put a finger up to her mouth and curled her head away from me. "Hello?" she answered in a voice she never used when I called her. "Can I call you back?" she asked and said a few mmhmms, yeses, and okays before she hung up.

"You are something else," I said. "I can't believe you weren't going to tell me."

"We're just testing the waters. You've been so busy that I didn't want to put something else on your plate." She shrugged. She picked up a dishtowel and started to dry the pans. "And we are working. I'm going to show him how to make my famous wilted lettuce."

"You don't have to sugarcoat your date with me. I'm just happy you two have finally realized what everyone else around town sees." I couldn't believe it. It was finally happening. My two good friends, together at last.

"What?" She drew back as though I'd insulted her.

"That you two do have chemistry outside of your jobs. Everyone sees it," I said, taking a bite of the bread.

"You mean like how everyone sees the chemistry between you and Finn Vincent, but y'all don't?" She stuck her hands on her hips.

Chapter Twenty-Four

Jolee sure did have a good comeback after I'd caught her about her secret little rendezvous with Ben Harrison, which made me happy since I knew they were perfect for each other.

"Hey there." As I left the food truck, I put the feelings that Jolee had stirred in me about Finn Vincent aside and walked up to Lulu and Jenny. "Did y'all get your afternoon cup of coffee?"

"I did earlier." Lulu smiled. "Jenny here tells me that you've been out at the Inn." Lulu put her hand on Jenny's back.

My eyes lowered to Jenny's face. She reddened from the forehead down to her neck. No, don't become one of those henny-hens, I wanted to scream, but I put on a thin smile.

"Anyways," Lulu waved her hand in front of me, "I did give her a Re-elect Lowry pin from your mama after she signed my new lease."

"New lease?" I asked.

"Deputy Vincent has decided to keep Cosmo, and I just can't have a cat in the apartment over the shop. Some of my customers are allergic to cats and the air ducts are connected, so I'm scared the cat hair will float around. I can't afford to lose any customers." She shook her head. "It's a shame too. I did love going to get my rent every month." She winked. "I timed it perfectly. If I showed up there around six a.m., Finn would answer the door with his jeans on, his hair wet," an evil grin tipped up her lips, her shoulders rose to her ears, and she gingerly closed her eyes, "and shirtless."

Her eyes snapped back open.

"But you know all that." Her button nose crunched. "At least that's what I'd heard."

"No." I laughed it off. "We're just partners."

"Yes." She wiggled her brows.

"Seriously, work partners," I insisted.

"Yes, dear." She gave me the ultimate "bless your heart" without actually saying it. She agreed in the demeaning way that only an elder could get away with. "Of course you are. And I also hear that he's looking at buying a house next to you."

There she went again with that smile. I glared.

"I'm not sure. We don't discuss our personal lives outside of the office." I sucked in a deep breath and turned to Jenny. "So you're planning on staying a while?"

"I am. I like the Inn. I wasn't sure I'd like cleaning, but it's not bad and there's not too many rooms," she spoke with a soft voice. "I'm busy now, but from what I hear it's just because of the estate sale, and we usually aren't that full."

"I'll be right back." Lulu hurried up into the boutique after the phone started to ring.

"I'm glad you are staying." I nodded. "And living here will be a lot of fun. I hope you decide to come to a craft night."

"Lulu was telling me about it. I think I'd like to come." She glanced over my shoulder, watching Jolee's truck drive off. "Tonight I'm going to the council meeting. This is a nice small town. Not that where I came from was huge, but everyone there's known me all my life, and there weren't many men there."

"There's not many here." I chuckled and took a sip.

"Finn Vincent is cute," she replied.

Coffee spewed from my mouth as I choked.

"Unless there is something going on between you two and you were lying to Lulu." She pointed behind us to the inside of the shop.

"No." My eyes felt as big as a full moon. I shook my head. Hell yes, I wanted to blurt out. There is something there, he just doesn't know it.

"Keep it together, Kenni-bug." Poppa ghosted next to me. "Let's go talk to Sean Graves so we can get Beryle's MG towed. Stay on track. We're burning daylight."

"It was good seeing you." I inhaled deeply through my nose to keep my wits about me.

Stiffly, I turned around and tried hard to blink my eyelids. I swear my eyeballs were frozen three times their original size.

"I'll see you tonight," Jenny called at my back.

"Yep!" I hollered and got into the Jeep. "Holy cow." I sighed deeply and turned the key to start the engine.

"We can deal with that later." Poppa sat in the front seat. He pointed north. "Get going."

There was silence between us the entire way to Graves Towing. Not that it was that far away, but my mind was.

The tow company was on the far edge of the north side of town before the county border. Sean Graves was a third-generation family owner. To a town visitor, the tow company would look like a farm with a big white farmhouse. The Graves were good about keeping their company nice and neat.

Around the property was black Kentucky post fencing, but around the actual tow lot full of cars was a chain-link fence with security cameras all around. You couldn't see the tow lot from the street; you had to drive up the driveway and go around the house to see the miles of concrete where they did their business. The land and house had been in their family for generations. It wasn't until Sean's father's management that they'd turned the house into the business and lived off property. I'd yet to see their home, but Finn had when he'd gone out there about the trespassing call we'd gotten a couple of days ago.

I pulled the Jeep around to the back of the house. I put the Jeep in park and headed into the house.

"Hello?" I called after I'd opened the door with the open sign and walked in. "Hello?"

"Here I am." Leighann Graves came out of another room, tucking her shirt in. "Daddy's out on a call and I'm answering phones."

"Looks like it." My eyes scanned over her shoulder. There was a shadow casting down into the hallway from the room Leighann had just come from. "Manuel, you can come on out now."

"Huh?" Leighann tried to play off her decision to make the most of her being alone.

"I can see your shadow," I called out to him, ignoring her. "And I don't think you want me to call Sean."

"Listen here, Sheriff." Leighann stepped up, and so did her voice. "What can I do for you? Unless you've got some towing business, then you can leave."

"Seeing how your father has called about Manuel trespassing before, I do have a right to be here to check it out." I rocked back on the heels of my shoes and rested my forearm on the butt of my gun. "So I suggest you get him out of here now. Understand?"

"Yes, ma'am." She chewed on her bottom lip.

"Fine." I pulled a business card out of the front pocket of my shirt. I picked up a pen from the desk and quickly wrote Sean a note about the car. I handed it to her. "Make sure you give this to your dad. It's official business."

"I'll call him right now." Her face relaxed. She seemed a bit relieved. "And I'll take care of the other thing." She tilted her head toward the door.

"Bye, Manuel," I called out. "Bye, Leighann."

"You know what?" Leighann stopped me. "Just wait until you fall in love. You'll see that it isn't easy to stay away from each other."

I gave a sympathetic grin before I headed out the door. My heart took a little dip. I felt it more than she knew.

Chapter Twenty-Five

Beep, beep. The walkie-talkie chirped right before Betty Murphy's voice came over the speaker with an urgent plea, "Calling all units, calling all units!"

"I'm here, Betty," I answered and waited to turn the engine over in the Jeep.

"I'm here too," Finn answered right after me.

"Oh, good, both of you." There was relief in her voice. "Darby called from over at the Inn. She said that someone tore up Hattie's room."

"What do you mean 'tore up'?" I asked and started the engine.

I turned the windshield wipers on and put the Jeep in gear.

"As in ransacked. Shuffled through," Betty answered back. "I didn't get all the details because Darby was so upset. She said to call Kenni right now."

"I just got to the Lemar residence. Lonnie's car is here, so I'll get his statement and then head over," Finn said.

"Betty, call Darby back and tell her we are on our way." I clicked off the radio.

With the beacon suctioned on the top of the roof and wipers moving as fast as they could, I headed right on over to the Inn.

The Inn had looked much different twenty-four hours ago with the sun shining on the amazing autumn leaves. Now, the rain and blowing wind had knocked off what remaining leaves were left on the branches, pasting them to the ground, damp and brown, making the road slick.

Finn was still in town checking out the Lemar residence to see if Paige was in fact home and had not been kidnapped by the killer.

After I put the Jeep in park, I scooted up the front steps of the Inn and in the door. Darby was sitting on the top step next to Hattie, and the reserve officer was standing up next to them. A few of the Inn's guests were in the gathering room on the right.

"They don't know about it," Darby whispered, tilting her head toward the guests. "I figured if any of their rooms were destroyed like Hattie's, they'd tell me."

"Why don't you take Hattie into the kitchen while I go look at the room," I suggested.

"I'm telling you," Hattie said, "it's that darn critter. It's lurking its ugly head, just like Sister said."

"I'll go look," I assured her. I gave a gentle pat on her back once Darby had her standing. I turned my attention to the reserve officer. "You can come with me."

I moved my bag to my left hand and used my right to hold on to the railing. My shoes were slippery from the rain, and I wasn't about to take a chance of falling down these hardwood stairs.

"Where were you when this happened?" I asked, knowing good and well he was there only to keep Hattie safe, which apparently, he'd done.

"Hattie wanted to go sit on the porch and listen to the rain," he said as we made our way down to Hattie's room. "I didn't see any harm in it. Darby had brought us some tea and cookies. I put a blanket around her legs, and we were out there for about thirty minutes. That's when the rain started to blow on the porch and I told her it was time to come in."

I opened the door to Hattie's room. The lights were already on, giving me a good idea that someone was looking for something. The cushions on her couch were flipped off. The TV stand doors were open and all the items that she'd had in there were strewn all over the floor in front of it. The kitchenette drawers were all pulled off their brackets and thrown on the floor with the contents of each of them half out and half in. There wasn't a drawer left in the place that was untouched. Including in the bedroom.

All the paper towels, plastic grocery sacks, and anything else underneath her bed was exposed from the flipped mattress and box spring. The curtains on her window had been jerked down.

"They destroyed the place," the reserve officer said. "I haven't touched anything. I saw that it'd been destroyed, and I took her back downstairs to find Darby."

"Thanks." I sucked in a deep breath. "I'll take over from here. Can you do one thing for me first?" I asked, not waiting for him to answer. "Go find out from Darby who the guests next door are. I'd like to talk to them."

"Okay." The officer left the room.

I opened my bag and took out my camera along with some evidence markers. I slipped on some gloves and started to work.

"This is awful." Poppa stood in the kitchen and looked around.

"Yeah. And this wasn't some random break-in. Whoever did this knows that Hattie is Beryle's sister and was looking for something." It was a big theory I'd had, and it fit the circumstances. "At least I'm going to investigate it that way."

After I took all the photos, I dusted for fingerprints. In the meantime, the officer came back and told me that Jenny was staying next door until she found a place to live. How convenient, I thought, wondering if Betty had gotten any more information about Jenny.

Poppa ghosted around me and watched and looked as I continued to work around the rooms.

"Someone was just angry once they got into her room." I pointed to the curtain rods that had been jerked out of the wall. The screws had even been yanked out of the wall, drywall crumbles on the floor.

"They seemed pretty confident that they'd get whatever it was they were looking for, and when they didn't, they went nuts, just like they did on Cecily and Paige." Poppa only confirmed what I was thinking.

"I can't wait to bring them to justice," I stated.

After I felt confident that I'd gotten all I was going to get of the fingerprints, I inspected them a little more closely.

"They're all Hattie's." Poppa had already gone around the room and took a good look himself. "They're all the same. Not a one different."

"This is just impossible." I pushed a piece of my hair off my forehead with the back of my hand. "Hattie's prints are everywhere, and not a single one is from anyone else. This person is good at covering their tracks, I'll give them that."

I hesitated to put police tape across the front of the door, not wanting to alarm the other guests, because I was 99 percent sure that this was an isolated incident that had to do with the investigation. Instead of putting the tape on the outside of the door facing the hallway, I took two of Hattie's kitchen chairs and stuck them a few feet apart just on the inside of the apartment and strung the crime tape all over them.

"What is this?" Poppa asked with his hands on his hips. "Hillbilly policing?"

"This," I snapped the edge of the tape, "will hopefully keep anyone out who shouldn't be in Hattie's room."

"You're right. No one but Hattie should be in here," Poppa said.

"I'm going to head downstairs to see what I can get out of Hattie." I grabbed my bag and checked my watch. "I wonder where Finn is." I turned to ask Poppa, but he was gone.

I headed down the hallway and down the stairs where the guests were enjoying pre-dinner drinks before Darby was to serve supper. When I swung the kitchen door open, there sat Mama, along with Darby, Hattie, and the reserve officer.

"Have you seen Deputy Vincent?" I asked and looked around the kitchen.

"No." Mama dragged her hand up to her chest before she fanned her face. "Trust me, I'd know if that man was in here."

"Mmm-hmmm. The kitchen is already hot, but he'd make it hotter." Darby continued the joke with Mama.

"Hot, hot," Kiwi repeated from his perch in his cage in the

corner of the kitchen.

"Seriously." I tipped my head and looked at them. "This is an investigation, not a Chippendale show."

Hattie looked content sitting at the table with a plate of Mama's famous ribs, mashed potato pie, and wilted lettuce. The reserve officer had his own plate too.

"Mama, you sure outdid yourself tonight." I couldn't help but stand over Hattie's shoulder and take a nice long whiff.

"Honey, did you just give your mama a compliment?" she asked and winked.

"Why, I think she did." Darby smiled. "So," Darby looked at me, "did you see anything up there?"

"It's just a shame that someone would come here and break in." Mama stepped next to me and put a hand on Hattie. She whispered, "Especially since her sister is dead and all."

"How did you know?" I jerked around.

"Honey, secrets in Cottonwood?" Her brows lifted.

I slid my eyes over to Darby. She wouldn't look at me.

"Darby," I scolded her. "Why on Earth didn't you keep Beryle's secret a little bit longer? I mean, you kept it for all those years."

"Kenni, I have no idea how I'm going to have Hattie's living expenses paid for," she said.

"I did find out that there's a fund set up at the bank and Hattie's got plenty to take care of her expenses. Wally is just finishing up the paperwork, and I'm sure he'll be in touch soon." I needed to put her mind at ease.

"I'll be sure to give Wally a call." She walked over to the stove and pulled out a tray of Mama's ribs from the oven. They looked nice and bronzed. The edges of the sauce were tinted a little browner. My mouth watered.

"I've got to have a sounding board, and your mama has a good ear." She nodded.

"It's a talent," Mama said proudly. "Besides, I'm not going to say a word." She made a turning key gesture in the middle of her lips before she tossed the imaginary key over her shoulder.

It was petty to get into it with them. Darby had already let the cat out of the bag, and it was only a matter of time before the cat sprinted all over town and told the news. Not saying that Mama was the cat, but somehow someone with very big ears tended to hear things that weren't meant to be heard. In my personal life, I lived by Poppa's rule that if you didn't want it out in the world, you didn't speak it.

"Can I have a cup of coffee?" I asked Darby before I helped myself. "I've got the afternoon slumps and coffee helps me think."

"Sure, honey." She made me a cup of coffee while I sat down next to Hattie.

"Well?" Her big brown eyes looked over at me. "Was it that darn critter?"

"I don't know," I said matter-of-factly. "But I do know that someone thinks you have something of importance in your room."

Darby set the steaming cup of coffee in front of me, and I curled my hands around and mouthed "thank you" to her.

"Did your sister, Beryle, ever come to see you?" I asked.

"I came from Beryle's and couldn't find the book. Couldn't find the book. Glad she's dead," Kiwi chirped.

All of us looked over at Kiwi. This was the second time I'd heard the bird say it. The first being before there was a killer walking around Cottonwood.

"She only went by Sister to Hattie." Darby started to answer, but I stuck my hand up for her to stop. "Crazy bird."

"Hattie, did Sister ever come see you?" I asked.

"Not for a long time. When she did, she was older like my mom." Hattie patted her wrinkly hand on the table. "Mom was always so pretty. I took after my dad. Bigger. Broader." She smiled.

Looking at Hattie, she reminded me of a little old granny. No one would know that she had special needs. She took good care of herself. It was like she'd been a dementia patient since childhood.

"I bet you were so happy to see her." I offered her a smile back before I lifted the mug for a drink.

"Oh yes." Her eyes sparkled. "I enjoy every visit. But she

doesn't get to come around often. Today she would've enjoyed the rain. When we were little girls we used to sit in her car and let the rain plop down on the roof. It made the funniest noises."

"I bet it did." Sadness swept over me when I realized she had no clue that Beryle had died. I couldn't imagine how she was going to feel.

"She'd paint and I'd talk." She tapped her fingers. "I'd talk and she'd paint."

"Do you remember the last time she came to see you?" I asked.

"Yes. She was mad." Hattie's face hardened. Her eyes dulled.

"Did she tell you why she was mad?" I asked and glanced up at the clock on Darby's stove. Finn should've arrived at the Inn by now.

"She kept saying how people were frauds and she couldn't trust anyone." Hattie shook her head. "She told me she loved me, and she always made sure she told me she was sorry about how Mom and Dad sent me away."

"You enjoyed your old house." Darby was good with Hattie and keeping her calm.

"I like it much better here." Hattie looked up at Darby. "Here I don't see the critters, I just know they're here. There, I saw them."

"It wasn't the nicest of places, the estate, but the Stones didn't have many choices back then." It was interesting how Darby took up for the Stones. "They did the best they could, according to Beryle."

"You don't have to worry about that here." I finished up my coffee and Darby rushed over to refill it.

"You said that she said someone was a fraud. Do you know who she was talking about?" I asked.

"I didn't listen to her much. *The Price Is Right* was on and she knows I love to watch that show. But she kept saying how she was going to come clean about the person. Something about a book at our old house, and she asked me about the hiding places we used to have." Hattie shrugged and pushed her plate away. "That was a mighty good meal. Can I go back up to my room now?"

"Dear." Darby's eyes dipped with worry. "Jenny is off today, and I don't have help right now."

"Hiding places?" I asked Hattie, wondering if it would be a good idea to take her to the estate and see if she could show me some, though she'd not been there in years. "You and Sister had fun hiding places?"

"Hiding places," Kiwi squawked. "Freeze! You're it!"

"Kenni." Darby's voice held a warning.

"Would you like to go see those hiding places?" I asked.

Hattie nodded her head and stood up. She walked over to Kiwi and opened his door. He jumped on her outstretched arm.

"Can she take Kiwi?" I asked. "He won't fly off or anything, will he?"

Darby walked over and stood at the door between Hattie and me.

"I think you need to call Dr. Shively to make sure this is okay." Darby gave a good suggestion.

"I've been meaning to call her. Good time now." I pulled my phone out of my back pocket and scrolled through my contacts, hitting Camille's name when I found it. I made a mental note to ask her about Paige being released from the hospital.

Darby and Hattie, with Kiwi perched on her shoulder, stood next to the door, both watching me. Mama continued to work on plating the food for the guests, and she'd even gotten the reserve officer to start taking the plates out to the dining room where the guests had already seated themselves.

"No answer." I was a little disappointed, but I was also on a mission to solve this crime. "So, I'll keep trying." I put my hand on Hattie's back. "You ready?"

"I don't know, Kenni." Darby was on my heels.

"I know that I need to know where this manuscript is, if there is one, because that is why someone broke into Hattie's room. If it was a break-in and not just a let-me-look-around." I leaned into Darby's ear. "Just how well do you know Jenny? Think about it. She shows up here on the day of the murder. Just a little convenient that Paige worked here too." I pulled back and gave her a long stern look before I cocked a brow. "I've got Betty looking into her past just in case somewhere along the way she knew Beryle."

Darby's chest lifted when she took a deep inhale as she contemplated my words.

"I do take people at their word, and I didn't check her references," Darby's words faded. "Oh, dear. Maybe I need to call those references."

"Let me know what they say. Do you have a raincoat?" I asked Hattie.

She pointed to the coat tree next to the front door and walked over to retrieve it. She used an umbrella to keep her and Kiwi dry. We headed out to the Jeep and got in.

"I sure wish I was sitting with Sister in her car." Hattie stared out the passenger window. Kiwi made a perch on the back of the seat.

The rain beat down around us. The sky had turned to night. The old curvy road between the Inn and the Stone estate was slick as cat's guts. My tires skidded off the road just as I swerved to miss a deer.

Hattie grabbed the door handle as the Jeep jerked to the right and then to the left. Kiwi flapped his wings, sending feathers all over.

"Are you okay?" I asked Hattie once I'd gotten the Jeep safely stopped on the side of the road. I noticed Kiwi's nails had made a few holes in the seat, but that was okay as long as he was safe too.

Her eyes were big and round. She nodded quickly. She gulped.

"Good." I looked in my rearview to see if I saw the deer. I knew I didn't hit it.

I turned over my right shoulder to look out the back window at the white billowy figure coming toward the Wagoneer.

"Poppa?" I asked, wondering if he had ghosted outside. The figure got closer and came into view. "Paige?" Disbelief swept over me. I shuddered.

Chapter Twenty-Six

I grabbed a blanket off my backseat and jumped out of the car.

"Paige!" I screamed when I saw that she had blood all over the front of her hospital gown. "You're safe," I said and wrapped the blanket around her cold and shivering body.

"Sterling, Sterling," she whispered over and over, her eyes blank. She looked to be in shock.

"You're safe," I assured her and put a steady arm around her shoulders.

As I walked her back to the Jeep, the rain continuing to bat at us, I glanced over my shoulder to see if anyone was following her.

I opened the backseat passenger door and helped her into the seat. With the blanket still around her, I hooked the seatbelt around her.

"You're going to be fine." I looked her straight in the eyes after I'd given her a onceover. Her previous wound looked like it'd opened up, and the blood on her gown looked like it'd come from the blood dripping down her face.

It took me a minute to compose myself once I got in the driver's seat. Hattie had turned completely around in the seat. The seatbelt pulled taut.

"You okay, Paige?" she asked.

Slowly Paige dragged her chin up. Her hair was matted to her head. She didn't acknowledge Hattie. She just stared at her.

I hit the button on the walkie-talkie.

"Finn! Finn, where are you?" I asked.

Paige shivered from the backseat. I wasn't sure if she shivered from the cold rain that saturated her or the fact she was running out of the woods in a dead sprint and scared to death. I turned the heat up in the Jeep. Hattie and Kiwi continued to stare at Paige.

"Finn, come in," I said again, giving him another minute.

When he didn't answer, I took my phone out and called him. It immediately went to voicemail.

"Paige," I turned around, "I'm going to call Lonnie."

She didn't move.

I scrolled through my contacts and found Lonnie's name and hit send. It went to voicemail too.

"Paige." I tried to get her attention. "Can you tell me where Lonnie is?" A sick feeling covered me. She didn't answer. "Can you tell me who took you out of the hospital?"

There was a crack of thunder, followed up by tendrils of lightning spreading in different directions across the sky.

I called Camille Shively again.

"Hello?" she answered.

For some reason, it made me feel a little better. For a moment, I'd been feeling as if I was all alone in a scary movie.

"Camille, it's Kenni Lowry." I didn't wait for her to answer. "Did you discharge Paige Lemar from the hospital?"

"I was in the process when I found out that she'd left with Lonnie. I've been trying to call them all night, because it's imperative she takes her infection medications." Camille made it sound so much better than it was.

"Listen," I took my voice down a notch because Paige Lemar was in shock and she needed something, "long story short, I've found Paige wandering around in the rain between the Stone estate and the Inn. I've got her in my Jeep. She's in shock."

"Get her out of the rain and into some dry clothes. Cover her up and I'll be right over. Where are you taking her?" Camille asked.

"I was heading over to the Stone estate and it's closest, so I'll just take her there. See you soon." We said our goodbyes, and I jerked the gear into drive.

"Glad she's dead," Kiwi squawked on his way back over to Hattie's shoulder. "Dead!"

"What did you say?" Paige found her voice. Her eyes blinked a few times. "Kenni?"

"It's okay, Paige." I turned the car into the estate driveway. "Dr. Shively is on her way. You'll be okay. You're in a bit of a shock."

"Shock. Shock." Kiwi's feathers stood up on end.

I pulled up to the house as close as I could.

"Hattie, you stay right here while I get Paige into the house," I said and she nodded.

I grabbed the umbrella and jumped out of the Jeep.

Paige had already opened the door and had the quilt tucked up and around her. She was still shivering.

"Lonnie. Where is Lonnie?" she asked in a quiet voice. Her eyes dragged up to the front of the Stone estate. "Beryle? Are you bringing me to work?"

"We're going to go in and get some dry clothes on." I nodded. I held the umbrella with one hand and curled an arm around her shoulder to guide her toward the house.

Once I got us inside, I figured Beryle wasn't going to be using her bedroom anymore, and Finn and I had already combed it for any evidence. Paige needed a bed and dry clothes.

"Kenni. Am I going nuts?" Paige asked. She stood in the doorway of Beryle's en suite bathroom with the blanket tight around her.

"No, honey." I took a pair of Beryle's flannel pajamas out of her dresser and walked them over to Paige. "You've been through a lot, but it's all over now," I assured her.

She was fragile and in shock. This wasn't the time to question her about Lonnie or how she'd gotten out of the hospital. I'd wait until Dr. Shively gave me the okay.

"You need help changing into these dry clothes?" I asked.

"I'm okay. Can you call Lonnie and tell him I'm here? He worries so much about me." Her face was stone, but her mouth softened. "Especially when Beryle needs me to read for her. She takes so long."

"Sure, Paige." It was apparent she was not in her right mind. "I'll be right back."

I was in bit of a pickle. On the one hand, I had Paige here in shock, and on the other, Hattie, who was outside with Kiwi. There was no way I could leave her out there much longer.

"Betty?" I called over the dispatch. "Are you there?" I walked back out into the rain to get Hattie and bring her in.

It would be nice if I could get Paige to sleep in the bed while I followed Hattie around and looked for some secret compartments.

"Alrighty, you two," I said as I swung the passenger door of the Jeep open with the umbrella positioned slightly over the roof and the open door. "Hattie?" I stared into an empty car. "Shit," I muttered and looked around. "Hattie!" I screamed into the rolling thunder.

"Here, Kenni!" Poppa stood by the barn, where the door was open, the broomstick on the ground.

"What on Earth is she doing in there?" I shook my head, throwing the umbrella on the ground and running over. "Hattie?" I called into the dark barn.

"Where is it?" Kiwi squawked.

I flipped my flashlight off my belt and shined it over to the car, where a drenched Kiwi was perched on the convertible top, Hattie standing next to it.

"Hattie? What are you doing?" I asked. "We need to go into the house. I'll play hide and seek with you. Remember you were going to show me your hiding places with your sister?"

"Yes. We loved sitting in the rain." She turned back to me. "She'd paint. I'd talk."

"You said that." I put my hand on her damp shoulder. "Let's go on, and maybe we can take a ride later."

"Imposter." She repeated the word that Beryle had painted on the canvas I'd found earlier. "Sister imposter."

"Your sister was a good person." Poppa stood next to her.

"Good person." Kiwi lifted a claw into the air toward Poppa.

"Why is it that animals and children can see me?" He bent

down and looked at Kiwi. "Who killed Beryle?"

"Glad Beryle is dead!" Kiwi put down the claw and lifted the other one up. "Dead."

Hattie jerked on the handle of the door. "Open the door. Sister painted."

"I know she did, but she's not in there." I took the key out of my pocket so I could show her. "Good grief." I looked at Poppa, who was still trying to talk to Kiwi. "I've got Hattie out here and Paige in there. I can't get a hold of anyone at the office. "

I opened the door of the car and Hattie jumped in. I decided to let her get in to be satisfied that Beryle wasn't in there. I took my phone out of my pocket and dialed the Inn. If I couldn't get in touch with Finn, I'd use the reserve officer, since he was over there doing nothing while I had Hattie.

I didn't have any bars. Cell service was already spotty in Cottonwood, but the trees and down in the gully near the river really didn't allow for cell towers to be built.

"Okay, I'll wait for Camille. Once she's here, I'll let her stay with them while I go back to the Inn and grab the reserve officer. When I get him here, I'm going back to town to find Finn and Lonnie," I said, my head down, continuing to hit the dial button in hopes I'd catch a random signal. "Hattie." I gave up and put my phone in my pocket. "See, your sister isn't here. Come on. We need to go see Paige in the house."

"I came from Beryle's and couldn't find the book. Couldn't find the book. Glad she's dead." Kiwi walked around and around on the convertible top. "Sister's dead."

"No, she's not," Hattie said from inside the car. She grabbed the draped canvas and got out of the car. "No, she's not," she leaned over the roof and said to Kiwi.

"Where is the book?" Kiwi asked.

"I told you I don't know what you are talking about," Hattie said to Kiwi like they were actually having a conversation.

"Hattie." I put my hand on her shoulder.

"Wait," Poppa said. "I think we have something here."

"And I told you she's dead, so give me my manuscript." Kiwi danced back and forth on his feet. His head bobbed up and down.

Hattie put the draped canvas on the barn floor and leaned it up against the car. She bent down and took the canvas out of the drape.

"Hattie, why don't we leave the canvas in the package for safety?" I reached for the canvas and she smacked my hand away.

"Imposter," Hattie said through gritted teeth. "Imposter!" She flipped the canvas around and ripped off the brown paper that was stapled to the back.

"Shut up!" Kiwi screeched just as the thunder shook the barn and lightning lit up the inside, giving the person standing at the door a long and lean shadow.

A pack of papers held together by a binder clip fell on the ground from the back of the canvas.

"I'll take that." The shadow's voice was angry like the nighttime sky. The sky cracked again, lightning flashed, and the eyes of Paige Lemar glowed with an inner savagery. The shotgun from my Jeep pointed at Hattie.

Chapter Twenty-Seven

"Paige," I took a step forward, "what are you doing?" I asked, knowing she'd completely lost her mind.

Her eyes were dark with emotion.

"I've come for the manuscript." She walked forward, my shotgun still pointed directly at Hattie. She took one hand off the gun and curled her fingers in and out. "Gimme."

"Nuh-uh." Hattie shook her head and pulled the paper-clipped papers to her chest.

"Everything is fine." I took another step forward. "Paige, honey, you've been in an accident, and Dr. Shively is on her way now. And so is Lonnie," I assured her.

"Kenni-bug, I don't think she's doing this because she's in shock." Poppa wasn't making sense.

"They aren't coming." Paige laughed in a deep jovial way. "None of them are coming to help you. That's mine. All of this is mine."

"Paige, are you telling me that you're behind the murder of Cecily Hoover?" I asked, trying to sort out what was going on.

"Murder. That is just such a yucky word. I made the world a better place." Her wide-eyed innocence from earlier was merely a smoke screen. Now those eyes looked at me, dark and insolent.

"Wait." The word popped out of my mouth, trying to stall. "How did you make the world a better place by killing someone?"

"Maybe I've given you too much credit." She now pointed my shotgun at me. "I thought for sure that you'd figured all of this out."

My head was spinning around so fast that I couldn't remember if I'd put shells in the gun or not. The darn thing had been in my backseat for so long. I rarely used it. When I did, it was just for a shot or two in the air when I'd gotten a coyote call from dispatch.

"But you were hurt at Ruby's." I stepped in front of Hattie who'd eased down into a squatting position with the papers tucked in her body. "Your head."

"Yeah. Who knew that Cecily would be able to fight back and take a swing at me before I could finish her off." She held her hand out. "Give it to me, Hattie."

"Why?" I asked, buying time to figure out what I could do to turn the gun on her.

"Are you kidding me?" she asked with vehemence. The sky lit up behind her, and the thunder rumbled off into the distance. "She left behind a tell-all manuscript that would not only expose her for who she really was, but expose me."

"Are you the one who fed her all the gossip in Cottonwood to make the plots?" I asked. "It would make sense because you were her friend."

"Friend? You mean her ghostwriter?" She looked at me. Apparently, I had a look of shock and awe on my face. She said, "You don't know, do you?"

"I don't." It wasn't time to sugarcoat anything. I had no idea what she was talking about. All I knew was that she was the killer, and I had to get Hattie out of here as quickly as possible. Alive. "The only thing I know is that Beryle had been using Cottonwood secrets as her plots and changing the names. Like with my Poppa."

"This ought to be fun." She smiled. "I really enjoyed catching him and Viola White in the sheriff's department when Lonnie was his deputy."

"Don't listen to this crap, Kenni-bug." Poppa danced on his toes with his fists in the air. "I'm a southern gentleman and I'd never hit a lady. But she's no lady."

"Beryle Stone didn't write a single word. Not a word. But she did start somewhere." She dragged the barrel of the shotgun in a motion that told me to sit down next to Hattie.

I did what she asked, just like we'd learned in the academy. Hattie looked up at me from her crouched position on the floor.

"My mother worked for her family as their housekeeper. I had to come to work to help my mom. Really, I was Beryle's playmate. Beryle was always making up stories, but they were boring. I would tell her to add this and add that, which made her stories better. I was a senior in high school when my mother died. I still came and worked for them, picking up more cleaning duties. Do you remember those grocery magazines where you could send in short stories for publication?" she asked, as if we were just enjoying a cup of coffee, not her holding me at gunpoint.

I shook my head no. I shifted, hoping to get my hand on my gun.

"Ah, ah." She moved forward. I winced when she stuck my own gun in my gut. She reached down and flipped the holster snap, taking my pistol. "I'm old. But not stupid."

"I never said you were." I wanted to butter her up as much as I could.

"Anyways." She tossed my gun into a barn stall. "Beryle sent in one of the crazy short stories I'd helped her write and some publisher read it. They contacted her, and that's when she told them she had some big story ideas. She didn't. She lied. She used all of my ideas. Her father let her when I went to him and told her. To keep me hushed, I was paid handsomely by them with each book idea."

"Tag, you're it," Hattie whispered.

"Shut up!" Paige yelled back.

"Shut up, shut up," Kiwi said. I could hear his little claws hitting the roof of the car and secretly prayed that he'd suddenly take flight and land on Paige's eyeballs.

No such luck. Paige just kept on talking. I adjusted myself up against the car, my shoulder with my walkie-talkie leaning against the door.

"What about Hattie?" I asked.

"Her." Paige's nostrils flared. "It wasn't just me that Beryle's father was giving hush money. He paid the facility where they'd put Hattie too. When the money stopped coming, they found Beryle and told her about Hattie."

"That's when Beryle brought Hattie here." My jaw dropped as more and more of the puzzle pieces started to fit together.

"Now you're using your noggin." Paige tapped her temple.

"You got paid more money to take care of her." All of what Darby was saying fit. "And you still fed Beryle the gossip that gave her the ideas for her novels."

"I renegotiated." Paige strolled back and forth, haphazardly rolling the butt of the shotgun under her arm. "I started to get half of her advances to keep my mouth shut."

"So, you were blackmailing her? No wonder Beryle wrote this." I pointed to the hidden manuscript we'd found.

When she turned away me for a moment, I slid my hand up to my walkie-talkie, turned off the beeping option, and leaned closer to the car so the talk button was pushed in, in hopes that Finn or Betty would just so happen to hear the conversation and maybe come save us.

"What happened? Why would you kill Cecily?" I asked again, just in case someone was listening on the other end.

"Kill Cecily, kill Cecily," Kiwi shouted.

"Shut up, you dumb bird. I've been waiting to do this for a long time." Slowly, Paige dragged the shotgun up to her chin level and pointed it at the bird. She got eye level with the sights and curled her finger around the trigger.

"Paige!" I stood up between Kiwi and Paige. I sucked in a deep breath. "I can't believe I'm doing this for a bird. You've got to turn yourself in."

"No. No, I don't." She shook her head from behind the gun. Her arms trembled, which gave me a little hope that she wasn't used to holding a heavy shotgun and that her aim would be off. Really off. "Here we are. You're about to be killed by your own shotgun. I slipped it under that warm quilt you gave me." A deep laugh escaped her. "What type of sheriff leaves her gun sitting on her backseat?" She made fun of me. "I mean, seriously, you're the sheriff? If I didn't hate Lonnie so much, I'd help him get elected, but right now I need that manuscript. I need it now."

"What is in there that's so important that you wanted Cecily dead?" It was the moment I'd been waiting for.

Poppa pointed to the painting.

"The painting. The painter. *Crimson Hearts*." My mouth dried. "Beryle and Lonnie?"

"Wouldn't you like to know that you're right." She jutted the gun forward, pointing away from Kiwi and instead at me. "'I hear Beryle wrote a tell-all. I heard that Beryle knows a lot of secrets.' Blah, blah, blah."

"Beryle knew she was dying of cancer." I was pushing my luck, but if I was going to die at the hands of Paige Lemar—and she obviously wasn't scared to kill me since she'd already killed Cecily—I wanted answers. "She had nothing to lose, and she'd have a clean conscience."

"Things in my world aren't as pretty as you'd think. And Lonnie," she scoffed. "He's no innocent man in this." Her hands were visibly shaking. "He's just as much of a murderer as I am. He killed me years ago." She pounded her chest with a tight fist.

Paige dropped the shotgun to her side. She paced in front of Hattie and me with the gun pointing down.

"I'll never forget it. Never." She looked down at her feet as she walked. "When Beryle was on her deadlines, she'd come back here to stay. No one knew but me and Lonnie. I'd bring Hattie here to visit her while I'd come and work. Lonnie would go to the sheriff's office with Elmer." She referred to Poppa, Elmer Sims. "At least that's what I thought he was doing. Until one day I got what they call the writer's block. It was the last novel I did for her. *Desires of the Heart*."

"That was the movie from the early eighties, right?" I recalled Lauren Bacall had played the part in the big-screen version. It was likened to *Gone With the Wind*, only a modern version for that time.

"It was." A single tear dripped down her cheek. "I knew it was good, and Beryle had promised me all sorts of things. So, I was working on the last scene, and I wanted to make it perfect. I got stuck. I put so much pressure on myself, so I decided to go for a walk." She pointed to the car. "It was right there that I found them. Beryle and Lonnie. It was like she wanted my life and I wanted hers. She took whatever it was she wanted."

Poppa ghosted himself next to the car. "Kenni-bug, I remember now." Poppa ghosted next to Paige. "Lonnie wanted to leave Paige for Beryle."

"I was working my fingers to the bones to help give her the celebrity status she was used to. The publisher loved the chapters, and they knew it was going to be a big success." She gulped. Her eyes filled with tears. "I just wanted to come out for some fresh air. I noticed the barn door was open and I walked in. The car top was down and there they were. Kissing, embracing each other." Her voice faded off, as did the memory.

"I'm so sorry, Paige." There were no words to comfort her.

"I'm not sorry for them." Her sad features hardened back into the angry stare, pursed lips and harsh words. "They deserved everything I did to them."

"Are you talking about Cecily and Beryle?" I asked.

"No. Beryle and Lonnie." A disgusted tone spat out of her mouth. "I've been threatening all these years to expose their affair. Every chance I got, I emailed Beryle, called her and threatened her. Lonnie continued to beg me not to. He was a productive member of society. A deputy. One day to be sheriff. Only your poppa refused to die, and Lonnie accepted that. I was going to go ahead with the divorce and sue Beryle for what was rightfully mine. My money."

The rain had started up again, this time pounding so hard on the barn roof that Paige had to yell louder.

"She came back to Cottonwood and brought little Cecily with her. She told Cecily they were here to clean up a little mess, sell the estate, and give the money to the charities. She quickly set up all the necessary paperwork with Wally Lamb so she could die with nothing hanging over her head. Only I knew the little secret about Hattie and what would happen to her reputation if the adoring public knew she'd kept her sister a secret all these years and that I was her ghostwriter, not to mention the affair. That's when she told me that she was here to make good on her life with the people she left behind, including Lonnie. She was going to expose him right here before the election with this tell-all. She was even going to list every book with the real-life people behind the characters and expose their secrets." Her face lit up with pride. "I stayed with Lonnie all these years. I've waited a long time to be the sheriff's wife. I put up with his affair, and I wasn't about to let her waltz in here and ruin it again for me."

The thunder rolled over top of the barn. The rain poured like a waterfall from the loft through the hole in the ceiling into the guts of the barn. With each lightning strike, the barn lit up.

"Wait." I stalled for more time thinking, there was no way I was going to get out of this one, and if I did, I could read Edna Easterly's headline now: *Sheriff Taken Hostage By Own Shotgun.* "I'm confused. Did you talk to Beryle recently?"

"The cancer claimed Beryle before I could kill her. I was never going to let her live. I figured the threats were over. That's when the stupid bird picked up on me talking to Hattie." She pulled the shotgun up to the roof of the car, and with her eye on the sights aimed at Kiwi again. "I decided to be sure there wasn't a manuscript to check out the house for myself. That's when I met Cecily. Cecily insisted there was a secret tell-all and though she never said it, I could see in her eyes that the secret was my secret." She chuckled. "Wally Lamb didn't waste a moment getting Beryle's things out of here and letting Ruby Smith know that she was the executor because Hattie couldn't be. It was then that I wondered if Beryle had decided to put the manuscript in one of her antiques, that way someone would happen upon it and sell my life's secrets along with my money just because they found it. Beryle was conniving. She'd do that, you know."

I nodded just to agree with her. There was no way I was going to be able to convince this crazy person of anything. I could see it in her eyes. She was on a mission to kill anyone in her way of getting the manuscript.

"I told Cecily to meet me at the antique shop. I'd lied and told her that the estate would get a lot more money for Hattie if we found the manuscript and sold it. We went inside and looked around. We went into the storage room where Ruby had left the inventory sheet to make sure we'd checked all the furniture," she said.

"Yep. That's where that feather you found came from. Paige worked at the Inn all day. She's pretty much in charge of Hattie, who Kiwi practically lives with. The feather must've stuck on Paige's clothes and when she went to the antique store, the feather floated off her during the scuffle." Poppa paced behind Paige. He rubbed his chin. "Now I need to figure out how to get you out of this pickle."

I glared at him as he ghosted away. Leaving me wasn't going to help at all.

"It was then that I knew it was time to kill Cecily. I grabbed the ax and hit her over the head. I never figured she'd fight back. She swung her arm and knocked the ax out of my hands. She hit me with the handle. That's when I was knocked out." She shrugged. "Apparently, she didn't have enough gumption to kill me, so she dragged herself out into the alley and died." She looked up at the falling rain through the loft. "When I woke up in the hospital, I was surprised you didn't know it was me. I thought I was off the hook. Then Lonnie..." Disgust fell from her lips.

"What about Lonnie? Where is he?" I asked.

"He's an idiot. After you left the hospital, he started using his investigative skills. He started to put two and two together. He stood in my hospital room and solved every single detail. He had a leg up on you because he knew he'd had the affair with Beryle. He claimed it was a perfect motive for me to kill her. He told me that I'd now ruined his run for the sheriff's office and he was going to turn me in. I wasn't about to let that happen." She *tsk*'d.

She threw her head back and let the rain that was falling from the loft pound down on her.

"Lonnie left and I slipped out of the hospital. Not like Cottonwood is so big that I couldn't make it home on my own. There he was. Sitting by the fireplace, his phone in his hand. When he saw me, he told me that he'd just spoken with Finn Vincent, and Finn was on his way over to get Lonnie's statement."

Suddenly my heart fell. Finn. What did she do?

"What?" she asked. There was a look of satisfaction on her face. "Did that get your attention, Kenni Lowry?" She laughed out loud. "Funny, I'd heard something about you and Finn at the church group. I was a bit nervous since I knew I needed to attend to have an alibi, so I didn't get the full story, but it seemed that you were being a little town floozy right in front of Ben's. Your poor mama. Such a shame."

"Say cheese!" a voice called from the front of the barn.

Hattie looked up and smiled while Paige and I turned toward the voice. A click of a camera flashed so brightly, I looked away. When I did, I saw that Paige had brought her arm up to shield her eyes. I scrambled to my feet and let the adrenaline of how mad I was from her words about Finn take over. With a thud like the rolling thunder ahead, Paige went down with me on top of her. The shotgun, my shotgun, skidded across the floor.

"I've got you covered." The sweet sound of Edna Easterly's voice rang above the clapping thunder, right before the yellow flashing light of Graves Towing's truck lit up the inside of the barn through the open doors, giving me the light I needed to get Paige Lemar into handcuffs.

Chapter Twenty-Eight

"Edna, I don't know why you're here, but I'm sure glad," I said after I'd used Sean Graves's phone to call Betty at home to tell her to send an ambulance.

Luckily, Paige hadn't hurt Lonnie or Finn; instead, she'd cuffed Lonnie to the foot of their claw foot tub with his own handcuffs and used his gun to cuff Finn to their bed post, something I kind of wished I'd seen.

"You can thank Jetter." Edna pointed to the visiting tabloid reporter who was giving her statement to Finn, who'd been released and headed right over. "She's been following Beryle Stone around for years, since her mother retired from the tabloid. She took over for her. Her mother was obsessed with Beryle Stone and her reclusive life. She was even on the trail of Hattie being the sister after she'd traced money from a bogus charity going back to the Inn. She'd also been hot on the trail about a ghostwriter but never figured it was Paige. Somehow, she used her contacts to find out about the results of the Kim's Buffet tape. She'd also overheard at the diner how you were looking for Sterling. She found him. He told her he saw Paige and Cecily arguing. He'd hidden by the dumpster, and when Cecily stumbled out of the shop all bloody and half dead, he got spooked and ran off. He's been in hiding because he wasn't sure how to tell anyone that it was Paige."

"And that's how the video got him and why we couldn't find him." I tried to wrap my head on exactly how they had gotten here. "How did you know to come to the barn?"

"Jetter said it was the strangest thing. She was in her room at the Inn working on the article. Sterling was with her, using her room as a safe haven until she figured out how to get him to open up to you about that murder. She said the papers on her desk flew around like the wind had hit them." Edna continued, but it was Poppa standing behind her that had caught my attention.

He'd hung his thumbs in his belt with a big ol' grin on his face.

"That was me." He pointed to himself. "I blew them papers off to make the hospital information float right on top of her laptop. I made her think about Paige and if she'd woken up yet." Poppa tapped his temple. "Jetter called the hospital and they told her that Paige was no longer a patient. They left out the part that she'd skipped out. But she was smart enough to go by the Lemar place. She thought she was going to get an exclusive from Paige and what happened that night at Ruby's shop before she turned her in. Sterling went with her."

"They happened to go in the house when no one answered." Edna's voice overtook Poppa's, so I diverted my attention back to her. "That's when she saw Lonnie and Finn all tied up." She leaned in and whispered, "Between me and you, I'd have taken a few pictures of that hunk Finn just for my records." She winked. "If you know what I mean. In handcuffs and all."

"How did you get here?" I asked, rushing the story and trying to get the image of Finn handcuffed to a bed out of my head.

"Jetter called me and told me what she'd found and how the reserve officers were on their way over to get her statement. She said that Finn had mentioned something about you and Hattie at the estate. We decided I'd come to the house to see if I could uncover anything about Hattie, and that's when I noticed the barn door was open. That's all she wrote."

"We didn't see your headlights because the lightning was so bad." I never thought I'd say this to Edna. "I'm so happy you have that new crazy flash camera."

"Well, I will forgive your harsh words. But I want an exclusive for the *Chronicle*." She patted the camera hanging around her neck.

"You drive a hard bargain, Edna." I teased. "Go on. Take all the photos you want. This case is closed."

Chapter Twenty-Nine

Knock, knock. I lightly tapped on the door of my new neighbor's house.

"Come in!" Finn Vincent's voice echoed through the house and out of the screen door. Music blared from inside. Paint fumes drifted out to greet me.

"Just moved in and already feeling at home enough to yell 'come in'?" I mimicked him.

He stood on the ladder in the family room with a paintbrush in one hand and a paint can in the other. He had on a pair of blue faded jeans and a white V-neck tee.

"Don't just stand there. Grab a brush." He turned back to cutting in underneath the ceiling.

"I don't do painting. Unless it's my nails." I wiggled my fingers in the air. "Mama took me to Tiny Tina's. She said I needed a good spa day since we solved the murder and Lonnie told everyone at the council meeting last night that he wasn't going to run against me for sheriff."

Finn got down off the ladder. The air between us seemed to electrify. My heart hammered inside my chest. I felt like a breathless eighteen-year-old girl.

"I heard." He took another step closer to me. "Which means this was a good investment, since we'll have another term together."

"Yes," was all I could make come out of my mouth. He was so good-looking, it made my mind mush.

"It seemed that the whole town went nuts over a few things in

Beryle's book." He wiped his hands on a towel and walked into the kitchen. He grabbed a couple of beers and handed me one.

"She only really told on herself and how she didn't write the books. I guess it was sort of a confessional. And how she did want to come clean with the affair." We clinked our beer bottles together and both took a drink. "The publisher told Ruby they were still going to publish it, and the royalties will go to Hattie's fund."

"I saw Darby at Ben's this morning, and she said that Preacher Bing signed all the money over to the estate, which is Ruby, and Ruby will pay all of Hattie's bills like Beryle did," Finn noted.

"I'm glad Hattie is able to stay and not uproot her life." There was something so sweet and kind about Finn and how he did care for the people of Cottonwood.

Now that there wasn't a case to focus on to keep my mind busy, I couldn't stop looking at him.

"Now that I live practically next door, we'll be seeing a lot more of each other outside of the office." He took another step closer to me. He gazed down at me and ran his hand down my hair, making my skin tingle. "I think we make an excellent team."

As if there was an invisible string pulling my lips to his, I curled up on my toes. Our lips met. The kiss sang through my veins.

"We do make an excellent team," I whispered before he pulled me into his warm strong arms and kissed me again, this time with more passion.

"Oh, my stars!" Mama's voice sang out from the open front door.

"Mama. Have you no shame?" I jumped away from Finn and curled my lips together.

"I waited outside like you said." She smiled like a beauty queen that had just won the big title.

"I did, didn't I?" I looked at Finn. "I'll be right out, Mama."

Mama clasped her hands together and twirled around on the balls of her feet. She shut the door behind her.

"I'm sorry," I said.

"For what?" He winked. "Dinner tonight? A real date."

"I'd love to," I answered, wishing it was already suppertime. I pointed to the door. "I better get out there and calm Mama down."

"Yep, she's probably already booked the church," Finn joked.

I shook my head and walked out the door, briefly stopping on the other side.

The thought swirled in my head. I wouldn't mind being a summer bride.

TONYA KAPPES

Tonya has written over 20 novels and 4 novellas, all of which have graced numerous bestseller lists including *USA Today*. Best known for stories charged with emotion and humor, and filled with flawed characters, her novels have garnered reader praise and glowing critical reviews. She lives with her husband, three teenage boys, two very spoiled schnauzers and one ex-stray cat in Kentucky.

**The Kenni Lowry Mystery Series
by Tonya Kappes**

FIXIN' TO DIE (#1)
SOUTHERN FRIED (#2)
AX TO GRIND (#3)
SIX FEET UNDER (#4)

Henery Press Mystery Books

And finally, before you go...
Here are a few other mysteries
you might enjoy:

DOUBLE WHAMMY

Gretchen Archer

A Davis Way Crime Caper (#1)

Davis Way thinks she's hit the jackpot when she lands a job as the fifth wheel on an elite security team at the fabulous Bellissimo Resort and Casino in Biloxi, Mississippi. But once there, she runs straight into her ex-ex husband, a rigged slot machine, her evil twin, and a trail of dead bodies. Davis learns the truth and it does not set her free—in fact, it lands her in the pokey.

Buried under a mistaken identity, unable to seek help from her family, her hot streak runs cold until her landlord Bradley Cole steps in. Make that her landlord, lawyer, and love interest. With his help, Davis must win this high stakes game before her luck runs out.

Available at booksellers nationwide and online

Visit www.henerypress.com for details

PILLOW STALK

Diane Vallere

A Madison Night Mystery (#1)

Interior Decorator Madison Night might look like a throwback to the sixties, but as business owner and landlord, she proves that independent women can have it all. But when a killer targets women dressed in her signature style—estate sale vintage to play up her resemblance to fave actress Doris Day—what makes her unique might make her dead.

The local detective connects the new crime to a twenty-year old cold case, and Madison's long-trusted contractor emerges as the leading suspect. As the body count piles up, Madison uncovers a Soviet spy, a campaign to destroy all Doris Day movies, and six minutes of film that will change her life forever.

Available at booksellers nationwide and online

Visit www.henerypress.com for details

MACDEATH

Cindy Brown

An Ivy Meadows Mystery (#1)

Like every actor, Ivy Meadows knows that *Macbeth* is cursed. But she's finally scored her big break, cast as an acrobatic witch in a circus-themed production of *Macbeth* in Phoenix, Arizona. And though it may not be Broadway, nothing can dampen her enthusiasm—not her flying cauldron, too-tight leotard, or carrot-wielding dictator of a director.

But when one of the cast dies on opening night, Ivy is sure the seeming accident is "murder most foul" and that she's the perfect person to solve the crime (after all, she does work part-time in her uncle's detective agency). Undeterred by a poisoned Big Gulp, the threat of being blackballed, and the suddenly too-real curse, Ivy pursues the truth at the risk of her hard-won career—and her life.

Available at booksellers nationwide and online

Visit www.henerypress.com for details

THE AMBITIOUS CARD

John Gaspard

An Eli Marks Mystery (#1)

The life of a magician isn't all kiddie shows and card tricks. Sometimes it's murder. When magician Eli Marks very publicly debunks a famed psychic, said psychic ends up dead. The evidence, including a bloody King of Diamonds playing card (one from Eli's own Ambitious Card routine), directs the police right to Eli.

As more psychics are slain, and more King cards rise to the top, Eli can't escape suspicion. Things get really complicated when romance blooms with a beautiful psychic, and Eli discovers she's the next target for murder, and he's scheduled to die with her. Now Eli must use every trick he knows to keep them both alive and reveal the true killer.

Available at booksellers nationwide and online

Visit www.henerypress.com for details

CPSIA information can be obtained
at www.ICGtesting.com
Printed in the USA
LVHW081603120319
610367LV00010B/199/P

9 781635 112504